Darkest Dawn

The War Scroll Series
Book 3

J.B. TUCKER

ISBN: 979-8-9908355-3-5

First Edition

Cover art by MeLisa Stone
Copyediting by Bitch'n Books Editorial

www.jbtuckerbooks.com

To my readers.
Thank you for going on this journey with me!

Darkest Dawn

In the beginning, there was darkness, an endless void blanketing space and time.

Darklings, born of dark energy, floated through and over the darkness as an ocean, not knowing warmth from cold, light from dark.

A great light cut through the void, a persistent flare shining into the deepest recesses of space.

Awakened, the darklings turned toward a new existence.

Their creator shrank from the light, its rays too painful to bear.

From a dark corner, The Void watched as its creations forsook their original Creator in favor of the light.

Watched and waited.

For in the end, it would pull its darling darklings back into its cold embrace once more.

Darkest Dawn

Chapter 1

April 19ᵗʰ

Deep within the English countryside stood a lonely cabin, its walls green with crawling vines. The humble structure was hidden within a copse of trees. Birds hopped from branch to branch of the surrounding birches, chirping and celebrating the return of spring on that rare sunny day.

Half a dozen uniformed attendants lined the edge of the warped wooden porch to await their high-profile employer. They shifted uncomfortably in the unseasonable heat as a pair of white Mercedes SUVs traveled down the overgrown country lane. When the tires crunched to a halt, a finely dressed woman burst from the driver's side seat.

"Where is he?" she cried out.

"Inside on the couch, ma'am," one said with a bow.

A man in a black polo and wrinkled khakis stepped out onto the gravel drive next and watched as his wife sprinted into the two-story log cabin. He adjusted his black-framed glasses and followed her inside.

A small boy sat on the sofa in the quaint living room, sucking his thumb. The woman rushed to scoop him up. She made little shushing noises as she rocked the toddler back and forth. Snot pooled on his upper lip as he cried.

The woman pulled away and searched the boy for injuries. He whined pitifully, wanting to be back in the warm cradle of his mother's embrace. "Shh. It's okay. Mommy's here now. You're safe. Shh."

"How is he?" the politician asked his weeping wife.

She raised her wet, brown eyes.

"Beyond the emotional scarring he'll carry for the rest of his life, he's fine." She sniffed.

Satisfied that the boy was unharmed—physically at least—the man's shoulders dropped, and he sighed heavily, releasing months of pent-up fear and frustration. His son would live. His relief was quickly overshadowed by the gravity of their situation.

The attendants removed the baggage from the back of the SUVs and began loading it into the humble cabin in a single-file line, heading straight for the basement. The politician watched as they descended the narrow staircase, bumping and scraping the walls with the luggage as they went.

He knew this day would come, had planned for it scrupulously. Yet as they prepared to leave humanity to fend for itself, his stomach ulcer flared up. He shook a pair of colorful antacids into his palm and tossed them into his mouth, trying to ease both his pain and his guilt.

The boy had been taken from his home in broad daylight

months ago, and the politician's stately wife had turned into an emotional wreck overnight. It had taken them a decade to get pregnant, and the boy was her pride and joy.

The emails began mere hours after his son's disappearance. Blackmail. Ransom. There was no thought of refusing the unknown terrorists' requests, of course. There would be no peace in the man's life until his son's return. Not to mention that the press would eventually notice his only child's absence. He couldn't afford the negative attention a kidnapping would bring. But the devils didn't want money, though the man had plenty to give. No, they wanted *favors*. Favors only a man with his position and power could give. Favors that would earn him a one-way ticket to hell.

The mysterious sender made promises, too. A place in the New World Order, a leader in his own right. It sounded like a damned dystopian novel. Though he had to admit, if the world were to end—with or without his help—he preferred to be on the right side of things. So, he'd complied, may God have mercy on his soul.

An older woman entered the room, and his wife handed their son to her. "Thank you, Cosette. Please take Charles below." She smoothed the wrinkles from her cream linen trousers and struggled to compose herself.

As the nanny passed the politician, she paused so he may greet his son. He placed a hand on the toddler's red, swollen cheek. "Alright there, my boy?" he asked. The toddler merely hiccupped in response. The man placed a kiss on the boy's forehead and nodded for the nanny to continue downstairs.

A broad-shouldered guard appeared at the top of the staircase. "Sir, your things are stored below, and we've done a final inventory."

"Very good." The politician held a hand out to his wife.

"Shall we, my dear?"

She squared her shoulders and took his outstretched hand. "If we must."

They descended the shag-carpet-covered steps into the basement, where a large steel door stood ajar. Bright halogen light poured through the opening. The twelve-bedroom underground bunker stood in stark contrast to the humble cabin above. The subterranean complex was as lavish as it was secure. It had all been part of the deal. The man would incite a conflict between Britain and the Middle East, and he'd receive his son–safe and unharmed–a secure place to ride out a nuclear winter, and a seat at the table when the dust settled.

Once the family and their servants made themselves comfortable, the dignitary nodded for his assistant to close the bunker. The young man pushed the steel door shut and pressed "lock" on an electronic panel. The metal bolts inside the thick door frame slid into place.

The screen turned red, and a five-second timer unexpectantly appeared. It ticked down steadily. The assistant turned to the group, brows knitting in confusion. "Sir…"

Five. Four. Three. Two. One.

White blinding light filled the bunker mere moments before the explosion. The politician's final words were, "Those bastards."

Chapter 2

Kirie

3 weeks earlier

woke to my face plastered to a cold bus window. The world beyond was dark, though I couldn't guess the hour. Stretching, I shook off yet another ugly vision. This one featured a ruined downtown city with an orange-tinted sky. Crowds of people covered in blood and dirt were bowing to a massive wall of shadows. Their fear and desperation stank of sweat and copper. I rubbed my arms, trying to wipe off the terror-filled scene, but it clung to my skin like a stain.

"Bad dream?" Luca asked, leaning his shoulder into mine.

I soaked in his warmth. I still couldn't believe he was sitting right next to me, holding my hand like it was something precious. Just a few days ago, I was convinced he hated me.

Now I felt something quite different coming from him through our newfound connection, a connection that shouldn't exist—hadn't existed in the history of The Society of Light, as far as anyone knew. It was impossible to process all that had happened in the past several days. Arin was dead. Diako was a traitor. Luca loved me. A mixture of conflicting emotions—fear, grief, joy, and excitement filled my chest like an overfilled balloon ready to explode.

I looked up into his gem-green eyes and nodded. He knew it was much more than just a dream. Since we'd left the Iranian mine, the dark energy known as The Void had continued its assault on both our minds, adding yet another layer of exhaustion to our already depleted bodies.

As we travelled across Europe, Luca and I made sure to take only small buses and trains, keeping our hoods up and faces down to avoid the occasional security cameras along our route. Just as Finn instructed. We'd only been on this particular bus for a few hours, and I was ready to swear off public transportation for life. The seats were torture devices for my lower back, and the pungent smell of the lavatory one row back burned my nostrils. Sadly, flying commercial wasn't an option. Airports meant flight records and government oversight. So, it was public transportation all the way to London.

Staying in hotels was also out of the question. Instead, we slept on the trains and buses whenever we could. My neck hurt constantly from sleeping upright, and my hair was thick with grease since we hadn't bathed in days. Luca and I kept one eye on the road and one over our shoulders—a necessary precaution since we were running from not only The Order, but The Society of Light as well. It was a crappy way to backpack through Europe.

An old woman sitting across the aisle shot me a side-eyed

glance. Though no visible shadows clung to the woman's skin, my heart raced. We were being hunted, and everyone was a potential Shadowman. I pulled my black hood over my head, sinking deeper into the cracked vinyl seat. Nudging Luca with my elbow, I nodded at the woman. Luca turned and glared at her, positioning himself so that his broad shoulders shielded me from the maybe-shadow. The old woman recoiled from his glare, turning her face to the dark window without another glance.

"What do you think?" I motioned to the woman. Again, she seemed so normal and unassuming, but I'd been fooled too many times before by average faces and placid expressions to take anything for granted.

"We'll get off at the next stop," Luca turned and whispered. "Just to be safe."

An hour later, we stood on the side of the road, clouds of our breath obscuring the bus's red taillights as it faded from view. Luca took hold of my hand and I sighed with relief. The woman hadn't followed us off the bus. False alarm.

I looked around, trying to get my bearings. We were standing along a rural road in a small French town, still hundreds of miles away from Finn's safe house. Gravel crunched beneath our shoes as we trudged toward the nearest train station, our bodies sore and travel-worn. Our next stop was the Channel Tunnel, and then on to the UK.

The closer we got to London, the quieter Luca became. I supposed it made sense. It was where he lived with Donovan, forced to do inhumane things for ten years in a twisted effort to turn him dark. It was clear that Luca still bore the shadows from that period of his life. Sometimes I could even see them clinging to his skin. So I stayed close to his side, hoping my presence would keep the darkness at bay. I looked up at him again and bit my lip. It didn't seem to be working.

The rest of our trip was uneventful, and we were both relieved when we finally made it across the channel, past London's city limits, and into the British countryside. That was until we arrived at the address Finn had given us.

I expected the safe house to be a small country cottage. Instead, we stood in front of a Tudor-style gatehouse that looked as though it had been ripped from the pages of a children's fairytale book. It sat at the end of a long, gravel lane lined by mature trees that presumably led to our final destination.

I looked around for another house along the road, sure we were lost, but there were none. What kind of house had its own gatehouse?

"Are you sure we're in the right place?" I asked.

Luca took the folded paper out of his pocket and reread it. He shrugged and said, "This is it."

Luca interlaced his sweat-slicked fingers with mine, and we began trekking up the long country lane, my travel-weary feet screaming with each step. I stared in wonder at the rolling green lawns that stretched out on either side of us. It looked like the set of the opening credits of some regency romance movie—beautiful in an unrealistic and untouchable way.

It was nearly April, and spring had arrived in England. The air had lost a bit of its sting, and tiny green blades of grass were pushing their way through the thawing ground, delicately nudging winter aside. Something tight loosened in my chest at the thought.

When the house finally came into view, my breath caught in my throat. Luca and I stood side by side, staring up at Finn's "safe house." Instead of the covert cottage I'd envisioned, we faced a massive three-story mansion. Like many of the historic buildings we'd seen passing through London, the cream-colored stone exterior was stained by rain and age. Half a dozen towers topped each corner of the enormous complex. I gaped at the sheer volume of the place. It was more than a mansion; it was a palace.

I turned to Luca in question. "Finn's safe house is a castle?"

Luca, still staring at the edifice, shook his head. "This is mental."

"Totally crazy," I agreed.

I turned my focus back to the palatial structure, surprised someone as understated as Finn would pick something so large and conspicuous for his safe house. I supposed that was the brilliance of it. No one would guess from the outside that it was anything other than an old country estate, large and ridiculous as it may be.

Luca sighed in resignation. "Come on. Let's go inside. I'd kill for a bath." I didn't protest as he pulled me toward the entrance. Heaven knew we both needed to bathe.

We walked beneath the arched doorway to a tall wooden door. I stepped forward and took hold of the stamped metal handle. Locked.

"It's about time you showed up," a wizened voice said from behind, causing me to nearly jump out of my skin.

Luca and I swung around, hands raised and lit—a knee-jerk reaction from being constantly on guard and on the run. A woman in her late seventies rounded the corner of the massive building. She wore a raincoat, rubber boots, and a pageboy hat atop her white hair.

"Now, now. I'll have none of that." She swatted our hands away as she walked past us to the front door. I glanced at Luca, brows raised. The older woman hadn't even flinched at our illuminated palms. Cool as a cucumber, she pulled a key from her pocket and unlocked the massive front door. It groaned plaintively as she pushed it open. I edged closer to Luca whose eyes were affixed to the strange woman.

She turned back to us and huffed. "Well, don't just stand there. Come in."

Luca lifted a shining palm once more, aiming his intense light at the woman. "We're not going anywhere until you tell us who you are and what you're doing here," he demanded.

"Fine." She huffed again. "Name's Nora Walker, and I work for Mr. Bellamy. Now, put that hand down, Mr. Durant," she scolded.

Startled, I stared up at Luca, searching for a sign of recognition. Instead, confusion flared through our bond. Luca honestly didn't know the tiny woman before us. Still, he lowered his hand at her stern expression like a cowed schoolboy. "How do you know my name?"

"Mr. Bellamy told me to expect you, of course. Did I not just say I work for him?" She sniffed and waved us toward the entry once more. "Now, come on in. Mr. Bellamy will be glad you made it here safely."

Nora led us into a spacious foyer decorated with marble busts and gold gilded furniture. We followed her up a flight of red carpeted stairs to a set of arched glass doors. Nora pushed them open and led us into an extravagant two-story room. Soft sunlight filtered in through a coffered glass ceiling. In the middle of the room sat twin red couches framing a grand fireplace. The second floor was lined by arches exposing the hallway above. It was as though we'd been transported back to the Middle Ages.

"This is the Grand Hall," Nora stated, waving a hand half-heartedly at the space as if it were nothing special.

Luca began to wander about the room. I followed, careful

to never turn my back to Nora as I took in the art and antiques. Finn hadn't mentioned an employee. To be fair, he didn't have much time to do anything but give us the address and shove us out the door. Still, how did we know she wasn't a Shadow luring us in? She could be anyone.

"What do you do for Finn, exactly?" I asked, casually examining an oversized painting of a group of patrons praying to the Pope.

"*Mr. Bellamy* and I have known each other for many a year." She emphasized Finn's last name as if chastising me for being informal. I could have told her that Finn was my father, and I'd call him whatever the hell I wanted, but I thought it was wise to hold my tongue. She continued, "He bought the estate several months ago with the intent to restore it to its former glory, a great feat to be sure."

I took in the Grand Hall. Subtle evidence of a restoration was everywhere. A drop cloth lay on the floor in the corner, and a ladder was propped against a half-painted wall.

"Why would Mr. Bellamy want to restore a castle? Was he planning to live here?" Luca asked.

"That's Mr. Bellamy's business, now, isn't it?" she said, shrugging. "And it's a family estate, not a castle. This is Mentmore Towers. The Rothschilds built this residence back in the late nineteenth century." I looked at her in surprise. The house looked at least several hundred years old with its high towers and Gothic style.

"I would have guessed Elizabethan Era," Luca said.

"Yes, well I believe the family preferred seventeenth-century architecture to that of their day. Pretentious bastards." She lifted a haughty chin.

"I think it's beautiful," I said with a shrug. Sure, the style was old and stuffy, but the Rothschilds had obviously spared no expense when building their home. Antique furniture, vases, tapestries, gold chandeliers, all of it was extravagant. The home was a museum of sorts, and I couldn't help but appreciate the craftsmanship.

"Ha! This pile of shite?" Nora scoffed. She looked up at the walls in contempt. "The old bitty is determined to remain in disrepair no matter what I do. Fix one thing, and another thing breaks. It's a never-ending project. Don't know why Mr. Bellamy bothers." She folded her arms tightly over her rounded waist and sniffed.

My eyes traveled around the room again, and I had to admit the old woman had a fair point. Despite the obvious work and repairs, paint still peeled from the crown moldings and tiny cracks spread across the newly painted walls like spider webs. It was as if the house was protesting its owners' desertion by falling apart. If this house could talk, I imagined it would likely sound a little like Nora.

Nora clapped her hands. "Enough talk. Come, I'll show you to your rooms."

Luca and I obeyed Nora's command like good little soldiers and followed her out of the Grand Hall. There was something endearing about the old woman's snarky attitude. Perhaps it was the pure honesty in her lack of refinement. I had the sense that Nora would tell you exactly what she thought at any given moment. The Society was nothing if not full of secrets and false faces. Hell, even my mother had hidden things from me. Nora's apparent transparency was refreshing.

She led us up a marble staircase. Framed paintings of British monarchs lined the walls. In grand fashion, it branched into two staircases after the first landing. I trailed my fingers along the handrail, which was made from some kind of green stone, cold to the touch. Clearly, the owners really *had* spared no expense. Restoring a home this grandiose must cost a fortune. What was Finn thinking of taking on a restoration project like this when war was imminent?

We followed Nora down a tall hallway. One side was lined by wainscoting and art set in gold frames. The other side was lined by intricately designed archways that looked down on the Grand Hall. Though the ceilings were tall, and the staircases grand, the upstairs hallway felt dark and closed in. I imagined it was what walking through a medieval castle must have felt like.

Nora stopped in front of a tall wooden door. "This is your room, Ms. Sorenson. The shared bathroom is at the end of the hallway." I followed her into the room, and she gestured to a tall wardrobe along the internal wall. "Mr. Bellamy asked that I buy a few necessities before you arrived. I didn't know your size, so I did my best. I'm going into town tomorrow morning. Just write up a list and I'll make sure to get the things you need."

"Thank you," I said, folding my arms over my stomach. How long would we need to hide out in this place? I couldn't imagine living here long-term. The palace-like building hardly felt like a home, and my appreciation for the art would only stretch so far.

"Mr. Durant, if you'll follow me, your room is a few doors down, away from Ms. Sorenson's. Mr. Bellamy's orders, of course."

I stifled a groan as Luca dutifully followed the old housekeeper to his room. Finn was still trying his hand at parenting, it seemed. My temporary bedroom was newly renovated, and paint fumes still hung in the air. A queen-sized four-poster bed, an antique I guessed, sat in the center of the room, surrounded by matching end tables. The original windows remained, framed by white drapes. Simple elegance and understated wealth. It was the only thing Finn-like in the entire building.

Black-and-white photos lined the bedroom walls. I stood in front of one of them and studied it. It was a picture of the Grand Hall filled with men in military uniforms. Bags and boxes in varying shapes and sizes lay in heaps around the room.

"Knock, knock." I heard from the doorway. I turned to see Nora poking her head in and offered her a weak smile. My feet and back ached, and all I wanted to do was take a hot shower and fall into that giant bed.

"I'll be downstairs if you need anything. Dinner will be served at seven." With a nod, she began shutting the door.

"Wait, Nora. What's this picture of?" I asked, pointing to the old photo.

Nora shuffled in and leaned in. "Ah, yes," she said, tapping the pane of glass with a gnarled finger. "During World War II, it was common for the military to use country estates like Mentmore Towers to house troops and protect priceless art and furniture from Buckingham Palace from harm. Perhaps it will do the same in the next world war."

"Next world war?" I asked, brows raised.

"I imagine that's what we're headed for. The final battle between the forces of Darkness and the forces of Light is nigh. It will be a war unlike the world has ever seen."

I looked down, my tears stinging my eyes as the images The Void had forced upon me surfaced in my mind. If The Void's grotesque visions were any indication of the future, humanity would not survive *this* world war.

"I'll leave you to freshen up before dinner," Nora said with a sniff. "Lord knows you need it, girl."

I pulled my hair around my shoulders, suddenly embarrassed by my dirty clothes and greasy hair roots. "Sorry. We didn't have time to clean up on the way."

"I expected not." Nora nodded and stepped back. "Dinner will be at seven sharp. Don't be late." With that command, Nora shuffled into the hallway and shut the door.

I stood in the center of the room, uncertain what to do with myself. It was the first time I'd been alone since Arin showed up at my apartment in Rome. The silence pressed uncomfortably against my ears. It felt like years had passed instead of days. Time had ceased to exist down in that horror-filled mine, and the loss of time made me uneasy.

I patted my back pocket for my cell phone, intending to look at the date, only to remember that Luca and I hadn't brought our phones with us. We had to remain off grid so both The Society and The Order couldn't trace us. Obviously, that meant no Internet, no communication with the outside world, and no leaving this creepy, over-sized house. I'd never been addicted to my phone, but not having a connection to the outside world felt isolating. I was used to being separate from my peers. At school, I'd been too strange. In training, I'd been too old. Despite a lifetime of isolation, however, I'd at least been able to find connection through the Internet. I thought of Parisxxxi8, my online friend. Would we ever speak again? Would he survive what was coming?

Luca and I couldn't stay locked away from the world forever. Before long we'd lose our minds. There was a war brewing out there, and prepared or not, I knew Luca and I were destined to play a part in its outcome. We couldn't hide from it even if we wanted to.

With a sigh, I pulled a pair of light blue pajamas from the antique wardrobe and headed down the hall to the small, shared bathroom to wash the several days off my dirty skin.

Chapter 3

Kirie

**fter** Luca and I had scrubbed the bus and subway grime from our bodies, Nora called us down for dinner with an authoritarianism that rivaled Bert's. It almost made me miss the sadist. Almost.

Nora informed us that the formal dining room was in disrepair, so we'd be eating in the kitchen for the foreseeable future. It was tucked away from the owner's side of the home, a space intended for the help, not the wealthy owners or their friends. Unlike modern American kitchens, this one was a small, uninspiring space with industrial-sized appliances and utilitarian cabinets. The room was clearly not intended for guests with its old wooden table and mismatched chairs.

"Here we are. Toad-in-the-hole," Noar said, placing a

square casserole dish in the center of the table. *Toad in a what?* Luca laughed and squeezed my knee when I gave the dish a skeptical look. I'd assumed British food would be different from what I was used to, but toads?

Nora cut into the suspicious dish and set a square onto our plates. I sighed a breath of relief when it turned out toad-in-the-hole was just sausages baked in pancake batter—no amphibians in sight. Nora then piled a heap of pickled veggies on our plates, and I crinkled my nose at the sour-smelling side dish. I already missed the simple Italian food I'd grown accustomed to.

I wondered what my younger classmates were up to. It was the first time I'd missed training since I joined The Society of Light. My absence couldn't have gone unnoticed. Had Daiko already told everyone Luca and I were traitors? Did my classmates believe him? Did they even care or had they simply moved on with their training? I couldn't blame them if they did. I was always the latecomer, their "plus one."

The next morning, Nora took us on a tour of the rest of the house. I learned there was an owner's wing and a servants' wing. The two sides of the home couldn't be more dissimilar. No expense had been spared on owner's side, though many of the rooms and their furnishings were in a state of decay. Entering the servants' quarters was like walking into a different universe. There were no chandeliers, open staircases, or wide hallways in this section of the estate.

I could almost see the ghosts of the servants dashing to and fro, carrying linens and dishes with harried, flushed faces as they rushed to do their employers' bidding. My heart ached for the disparity of the classes. What more could this wealthy family have done for their community with their ample resources? Instead, they built fancy mansions, caring little for those in their employ. But how different was The Society of Light, really? The secret organization fought Darkness in all its forms, true, but their combined wealth and influence had the power to ease suffering and end hunger on a global scale. Instead, The Society focused on dismantling their enemy, The Order. Were the Shadowmen simply their enemy, or were they also their *competition*?

Nora led us back to the owner's side of the estate and down a short hallway lined with two-story windows. We stopped in front of a pair of tall wooden doors. "This is the ballroom. It was a conservatory until the owners converted it into an event space in the 1880s. You'll find it serves a much different purpose these days," Nora said with a smirk. She shouldered open one of the heavy doors and stepped aside, raising an arm for us to continue through.

I'd imagined the typical ballroom I'd seen in movies with gleaming wood floors, tall windows, and oversized chandeliers. It was all of that, but much more. One side of the room was set up like the training facilities at The Centers of Light in both Paris and Rome, complete with training mats, targets, and signature wall of weapons. Finn had an impressive array of armaments, including knives, guns, and longswords that Liang would salivate over.

But that wasn't the surprising part. On the far side of the ballroom sat a giant metal cage. The metal grid stretched from floor to ceiling, forming a perfect rectangle. Mouth agape, I approached it slowly and peered through gaps to the interior. There was a line of desks covered by computer screens and various low and high-tech devices. It looked like something straight out of a spy movie.

"I recognize this," I said, running my hand across the cold metal grid. "It's a Faraday Cage."

Luca stood beside me and curled his fingers through the cage. His mouth lifted in a sardonic grin. "I still can't decide if Mr. Bellamy is a genius or just incredibly paranoid." Luca found the door and walked inside. He circled the makeshift room, taking stock. "Computers, landlines, satellite phones. There's even a generator in here. Dear old dad is prepared for everything, isn't he?"

I rolled my eyes at the dad comment, still uncomfortable with the title. I skirted the outside of the cage and nearly stumbled on a line of thick black cords running across the back side of the desk. "Looks like everything's been hardwired."

I followed Luca into the cage, instantly uneasy with the cell-like space. I quickly turned and checked the door for a lock. My shoulder muscles loosened a bit when I saw it closed with a simple latch.

The phone on the desk rang and I jumped, letting out a high-pitched squeak. Luca raised his brows at me and picked up the phone.

"Hello? Yes, she's right here." He held the phone out to me. I eyed it suspiciously. "It's okay," Luca insisted. "It's Mr. Bellamy."

"Oh, okay." I put the plastic receiver to my ear.

"Are you safe?" No hi, how are you? Finn needed to chill.

I looked around and snorted. "Of course, I'm safe. I'm standing in your super-secret Faraday cage in your super-secret castle."

That provoked a laugh. "What can I say? I have a thing for saving old buildings. Is Mr. Durant still nearby? I need to speak to both of you."

"Yeah, hold on." I searched the phone base and found the speaker button. Pressing it, I set the receiver on the desk. "Go ahead."

Finn wasted no time getting to business. "I've been looking into the intel on the computer you procured in D.C., Luca. I was able to find something interesting in the emails stored there."

I knew very little about the mission Luca was assigned to just before Iran. Everything happened so fast; the whole thing felt like a fever dream. From what I'd gathered, Luca had extracted intel that pointed to a uranium mine in the Middle Eastern country. It was the impetus for our disastrous non-sanctioned mission. I briefly wondered if Arin would still be alive if Luca had never recovered that hard drive.

"The anonymous sender targeted nearly every influential politician, CEO, and dignitary across the globe," Finn continued. "Each recipient was blackmailed into performing seemingly small, yet traitorous acts against their respective nation. On their own, these favors appear inconsequential, but when I looked at them as a whole, a pattern began to form. It appears that The Order is working to destabilize relations between the global nations."

Luca leaned forward. "To what end? Incite another world war?"

"Precisely," Finn replied.

My stomach twisted at the implications. Tensions between the nations were already dangerously high. Russia was at war with Ukraine. China was threatening to reclaim Taiwan. Israel was in combat with its neighbors, and the USA was in the middle of it all. If the Shadowmen were able to stoke that fire, World War Three was bound to follow.

I thought of The Void's plans to eradicate all energy and light from the universe. What better way to destroy life on Earth than to let us destroy ourselves? It was what we did best, after all. The Society wasn't just fighting dark energy; it was fighting human nature. For the first time since learning of the War Scroll doomsday prophecy and the battle between Light and Darkness, I wondered if the prophecy got it wrong and it was Light, not Darkness, that was destined to lose the seventh and final war in the end.

"Did you find any clues as to a timeline?" Luca asked, pulling me from my dark thoughts.

Finn let out a tired sigh. "Not an exact date, but I'll keep looking. The answer is within these files, I'm sure of it."

Luca shifted in his seat. "Sir, before you go, I must ask. How is Alena?"

I felt a stab of deep concern flare through our connection. Luca was scared for his friend. His anxiety was understandable. We'd run away from the Rome Center of Light so soon after we arrived, it was impossible to know how Alena was handling the trauma of her adoptive brother's death. None of us had had time to process what had happened.

Finn paused before answering. "Ah, yes. I meant to speak with you about that. The healers have tended to Alena's minor injuries, but she's struggling with Arin's death." It was a kind way to say Alena was messed up.

Luca's face tightened with worry. It was clear he still cared for Alena, but I no longer felt the sting of jealousy that used to accompany thoughts of the two of them. She was the only family Luca had left. If their relationship was important to him, it was important to me. Besides, I felt no romantic emotions interlaced with his concern for my former roommate.

Luca's hands knitted tightly together. "And Arin's sister?"

"Arabella has been evaluated, interviewed, and is now staying in Rome with the other children from Kirie's training group. Alena is unwilling to leave Arabella's side, so she's been helping run the daily training sessions. She's driving Bert crazy," he explained with a laugh.

I couldn't help but smile. I would pay good money to see Bert and Alena go head-to-head. "So my classmates are doing okay, then?"

Finn hummed in agreement. "Bert is keeping them busy, but they're feeling antsy like the rest of us. Little Aonani would try to take on The Order single-handedly if we'd let her. *She's driving her mother crazy.*"

I laughed out loud at the mental image that created. Aonani really *would* try to defeat the Shadowmen on her own. She was the most courageous person I had ever met. I missed her.

Finn cleared his throat, and his tone turned serious. "On the subject of Alena, I don't believe it's wise for her to stay with The Society, given her connection to you. I worry she's no longer safe in our ranks. So I decided to send her your way."

My stomach soured. True, I was no longer jealous of the girl, but Alena and I were to be roommates again? I was suddenly grateful Finn had chosen such a spacious building for his safe house. The more distance between Alena and me, the better. Here, she had plenty of square footage to be messy far away from me. A smile crept up my mouth when I thought of Nora's likely reaction to Alena's chaos.

"Alena's not safe? What are you worried about?" Luca asked.

"There's been some talk of a disciplinary hearing," Finn explained.

"But Alena didn't do anything wrong!" Luca growled. His skin began to glow.

Finn sighed. "I agree, but I worry Daiko will want to make an example out of her."

I put my hands up. "Hold on. Could someone please explain what a disciplinary hearing is?"

Luca's hands curled into fists, and he spoke through gritted teeth. "A disciplinary hearing is a court held to determine if an Agent of Light has acted against the interest of The Society. If found guilty, an agent can be disavowed and sent out into the world to fend for themselves. It's a death sentence, and it's barbaric."

I couldn't imagine Alena and Arabella living in the world on their own without any protection from The Society of Light. They'd be exposed to the Shadowmen that hunted them. Children of Light stood out. How long would they last before a shadow ended up at their door? It *was* a death sentence.

"Things are quickly changing within The Society. I fear no one will be safe within our ranks for much longer. The climax of this endless battle is quickly approaching. Rationality and fairness won't play a part in this war. You need to keep that in mind in the coming days," Finn warned.

We sat in silence, acid churning in my stomach. His heavy words felt like a doomsday prophecy.

Finn finally broke the silence. "Don't leave the estate. I'll call you with further instructions in the next few days. Be ready to go at a moment's notice."

"We will," Luca agreed.

Nora was ready with a list of renovation chores the moment we hung up with Finn, working us to the bone until evening. Dinner was yet another lesson on traditional British cuisine. The Yorkshire pudding and over-salted collard greens sat heavily in my gut when I finally fell into bed. I tossed and turned well into the night. Thoughts of Alena being put on trial and ousted by her own people made me sick. Where would she go? What would she do when all she knew was The Society of Light?

By 2 a.m., I gave up on sleep. I threw my blankets off and

went to the bathroom. Walking on the balls of my feet, I peered over the railing to the medieval room below. The full moon cast an eerie red glow into the space. It could easily be a set from a horror movie. I quickened my pace. As I passed Luca's door on my way back to bed, I heard him whisper my name. My heart jammed into my throat, and I nearly jumped out of my skin.

Hand to my heaving chest, I peered into his room. Luca's window was open, and the soft moonlight bathed his room in its celestial light. I found him propped up on one elbow in his queen-sized bed. Our eyes met, and he lifted the corner of his blanket—an invitation. I hesitated, my feet glued to the floor. I'd never been in bed with a boy before. Though it felt like ages ago, it'd only been a few days since we confessed our feelings to each other. Before that, I was sure Luca was either disgusted or indifferent to me. He raised an eyebrow, and my heart rate spiked. If I could take on a dozen Shadows, I could lie next to the beautiful boy I loved. My feet felt like concrete blocks as I forced myself to the side of the giant bed.

The corner of Luca's perfectly kissable lips lifted on one side. "I promise to be a perfect gentleman," he said in his posh British accent.

I took a deep breath and slowly slid in beside him. In one swift movement, Luca curled his arm around my torso and pulled my back against his chest. The moment our bodies touched, I felt my skin warm. Soft light radiated from both our bodies.

"We're like glow worms." I giggled like a moronic schoolgirl.

Luca laughed, too, and I felt the low vibration of it in my chest, making me shiver.

"Well, this might make sleeping a bit more difficult," he

said, nodding to the bright room. He pulled the comforter up until only our faces were showing, tamping down most of our light. "There, that's better."

His warm breath caressed the sensitive skin on the back of my neck. I sank into his dips and valleys. Somehow, his body was both hard and soft, like a sun-warmed statue. One of Luca's arms lay curled around my waist while my head rested on the other. I smiled. So this was the "spooning" I'd heard so much about. Without a doubt, it was my new favorite thing to do.

Luca's lips touched the bare skin beneath my ear, and a rush of heat pooled low in my belly. Perhaps there *were* better things to do with our bodies than spooning after all. My pale cheeks burned at the direction my thoughts had suddenly taken. I covered them with my hands, grateful Luca couldn't see my face.

"Sleep, my love," Luca whispered into my skin.

Though I wanted to stay up all night living in this perfect moment, I was worn to the bone. My heavy eyes closed and I drifted off to sleep, bathed in Luca's warmth.

We run,
We run,
We cannot stand these shadows!
Give us the sun.

We are not made
For shade,
For heavy shade,
And narrow space of stifling air
That these white things have made.
We run,
Oh, God,
We run!
We must break through these shadows,
We must find the sun.

"Shadows" by Langston Hughes

Chapter 4

Luca

Luca shot up in bed, a high-pitched scream still echoing in his head. Sweat covered his brow, and his heart raced. The filthy London streets slowly faded from his mind, and his half-painted room in Mentmore Towers came into view. It was still the wee hours of the morning, and the house was silent and dark. Luca glanced down at Kirie, still lying next to him, and released a breath, grateful he hadn't woken her with his distress.

Kirie lay on her side, her long hair splayed across the pillow like spilled ink. Even in sleep, he could see the light clinging to her skin. She stole his breath. Kirie was likely the most powerful Agent of Light The Society had ever seen, and yet she bore her gifts with such meekness. She wasn't stained from past sins the way Luca was. He knew he was selfish for wanting her. Selfish for reaching out to her with his soiled hands. Yet he couldn't help the constant pull he felt to her. Fighting their bond was as futile as fighting gravity.

Luca had never heard of a similar connection between two Children of Light. He both loved and hated it. Not because he didn't want to be close to her–he craved her skin, her lips, the warmth of her light every minute of every day to the point that it bordered on obsession. No, he hated it because Kirie didn't ask to be tied to a man like him. Though she'd seen her share of darkness in recent months, Kirie wasn't dark herself–not like Luca. She deserved a man free of ghosts and shadows.

Luca peeked at the antique clock on the wall that ticked loudly in an otherwise silent room. 5:28 a.m. He knew from experience he wouldn't fall back asleep. Needing to clear his head, he slipped out of bed, sneaking down the grand staircase and through the side door. As he stood at the top of the long stone staircase leading to the lawn below, Luca watched the sun peak over the horizon. Mist covered much of the countryside beyond, curling around trees and creeping over hedges. He could smell the early spring flowers and fresh grass, feel the damp air on his skin. Luca used to love the early morning British mist that always clung to the earth, thought it was classically romantic even; now the sight reminded him of the shadows creeping up inside him.

He felt Nora's presence before he heard her. She stood next to him and pulled her floral morning coat tightly around her rounded middle. They stood in companionable silence for several long minutes.

"Couldn't sleep?" she asked.

He shook his head. His nightmares had gotten worse since the battle in the Iranian mine. It was as though the torture and Arin's death had destroyed the tenuous control he once had over his own mind. The ghosts from his past were set free to wreak havoc on his thoughts and dreams. He knew Kirie felt his disquiet, but he couldn't put the pain and anxiety into words for her. He feared his ghosts would become more real simply by naming them.

Nora laid a hand on Luca's forearm. "I know about your past, young Luca, and I know what it's doing to you."

Luca's shoulders tightened, and he looked down at the old woman. "What do you know?" He hadn't meant to be rude, but the nightmare had left him feeling raw and irritable.

She peered at him through age-heavy lids. "I see the shadows clinging to your form. They're growing, are they not?"

Luca turned back to face the creeping mist and let out a frustrated sigh. "I'm trying to force them back, but it gets more difficult every day. I fear I'm losing my mind." He looked down at the housekeeper, surprised at his candidness with this virtual stranger. He'd only ever shared his fears of his eventual descent into insanity with Abbott on Recovery Island, the tiny piece of land that lay between the Atlantic and Caribbean Sea where he'd learned to control his shadows.

Luca expected Nora to reassure him that he wasn't losing his mind like Abbott had in those early days. Instead, she grabbed his hand and pulled him away from the house. Though her thin, wrinkled skin was soft beneath his, her grip was surprisingly firm.

"Come," she said in a tone that demanded obedience.

Giving in, Luca allowed her to lead him down the long stone staircase to a gravel pathway that had been newly laid in the yard. It circled the wide grass-covered grounds, leaving an open space in the center.

"This used to be a grand garden, you know, before the

estate fell into ruin. It was as splendid as it was ostentatious." The woman continued to pull Luca along, their feet crunching in the loose gravel. "Mr. Bellamy wants to restore the estate to its former glory, but I think a more natural garden would be best, don't you agree, Mr. Durant?"

"Yes, ma'am," Luca said dutifully, not sure where the woman was heading, either physically or verbally. They walked in silence for several minutes.

"I was an Agent of Light, too, once upon a time," she finally said.

Luca's mouth fell open, and he looked down in surprise at the tiny woman. She clicked her tongue and slapped his forearm. "Don't look so shocked. I was a brilliant agent, and I'll thank you to remember it," she said with a sniff.

Heat crept up his neck, embarrassed by his rudeness. He hadn't meant to react so openly—another sign that he was losing control of his emotions. "I'm sure you were. I meant no disrespect."

She snorted. "Relax, my boy. I'm just winding you up. I'm too old to be offended."

Luca smiled. Despite his initial misgivings, he was warming to the old woman. It was hard not to like her straightforward, brassy personality.

Nora continued, "I understand internal shadows. We all have them."

Luca shook his head. "Not like mine. Some days I fear I'm made of more shadows than light."

The woman looked to the sky and sighed heavily. "God give me strength. The young are so self-centered." She turned her gaze to Luca and pointed a nubby finger at his chest. "You're not the only one who has battled darkness, Luca Durant."

Feeling as though he'd just been chastised by the headmistress, Luca ducked his head in shame. "No, of course not…"

"I was assigned to the conflict in Vietnam back in the late sixties," she said, cutting him off. "The Society hoped we could help end the war by bringing light and peace to the area. As if men could be placated so easily," she said with disgust.

Luca understood her ire. Like most wars, the Vietnam War left a dark stain on humanity's story. It was a twenty-year conflict with no real winners and no moral high ground. Those who had fought in the battle often carried physical and emotional scars long after the war was over. He couldn't imagine the horrors Nora had endured there. "That must have been very difficult," Luca said, trying to infuse sincerity in his words to avoid sounding trite.

The woman nodded. "That it was. I saw things–terrible things–and they've haunted me ever since." She stopped and pressed a palm to Luca's chest. "Our experiences are imprinted onto our bodies. But you cannot move forward and do what needs to be done until you confront your past."

"You don't understand. You can at least comfort yourself with the fact that you were on the side of Light during your trials. I can't say the same."

"Good Lord, boy. No living soul is spotless. Even the brightest Agents have regrets."

"But I've done terrible things–things that can't be undone," Luca said, his eyes burning from unshed tears.

Nora leveled him with a knowing gaze. "No, they cannot."

Luca searched the older woman's face, hoping the answer to his ever-growing problem was written in the folds of her wrinkled skin. "How do I live through it?"

"By *walking* through it."

Luca let out a huff. It was just another platitude from a well-meaning elder. He'd been trying to move through life with his guilt and ghosts, and it had gotten him nowhere. "It's not that simple."

Nora leveled him with a glare. "I don't mean let it pass. I mean you must *walk* through your trauma in a literal sense."

Luca scoffed. "Walking? How does walking help anything but my health?"

Nora took his arm in her firm grip and shook it. "I'm not talking about exercise, you daft boy. You must walk alongside your trauma and guilt rather than stuffing them down. It's about exposure and acceptance. These feelings aren't going away. Your ghosts are a part of you now."

Luca blinked, startled by the woman's words. How did she know about his ghosts? Could she see them as well?

"My ghosts?" he said in a strangled voice.

"Selfish, daft boy," she repeated. "Do you think you're the only one who has them? I know a haunted man when I see one. Stop fighting them, and they will stop fighting you. You must confront your fears. You must *live* inside your guilt." She reached up and pushed his shoulder. "Now walk."

Luca, not knowing what else to do, took a tentative step along the gravel path. Then another. The housekeeper didn't follow.

Luca felt foolish as he walked along the circular path while the Nora silently watched. Perhaps he wasn't the only one who was losing his mind. He wanted to leave the path and hide from the crazy old crone. What could strolling in the English countryside do to combat the evil he had done? It was a colossal waste of time. Still, she watched him with a stern face.

So…he walked.

Luca felt like a clown the first few laps. As he circled the path for a third time, an apparition appeared in his peripheral vision. Chills ran up his spine. Luca's gaze remained fixed forward, instantly recognizing the energy of the ghost that walked alongside him. It was the five-year-old girl Donovan had forced him to kill all those years ago—his first kill. Donovan had unwittingly resurrected her ghost when he'd released his demons down in the mine. She'd been one of his constant companions as the Shadowmen had tortured Kirie and him. Since then, she'd starred in many of his nightmares.

She was his greatest sin—and his greatest fear.

Her presence stung him, and he desperately wanted to lock the memory of her away again in the dark recesses of his mind as he'd done for over a decade. But the housekeeper had commanded that he walk through it, whatever the bloody hell that meant. So, Luca took a deep breath and pushed forward, the soles of his shoes sinking into the thick gravel path.

Luca and the girl walked in silence for a time. As the sun began to rise and burn the mist from the ground, the little ghost gazed up at him. It was the same inquisitive look she'd given him when he'd come upon her on that London street. She'd been so innocent, so curious as he'd advanced on her. Luca had never forgotten the lack of fear on her face moments before he delivered the killing blow. The very memory of it brought Luca to his knees.

"I'm s-sorry," he sobbed. Sharp pebbles dug into his knees as he tugged at his hair and screamed. "I'm sorry!" Luca curled into himself. It felt as though his body was tearing itself apart, molecule by molecule. The pain was destroying him. How could a body survive so much guilt and shame?

He pleaded with the tiny ghost for forgiveness, but she simply watched him unravel with those curious eyes. There wasn't a speck of accusation in her innocent expression, which made it only worse. He wished she'd yell at him, condemn him. But she stayed silent, ethereal in her ghostly calm.

"Walk through it," Nora called. He looked up and found her standing at the top of the staircase, staring at him with a focused gaze that seemed to demand that Luca continue this insane exercise. Luca obeyed, pulling himself to his feet and shuffling forward. He continued to walk alongside the girl's ghost for what felt like hours, quietly sobbing. Slowly, the pain began to lessen somehow. The tightness in his chest abated, and his breathing regulated.

Luca finally stopped at the base of the long staircase leading up to the house and took a deep breath. Nora stared down at him and nodded. "That'll do."

Before ascending, Luca looked for the ghost and found her gone. He still felt her presence within him—perhaps he always would—but the pain had lessened. Luca accepted the part he played in the girl's death. He'd walked through the guilt rather than locking it away. Luca didn't understand how, but walking through his pain and guilt *had* helped. The crazy old girl was right.

The next day at dawn, Luca found himself on the misty path again. This time, a man appeared next to him. In life, he'd been a former Agent of Light. He was in his late fifties and retired from the field. Although he'd posed no real risk to The Order, Donovan thought Luca required practice. So he'd forced Luca to end his life, insisting he use knives that time, a dirty job that left Luca covered elbow-deep in blood. His skin itched just thinking about it. Taking a deep breath, Luca began walking the path with the man at his side.

"I'm sorry for what I did to you," Luca said. The ghost silently walked alongside him. "I imagine you had a family. They must miss you dearly. I'm sorry for that, too." The man turned and looked at him then, a light sparking in his vacant eyes. Though he didn't speak, Luca could feel the ghost's grief at the mention of his family. Luca felt it as keenly as if it were his own.

Tears ran down his cheeks, and Luca's knees nearly buckled under the guilt. With all his might, he straightened his spine and walked on, wearing a track along the pathway. Killer and victim trudged through their shared pain as the sun burned off the fog.

Chapter 5

Kirie

stood at the tall window that looked down on the lawn, my nails digging into the newly painted trim. My chest was tight as I watched Luca walk. He'd been at it for two days, waking me at dawn with his fear and grief. The acidic taste of his guilt and shame was sharp on my tongue as I lay in bed, listening to him toss and turn until he could stand it no more.

He'd been out there for over an hour already, and my arms ached to hold him. I turned to go to him and ran into Nora instead. I jumped back, my heart in my throat at her sudden appearance.

"You just turn yourself back around, little miss. I know what you're about, but there's no use going out there," the housekeeper said, peering out the window at Luca. "This is a path he must walk alone."

I wrapped my arms around my chest. "But he's in pain. I just want to be there for him."

Nora clicked her tongue and shook her head in disapproval. "You young girls are always wanting to fix the broken ones. It's natural, I suppose. But your love, as powerful as it might be, is not enough to heal the wounds in *that* boy's soul. You must give him space to fix himself."

Though her blunt words stung, I knew she was right. I wasn't quite delusional enough to think I could fix a decade of PTSD and survivor's guilt with a hug and some comforting words, but the instinct to go to him, to ease his pain in any way I could, was nearly overwhelming.

"How can I just stand here and watch him fall apart?" I asked, my throat thick with unshed tears..

"By trusting your young man to deal with his own business. He's stronger than you give him credit for." Nora patted my arm and began walking back down the hallway. "Come now"– she called over her shoulder–"you have a call."

My heart rate spiked as I hurried after Nora down the staircase to the ballroom. We hadn't heard from Finn since we first arrived at the Mentmore Towers, and I was anxious for news of any kind. The phone receiver was sitting on the desk when we entered the Faraday cage. "Shouldn't we get Luca?" I asked.

Nora pointed at the receiver. "Go on and take the call, girl, and I'll fetch your boy." The tiny woman had a way of making me feel like a misbehaving child.

"Yes, ma'am." I nodded dutifully and put the receiver to my ear. "Hello."

"How are things going over there?" Finn asked.

I sank into the metal chair and nearly groaned. My muscles

ached from all the scraping and painting Nora had us doing. "Your warden has us working day and night on this drafty old house for you."

There was a fondness in Finn's laugh. "That woman could lead an army. I fear I'm wasting her talents."

I snorted. "You should put her in charge of the new recruits. She'll have them ready for war before they're out of diapers." My eyes followed Luca as he passed by the tall windows to the side door, and my heart did a little flip.

I cleared my throat and focused on Finn. "What's going on over there? Are you still in Rome?"

"Officially, I'm in the States taking care of a few issues. Unofficially, I'm in a secure location tracking Mr. Daiko and gathering intel." His voice sounded worn and thin.

My brows pinched. "You doing okay? You sound tired." I couldn't imagine the pressure it took to not only run the most powerful organization in the world, but also save it from his co-leader's efforts to sell it out to our enemies. Like Luca and me, Finn was alone in this mess.

"Thank you for asking. I'm fine," he said, putting on an artificially bright tone.

I rolled my eyes. "Liar." He grunted but didn't defend himself.

The cage's metal hinges squeaked as Luca pushed through the ballroom doors. Through our connection, I could feel a lightness about him. Whatever darkness had been weighing him down, though not completely gone, had lessened during his morning walk. I didn't understand what Nora had Luca doing out on that path each morning, but it seemed to be working. I could kiss the woman for that.

I sat up straighter in the cold metal chair. "Luca's here."

"Good. Put me on speaker."

I pushed the speaker button on the phone's bulky plastic base. "It's Finn," I whispered. Luca pressed a kiss to my temple and slid into the chair next to mine.

"Good morning, sir," Luca said.

"Mr. Durant," he replied, all business again. "I was able to extract Alena and Arin's little sister. Travel arrangements have been made, and they'll be arriving today. Nora will pick them up in London and make sure no one is following them. It's more critical than ever that you all remain hidden. Do not venture out for any reason. Daiko's employing every resource to find you."

I leaned toward the receiver, brows pinched. "Won't bringing Alena and Arabella lead Daiko right to us?"

"I've laid a false lead. According to The Society, they're headed back to Canada for therapy. They're traveling in disguise so they won't be picked up on the cameras."

"Sir, have you spoken to Abbott?" Luca asked.

The last time I'd spoken to Abbott had been in the Rome Center of Light. I felt a twinge of guilt for not thinking of my old high school teacher. Had he been reprimanded for his part in the Iranian mission? My chest ached at the thought of him losing his position in The Society. Like most agents, he'd devoted his life to this work.

"I sent him on an assignment as far away from Daiko as I could manage. He should be safe for now."

Luca let out a breath of relief. "Thank you, sir. I appreciate it."

"Of course. Despite his recent lapse in judgment, Abbott is one of our finest recruiters. Now, on to business. I did another deep dive on those files you extracted in D.C., and I found something interesting. As you already know, The Order intends to start another world war. Given the missing uranium from Iran, it isn't hard to imagine what their end goal is."

"It's like our dreams," I whispered to Luca. He nodded grimly. During my time in the mine, The Void had shown us vivid visions of mass destruction–melting bodies, screaming children, charred and smoking cities. The room suddenly felt a few degrees cooler, sending shivers up my spine.

Finn continued, "As you might remember, there's a map in the files with red dots–targets, likely–that span the entire globe. We can assume they have enough uranium to create two hundred nuclear bombs, which lines up with the map we found. Clearly, they plan to bomb every major city on earth, which would force us into a nuclear winter."

"If we already have the map of the targets, can't we just use it to locate the bombs before they're detonated?" I asked.

Luca shook his head. "We only know which cities they plan to hit. We still don't know the exact location or the exact time the bombs will be placed. It's like trying to find hundreds of needles in a million haystacks."

"That's why we need more information," Finn broke in. "Thankfully, we may have an opportunity to find out what their plans are before it's too late. Which leads me to my new discovery. Deep within the files you retrieved, I found the word 'Bilderberg'."

Luca sucked in a breath. "Brilliant."

I turned to him, face scrunched in confusion. "What's a Bilderberg?"

"It's a meeting that's been held every year since 1954. Key world leaders from Europe and North America come together and discuss world issues," Luca explained. "The location of the meeting changes each year, as does the guest list. Society leaders and high-ranking agents have always been invited to attend."

Finn hummed in agreement. "Except this year, The Society leaders have somehow been left *off* the guest list. This is the first time we haven't been included."

I chewed on my thumbnail. Excluding leaders from the oldest and most powerful organization in the world for the first time felt like a declaration–a dangerous one. The Order was obviously preparing to make a big move. They'd successfully transported a massive amount of uranium out of Iran, and many of the nations were on the brink of war. Now, The Society of Light was being cut out of key world meetings? Things were moving quickly.

"This could be our chance to nail down a timeline. We need to get eyes and ears on that meeting," Luca said.

"Yes, we do," Finn agreed. "But it's not going to be easy."

"Why not?" I asked. "Doesn't The Society have, like, the most advanced spyware on earth?"

Though I didn't work in the tech department, I passed through the "war room" every day on my way to training. Giant screens lined that subterranean room from corner to ceiling, each displaying videos of every major city and beyond. It was the reason Luca and I couldn't go outside–they had eyes everywhere. Infiltrating a simple meeting didn't sound like a big challenge, given The Society's resources.

"It's not that simple," Finn said. "The Bilderberg Meetings are private and heavily guarded. No one who isn't on the list can get within a mile of the meeting location. They'll also employ anti-spyware, and cellphones will be banned. I suspect there will be Shadowmen present as well, given the context of the emails. If they even get a hint that an Agent of Light is nearby, they'll neutralize our tech."

"We don't have a choice," Luca reaffirmed. "You need to send in a team."

Finn sighed. "It's a bit more complicated than that. The climate within The Society has changed drastically over the last few days. Mr. Daiko has convinced everyone that the two of you are acting as spies for The Order. Unfortunately, Arin's betrayal has also become common knowledge, and Daiko is using it as an opportunity to have every agent monitored."

Heat rose to my cheeks. "But Mr. Daiko is the mole, not us!" My hands balled into fists. He was so *infuriating*. I wanted to punch the smug little man square in his smug little face.

"That might be true, but I'm unable to find hard proof of his defection. He's hidden his tracks well."

"But I saw his memories. I know he planted that tracker on my jacket in Rome so the Shadowmen could attack me. People died that day. Can't you do something to expose him?"

"It's your word against Mr. Daiko's. I don't think I have to explain the complex power dynamics involved. You're an unknown to much of The Society of Light. No one will take your claim seriously." Finn said it kindly, but my temperature still began to rise.

My skin lit up. Luca put a cold hand on my arm, quenching my anger slightly.

Finn continued. "Mr. Daiko has every available agent searching for phantom moles to cover his tracks. If he gets wind that we're sending in a team, he'll alert his contacts in The Order, and we'll lose our advantage."

"So, send us," Luca blurted. I nearly rolled my eyes at his rash suggestion. Finn would never allow it.

"That's the idea, Mr. Durant."

I stared at the phone, mouth agape. Was he kidding? I expected Finn to shoot Luca's idea down immediately. The meeting was bound to be crawling with Shadowmen and guards. Wasn't the whole point of going into hiding to stay miles away from any threat? This was the exact opposite of staying out of sight.

"We can't do it alone. We'll need tech and backup," Luca said, seemingly unaware of my outrage.

"I have a few agents I can trust. They'll meet you at the location with the necessary equipment."

"Whoa, hold on," I said, hands up. They were both barreling ahead like a freight train off its tracks. "Where are we going exactly?"

"The meeting is being held at the Frederiksborg Castle in Denmark in three days, so we'll need to move quickly."

Was he serious? "How can we possibly be ready by then?"

"Let me worry about the details. Alena and Arabella should arrive in the next few hours. Alena will join the mission, of course, so you'll need to get her up to speed as soon as she arrives. Stay by the phone and wait for my call."

I heard a light click, and the phone went dead.

I sat back in my chair, head spinning. Three days. Denmark. Shadowmen and security everywhere. Had Finn lost his mind? I put my head in my hands. "This is insane. There's no way this is going to work."

"Come here." Luca pulled my chair toward his, and I leaned into his chest. My body shook. The weight of the past month came crashing down on me. Tears stung my eyes. It wasn't only the threat we faced taking on this new mission, but also the unresolved trauma of the past few weeks. Everything I'd endured–the river, the mine, Arin's death–I wasn't ready to head back into danger.

"All done, then?" Nora called from the doorway. I jumped back, my spine hitting the back of the metal seat. I turned my head away from Nora's stare and wiped back my tears.

"We've been given our marching orders," Luca

confirmed.

The old woman nodded. "Good. Now stop blubbering and follow me. I have work for you to do."

Chapter 6

Kirie

Nora was a hateful woman.

Before she left to pick up Alena and Arabella, she tasked Luca and me with preparing their rooms. Nora, in all her sadism, decided Alena was to sleep in the room directly across from mine, with Arabella in the room adjacent. Suddenly, Mentmore Towers didn't feel big enough.

"I'm not gonna lie, I'm not super excited to sleep this close to Alena. It didn't work out all that great for us the first time."

Luca lowered the sheet and laughed. "Arin and I were taking bets which one of you would throw the other over the balcony first." His smile dropped from his lips. Grief flared through our connection.

My chest ached for him. I quickly searched for a way to distract him from thoughts of Arin. "Oh, yeah? Which one did you bet on, me or Alena?"

The corner of Luca's lips lifted. "Alena, of course. She's scary as hell," he said with a little shiver. He wasn't wrong. The only thing scarier than Alena's mean jibes was her mess. My skin itched just thinking about the clothes, books, and dirty dishes she'd piled up all over our shared apartment. If we'd been roommates for much longer, one of us *would* have tossed the other off the balcony.

An idea formed in my mind as I smoothed the corner of the sheet under the mattress. The estate was *full* of rooms. If *Luca* took the room across from mine, he could act as a buffer between us. There was no reason Alena and I couldn't maintain a little space–for everyone's sake. And it wouldn't hurt knowing Luca was closer at night.

I peeked up as he tossed a pillow onto the freshly made bed. "Why don't *you* take this room? You're much cleaner than Alena. Plus, if we put her at the end of the hall, she and Arabella can be closer to the bathroom."

Luca tsked his tongue and shook his head. "Nora would not approve. She seems determined to keep us chaste." His mouth twitched like he was fighting a laugh.

I rolled my eyes. It was true. Nora had done her valiant best to insert herself between Luca and I. I had no doubt it was on orders from my "father," Finn. It was more than a little annoying that he was still trying to play dad from so far away. "What's she going to do, throw us out? She practically worships Finn. There's no way she'd go against his orders to keep us safely tucked away at Mentmore."

Luca shrugged. "Fine. But I'm telling her it was *your* idea."

I picked up the last pillow and threw it at his face. "Brat."

We quickly transferred Luca's things into the room across the hall, moving as if Nora would appear at any moment to stop us. I silently reminded myself at least a dozen times that the old lady wasn't the boss of me. The others arrived just moments after we finished setting up the rooms. Luca and I shared a look.

"We got this." I nodded.

He pointed a finger at my chest. "You mean *you've* got this. This was your idea, remember."

I followed Luca down the central staircase, preparing myself for Alena's trademark foul mood. Instead of the fiery Italian I was used to, Alena appeared subdued and windblown. Arabella held tightly to her hand. Despite the days she'd spent under The Society's care, Arin's little sister was still pale and hunched over, her blonde hair hanging limply over her thin shoulders. We stood in awkward silence in the center of the Grand Hall as the newcomers silently took in the worn down, opulent estate. The grandfather clock ticked loudly in the background.

Alena was the first to break the silence. "Why is Finn's safe house a castle?" Nora snorted, and everyone thawed at once.

"That's what I said!" I exclaimed, my shoulders loosening.

Alena turned in a circle, frowning at the offensive building. "It's ridiculous."

"She's a nasty one, isn't she?" Nora huffed.

Alena turned to Luca with a worn smile. "Good to see you're not dead," she said.

"I'm happy to see you, too," Luca said with a half-smile. He pulled Alena into a hug, which she fiercely returned.

Nora made a show of lifting one of Alena's bags as if it weighed a ton. "Yes, yes. Everyone's alive and well. Now, come on you two." Nora nodded to Alena and Arabella. "Let's get you settled. You're both dead on your feet." She pointed at the three other bags, raising her eyebrows at us. Luca and I quickly stepped forward and dutifully grabbed the remaining luggage.

"She's not the boss of me. She's not the boss of me. She's not the boss of me," I chanted quietly under my breath as Luca and I lugged the heavy bags. He snorted in response.

We walked single file up the grand marble staircase to the residential wing. Luca stayed at the back of the group, clearly leaving me to announce the room change all on my own. I glared back at him and mouthed, "Coward."

Nora, Alena, and Arabella stood near the first door on the left, across from mine. "Here we are. One of you will stay in this room. Kirie's room is across the way."

I straightened my shoulders and reminded myself that I was an Agent of Light, trained for battle by the best instructor in The Society. And *Nora was not the boss of me.* "Actually, Luca's staying there now. We prepared the rooms near the bathroom." Turning my back on Nora, I led Alena and Arabella to the end of the hall. I felt the heat of Nora's glare on the back of my neck.

I first led them into the room on the left and set their bags on the wooden floor. Luca quickly dropped his load and ran out the door. I glared at his retreating back. Stupid coward. Nora waited for me in the hallway. She set her hands on her girthy hips and levelled me with her grittiest glare. "What are you about, girl? I told you to prepare the room across from yours."

Alena poked her head out of the room. "Actually, if it's okay, I prefer to be closer to the bathroom. And we don't need two rooms. Ari will sleep next to me. She has nightmares," Alena explained.

I watched Nora from the corner of my eye, expecting a fierce rebuttal. Instead, she pursed her lips and nodded. "Fine. Do what you like. I'm no one's mother." With one last glare, she retreated down the hall. Alena shot me a wink before helping Arabella unpack. I hid my smile behind my hand, feeling optimistic for the first time in days.

That night, I woke with a start. My heart was racing, and dread and adrenaline coursed through my veins. Moonlight seeped through the white drapes, casting the room in a celestial glow. I clutched a hand to my chest and tried to breathe. Something wasn't right. Sitting up in bed, I searched the darkness for hidden dangers. I expected a Shadowman to materialize from the dark corners, but nothing stirred in the night. Yet, the warning in my chest remained.

I realized the anxiety and fear weren't mine, but Luca's projected through our connection. I sprang from bed and padded across to Luca's room, heart pumping. I placed my hand on his door handle, and the door creaked open. Waning moonlight filtered in through the open drapes, highlighting his form on the bed.

He let out a low groan and his head moved back and forth, as if he was in pain. I rushed to the bed and shook his shoulder. "Luca," I whispered. "Luca!" I repeated, shaking him harder. No response.

Heart in my throat, I slid beneath the sheets beside him. He jerked in his sleep, but didn't wake. He seemed to be trapped in his own mind. I reached for the unseen tether connecting us, hoping to find the source of his distress. When I found it, there seemed was a shadow wrapped around it. My stomach sank. I recognized that particular tone of Darkness.

The Void.

Luca was stuck in a vision—or whatever the hell it was when The Void took over our minds. There was no fighting his control over us. He was noncorporeal, eternal, everywhere. Older than the sun, The Void was space and Darkness itself. Just like my shadow, there was no hiding from its invasive presence.

I wrapped my arms around Luca's rigid frame and pressed my forehead to his. His skin was cold and clammy. I closed my eyes and projected warmth and safety. My body began to glow as I held him tighter. Several minutes passed before Luca's muscles relaxed beneath my arms. I let out a sigh of relief. I slowly released him and moved to the edge of the bed, intent on returning to my room. Heaven forbid Nora find me in here and call my dad.

Luca sat up in bed suddenly, and I gasped out loud as he pulled me back into his chest. "Stay," he whispered into my hair. Luca's chin brushed against my neck. He'd stopped shaving since we left Rome, and his rough stubble scratched against my tender skin.

I sank back into the mattress, and Luca pulled me against him, wrapping his arms around my waist.

"What did you see this time?" I whispered in the dark.

"Same as before." Luca paused. "But different somehow."

"Yeah," I agreed. "They *do* feel different."

Though The Void had continued to show us the same scenes of destruction and devastation, the *tenor* of the visions had changed. They felt less like a threat, and more like a promise. The Void had also stopped demanding Luca's and my participation in destroying The Society of Light like he had in Iran. I was worried about what that might mean. If it no longer needed us to undermine The Society in its war against The Order, someone else must have offered to do that job in our stead. And I had a pretty good guess who that person was.

"It's like it's—I don't know—showing off, or something," I whispered. "Like it knows it's going to win."

Luca's biceps tightened around my middle. "It's the same for me." he sighed. "Tell me something good."

I turned my head, looking at him from the corner of my eye. "Like what?"

"Let's see." He hummed. "How were the past few months in Rome? Did you like the city?"

"I don't know, actually. Bert had me working day and night trying to catch me up with the others. If it weren't for my classmates, I would have gone insane."

Luca snuggled deeper into me, burying his face in my hair. "God, I love your hair. Tell me about your classmates, then," he requested, his voice muffled.

I smiled, thinking of my younger classmates. I missed them. Perhaps Eden less than the others. "Well, Dayton and Liang are preteens who love to drive Bert *nuts*. They're absolute rascals."

Luca chuckled. "I would love to see them test Bert. He's an ass."

"He really is." I agreed. "Then there's Dawn. You'd really like her. She's the calmest person I've ever met. Eden is a boy-crazy teen with an attitude. And Aonani is a little fireball with curls—my favorite of course."

We talked through the darkest hours. Luca laughed at my stories of Dayton's and Liang's antics and the pranks they'd play on Eden. In turn, Luca told me about all the places he'd visited. I ate it all up, having only travelled in the past several months to Paris, Rome, and Iran. Even then, I'd only seen the inside of a training room and a dusty old mine.

"I've never been to the ocean," I confessed. It had always been on my bucket list. Though I'd now flown over two seas and travelled beneath the English Channel, I'd never stood on the shore, never felt sand between my toes.

This seemed to piss Luca off. He rose up on his forearm and glared down at me. "Everyone," he'd proclaimed, "has a God-given right to visit the sea."

I laughed at his indignation. "Maybe someday." I leaned up and kissed the tip of his nose. Luca's smile slid from his lips, and we fell silent, likely both thinking of The Void's vision and our uncertain future. If The Order wasn't stopped, I'd never get the chance to visit the sea.

"Do you want to hear about the time Dayton pantsed Liang during training?" I asked, determined not to let thoughts of The Void ruin this moment.

Luca snorted and tucked himself back behind me. "Please. I can't wait to hear the story."

We finally fell asleep around three a.m., wrapped in the warmth of each other's stories.

Luca woke at dawn and slipped out of bed for his morning walk. I attempted to go back to sleep, but I couldn't seem to block Luca's stormy emotions as he confronted the darkness inside him along the garden path. Again, I tamped down my instinct to run after him and comfort him, though just barely. Nora was right; Luca had to face his demons on his own.

I tossed and turned until my stomach growled. With a sigh, I rubbed my sandy eyes and slipped out of bed, hoping to scrounge up an early morning snack before Nora got up for the day. I tiptoed on cold hardwood down the central staircase. The Grand Hall was lit with early dawn light as I passed, the red tint making the little hairs on my arms stand on end. I quickened my pace. A tall grandfather clock ticked loudly in the silence.

A light shone from the kitchen. I peered around the corner and saw Alena making a sandwich. I stood in the doorway, remembering a different kitchen in a different city. Things had changed so much in the months since we'd shared a flat in Paris. It felt as though the whole world had turned upside down. The Paris Center of Light was a crater in the ground, and Arin was dead.

"Stop lurking," Alena said without turning around.

I jumped. "Sorry. I didn't want to bother you." Heat climbed up my neck.

Alena turned and leaned against the counter with a plate in her hand. "So you thought you'd just watch me from the darkness instead?" She raised one perfect brow.

"Well, when you put it that way." With tentative steps, I entered the kitchen. "I was, um, just going to grab a snack."

Alena shrugged. "Go for it." She sat her plate on the table and sank into an antique wooden chair.

I crossed the kitchen and opened the giant industrial fridge. Nora must have picked up groceries on the way to retrieve Alena and Arabella, because it was full of meats, cheeses, and veggies. I began making a mini charcuterie plate, side-eyeing Alena as she quietly ate her sandwich.

"Couldn't sleep?" I asked, hoping to alleviate the awkward silence.

Alena shrugged and offered no explanation. I didn't push. She seemed different—more subdued. Though I didn't appreciate her brand of fire, it was unsettling to see that it had diminished since Iran. An unexpected wave of empathy washed over me. Unfortunately, I could imagine the grief Alena was experiencing. I remembered the dark days after my own parents were murdered in front of me. In those first few weeks, I'd been stuck at the bottom of a deep hole, a place where time didn't exist, only a cold, sharp pain.

Arin's death had likely hit her the hardest. They were siblings in every way that mattered. It had been fun to watch Arin pester Alena like a brother, like it was his favorite pastime. And she gave it right back. Despite their bickering, Arin's love for Alena was obvious, as was hers for him. Now that he was gone, Alena, Luca, and I belonged to an exclusive club no one ever wanted to be inducted into. The grief club.

I tentatively sat across the table from Alena, not sure whether she still actively despised me. Her dislike for me had been an instant thing, though I could never quite identify a point of origin for her ire. I supposed she hated me simply for existing in her space. I thought back on what she'd shared about her troubled childhood. In a world full of Shadowmen, Alena's formative years had been plagued by shadows of a different kind. Instead of shielding her like mine had, Alena's mother fed her to that darkness for money. Luca, Arin, and Abbott had clearly become her safe space, and I supposed I was nothing more than an unwelcome interloper.

I nibbled on a salty strip of prosciutto in silence. I didn't want to be at odds with Alena. She was important to Luca; therefore, she was important to me. I just didn't know how to cross the gulf between us. I popped a piece of swiss cheese in my mouth, unable to fully appreciate its sweet and nutty flavor in the uncomfortable silence. My chewing sounded absurdly loud to my own ears. Finally, Alena spoke.

"I keep thinking he's going to walk through the door one day. I still hear his voice down the hall, see his face in every crowd." Tears spilled from her tawny eyes as she curled in on herself, a queen deflated. "I don't know how to live without him."

It was painful to watch her in such a diminished state. The Alena I knew had always been so intimidating–gorgeous, larger than life, and scary as hell. But right then, she was just a fragile thing. Without thinking, I reached out and took one of her hands in mine. I expected her to throw me off. Instead, she held onto me as though I was an anchor in a hurricane. I felt her grief merge with my own, and together we cried, tears stinging our cheeks, until the sunlight peeked through the high kitchen windows."

Luca cleared his throat. "Should I call the police or an ambulance?"

"Neither. Join us." Alena extended a hand to the chair across from her. Luca slid into it.

"What was it like growing up with Arin?" I asked, needing to understand him better.

"Luca was always so serious dand in control, so Arin took the role of annoying little brother," Alena explained.

"He was always playing tricks on us," Luca joined in. "He used to drive us all crazy!"

We spent the rest of the morning crying, eating, and telling stories about Arin. Not even Nora, with her chores, dared to ruin the moment of grief and healing.

Chapter 7

Luca

The next morning, as Luca traversed the fog-covered path, Nora went to town, returning by noon with a van full to the brim of household supplies and dry-packed food. She promptly stomped through the front door, demanding that the four of them "earn their keep" by unpacking it all for her. The woman was an absolute tyrant. Still, Luca supposed helping around the house was better than waiting for The Order to make its move.

"I feel like we're preparing for the end of the world," Kirie grunted as she hauled a rather large package of toilet paper to a spare room off the kitchen.

Nora turned and glared at her. "Of course we are, you daft girl. Where did you think this was headed?"

Kirie's shoulders dropped. "It just seems like it's all happening so fast. I guess I just thought we'd have more time."

"There's no room to be naive, girl. You're an Agent of Light," Nora chided.

Luca wanted to tell the old woman to sod off, but he'd already dealt with his shadows that day—no use waking them again. Not every mind went straight to the worst-case scenario. Kirie was still a new agent and had an optimistic worldview. It was one of the things Luca loved most about her. Her hope made him believe that not *everything* was rimmed in darkness, that light could still prevail.

Nora went back to town twice more that day and again the next. Soon, they had enough provisions to feed a village for a month. Knowing what The Order had planned, Luca worried it wouldn't be enough by half. A nuclear war would lead to nuclear winter, which would lead to dead crops and a halt in food production. In that scenario, their stockpile seemed massively inadequate.

Arabella, travel-weary and generally untrusting, insisted on working alongside Alena each day. Nora put the two in charge of scraping the peeling paint off the baseboards in the office. They obeyed without complaint, which surprised Luca as he'd never known Alena to do anything without complaint. He hardly knew this new Alena. Luca worried that something essential in her had died with Arin in that mine.

After a long day of chores, they met in the library situated just behind the Grand Hall. The air reeked of a nauseating mixture of fresh paint and mold. Leather-clad books lined the shelves of the floor-to-ceiling bookcases that framed a marble fireplace. Above the bulky mantle hung a portrait of a pantaloon-wearing noble. Luca glared at it. It was offensive to the eye. Finn should have burned it the moment he took possession of the estate.

More than any other room in that bloody house, the library whispered of a bygone age obsessed with royalty and fine breeding. A time when proud men in tailored suits stood around that very fireplace smoking cigars and congratulating each other on their brilliance and worldly influence. Luca flared his nose at the tableau that image created. He struggled to understand why Finn chose to renovate such a pretentious building.

The man in question had at least had the foresight to install a closed-circuit television on the library wall. It only received four local channels, but it was better than sitting in the drafty silence of the Grand Hall. The medieval-themed room, though built with impressive workmanship, felt menacing, particularly in the afternoons when the sunlight cast a reddish glow on the dusty space. It reminded Luca of Hell, and he found himself avoiding the room more and more each day.

Luca lounged on a nineteenth-century sofa that was made for sitting at a ninety-degree angle only. The upholstery's friendly flower design belied its torturous nature. Luca stuffed a small throw pillow behind his back to relieve the stabbing pain growing there.

Alena sat on the couch next to him with her little shadow just feet away in a nearby armchair. Exhausted from the day's work, they sat in silence as the news correspondent droned on about the escalating tensions between Russia and the United

States. No surprise there. Tensions were high across the globe generally. Exhausted and sore from hours of housework, Luca tried to tune it out.

Kirie sat tucked in an armchair opposite Arabella's, reading an anatomy textbook that she'd managed to find on the library's shelves. Luca watched her turn a page, distracted by her mouth as she chewed on her bottom lip. He had a sudden desire to kiss that mouth. Then, he'd like to throw her over his shoulder and take her from this drab and drafty mansion and straight to a jet. Hidden away either by her mother or The Society, Kirie had seen so little of the world. She'd never felt the freedom of travel or the ocean's salty breeze on her skin. A light as bright as hers wasn't meant to be hidden. He hated the darkness for managing to do it anyway.

Luca's hands tightened into fists as he imagined the deaths of every Shadow that dared touch her down in that Iranian mine. Luca could still hear the echoes of Kirie's screams as they tortured her. He had plans for Ciara, especially. It was her fault Kirie had lost faith in Luca in the first place. If only he hadn't met Donovan in the Catacombs. If only he'd kept his damned phone in his pocket. They could have been together for months. He had plans for Donovan in the end, too. Luca's inner shadows swirled in excitement. They loved his darker thoughts, especially when he dreamed of violence. It was a drug to them. He shook his head and sat up straighter. *One must not give in to dark thoughts.* Another one of Abbott's lessons.

Alena shifted on the couch and let out a grunt of discomfort. He felt her pain...literally. Nearly every piece of furniture in that bloody house was uncomfortable. If money could buy anything, why hadn't the wealthy owners bought thicker cushions? Luca missed his couch back at the Paris apartment before his life had been blown to bits. God, he was being a melancholy brat.

Breaking news flashed across the screen in big red letters. China, Iran, India, and Russia had called an emergency meeting to address escalating tensions in the South Pacific. "The president of the United States," the reporter said in a serious tone, "has labeled this meeting 'a major threat to world peace,' and has moved to DEFCON 3."

Kirie closed her book and sat forward. "I don't understand why The Order is going to all the trouble of forcing the world into another war. If they have that much sway over the nations' leaders, why not just demand control over everyone's nuclear weapons? What's the point of enriching stolen uranium when there are already thousands of nukes in the world?"

Luca's mind spun in circles. He worried The Void didn't intend for anyone to survive, including its disciples, the Shadowmen. But didn't that make The Order's actions all the more nonsensical? If the end goal was simply to destroy all life, why not cut to the chase? Why all the pageantry of a world war?

"Actually, Kirie has a point," Alena grunted in frustration. "If they're just going to incite a nuclear war between the USA, Russia, and China, whyyyyyy do they need their own bombs?" Alena pointed a finger angrily at the TV screen. "Seems like we're fully capable of destroying the world without the addition of several hundred nukes."

Why indeed? Luca thought of the War Scroll, the prophetic script detailing the seven battles between the Children of Light and the Children of Darkness. Essentially, each conflict lasted approximately one thousand years. The Children of Light had already won three. The Darkness won just as many. According to the prophesy, the final and current battle between the opposing forces would determine the fate of the overall war.

After six long battles against light and life, The Void must have realized that mankind's instinct to survive was too strong. Even when the Darkness won a battle, it failed to accomplish The Void's main goal–the complete eradication of all life on Earth. Even the Shadowmen wanted to live.

"Perhaps The Order knew they could convince the diplomats to give up state secrets, but not their nations' nuclear codes," Luca said with a shrug.

Perhaps The Void needed assurances this time around. By promising the Shadowmen and corrupt leaders a dark earthly heaven where tyranny and depravity reigned, it ensured their willing cooperation in their own demise. Forcing the world into a nuclear war must be a fail-safe in case The Shadowmen chickened out. In the end, no matter how powerful The Void was, it had no real power over the Earth. The only power it had was the power mankind freely gave it.

This was just an elaborate play, one put on by The Void. Our world was simply its stage, and we its players.

"I'm bored with this nonsense." Alena sighed heavily, flinging a hand out at the TV screen. Luca smiled. Only she could make major world events sound dull.

Alena stood and walked to a black baby grand piano at the far corner of the room that looked to have been abandoned by its owners several decades ago. She sat on the creaky wooden bench and placed her fingers on the ivory keys, striking a discordant chord. Alena's lips turned down. "Out of tune," she said in her pouty Italian accent.

Pushing off the wooden bench, she lifted the instrument's curved lid, and her torso disappeared over the piano's edge, presumably to tune the instrument. Like all Agents of Light, his adopted sister had many hidden talents.

Arabella stood and pulled her armchair closer to the piano, so she could stay within sight of Alena as she worked. Arabella hadn't strayed more than a few steps from Alena since they'd extracted her from that hellish Iranian mine. Strangely, Alena didn't appear to mind, though she'd never particularly tolerated the company of other females before. Come to think of it, Luca hadn't known her to like anyone but Abbott, Arin, and him, and only on her good days. Luca supposed Alena had a good reason to hate people. Unlike the rest of their kind, it wasn't the Shadowmen who had hurt her.

Luca turned his attention back to the news. A Russian spy ship had approached British waters earlier that day, tracked by a Royal Navy ship. Obviously, they were mapping something, likely their underwater cables. When the reporter transitioned into a fluff piece about dog breeds, Luca turned his attention back to Arabella. She was a strange, gangly creature. Her long arms and legs promised her brother's height, though she'd likely never achieve his girth. Arin had been the biggest bloke Luca had ever known. She also didn't carry his light.

Arabella made him uncomfortable, all big-eyed and malnourished. Though she was clearly young and guileless, a tint of darkness clung to her hunched shoulders. It was an eerily familiar sight–like looking at his ten-year-old self in the mirror. He imagined this was what Abbott saw when he rescued Luca from The Order. Though Arabella hadn't done the horrible things Luca had, she'd clearly been traumatized by her time with the Shadowmen. Her eyes were haunted. In that way, they were the same. It made his skin itch uncomfortably to be near her.

Despite the discomfort he felt around the girl, it appeared that taking care of Arabella smoothed Alena's rough edges—humanized her somehow. For that, he was grateful. He'd put up with the girl's presence for Alena.

As if sensing the weight of his stare, Arabella turned to Luca, her gaze direct and emotionless—as always. She stood and wordlessly joined Luca on the long couch, thankfully maintaining a wide distance. Still, Luca shifted uncomfortably.

"Was my brother a bad man?" Arabella asked.

Luca started, surprised by the girl's clear, strong voice. He struggled to find an answer to her blunt question, but the words wouldn't form in his mind. Arin's betrayal was a fresh wound, and the pain of his recent death obscured any hope of rational thought. He understood his brother's motivations on a basic level, but the decision to turn on him and Kirie, to hand them over for slaughter, cut deep. He would have given his life for his brother a hundred times over. He wanted to scream at Arin for not coming to him for help. They would have figured it out together. Perhaps then he would still be alive. Now, all he could do was yell at his ghost.

Luca studied the little girl beside him. Arin had chosen to save her over everyone else. He supposed it made some sense, as she was the last member of his family. Luca had been orphaned at such a young age, so he didn't remember what it was like to have a family. Apparently, blood ran deeper than his love for his adopted siblings.

She was so frail despite the days of nourishment, and Luca supposed anyone would want to protect something so fragile and vulnerable. How could they not? It was human nature. Still, there had to be a better way, hadn't there? His thoughts were a whirlwind.

Luca cleared his throat and attempted a diplomatic answer. "Your brother was one of the finest men I've ever known."

Arabella scrunched her face. "But he gave you over to The Order."

A sharp pain twisted in Luca's chest. He swallowed hard. "True. Arin did a bad thing when he betrayed The Society of Light. But he did it to save your life." He looked to the corner of the room where Kirie, sensing his distress, sent love and comfort through their bond. Luca soaked in her warmth and turned back to the strange girl with the questions.

Arabella pursed her pale lips. "So, you don't hate him?"

Luca ran a hand down his face and sighed. "No, I don't hate him. We were like brothers. We loved each other."

"Perhaps that's why he's dead," the little girl said without emotion.

Luca sat up straighter, her words striking a nerve. "What did you say?"

"The Order says that love is a weakness. They say people who love are easy to kill."

Luca's heart rate tripled. Those were the *very words* Donovan would say when Luca was in his "care" all those years ago. He couldn't remember how many times Donovan had taught him that lesson. Luca's skin turned cold as the shadows inside him swirled in joy and agitation.

"Arin saved your life," he snapped. "His love did *you* some good, didn't it?"

Alena retreated from the inner belly of the grand piano and glared at Luca. "Luca, be nice," she warned. He glared back. She had to know he was right.

Arabella simply stared at Luca, seemingly unaffected by his rebuff. On some level, Luca understood her callous words and indifferent attitude. The little girl had never been in the light. She'd never experienced anything but fear, hatred, and sorrow. Again, Luca thought back on his younger self. He'd be very much the same after his time with Donovan. It wasn't until Abbott had shown him love that he was able to comprehend the complex emotion. Even now, Luca struggled to convert love into healthy relationships. Still, Arin had died so that the girl could live. The least she could do was pretend to be grateful.

"Look, The Order lies. You'll do well to forget everything they told you."

Unable to look at the girl a moment longer, Luca stood and walked out the door. Kirie caught up with him as he strode through the Grand Hall.

"Hey, hold up." She placed a hand on his arm. Like always, a shock zipped through him at her touch. The hair on his arms stood at attention like little soldiers. Luca could live a million years and never get bored with her electricity. "Are you okay?" she asked.

"Fine," Luca said with a shrug. How could he explain the pain and confusion that being near Arabella caused without sounding like a total ass?

"Luca," she sighed. "There's no use lying to me. I can feel your emotions, remember?" Kirie looked up at him with those giant blue eyes, and the swirling shadows inside him dissipated.

Luca took her face in his hands. "Sorry. I just needed a moment."

Kirie wrapped her arms around his waist and tilted her chin to meet his gaze. Luca had never seen eyes so blue. They drew him in the moment their gazes met at her parents' funeral, and he'd never been the same since. They were the exact color of the Caribbean Ocean–a color she herself had never seen. Would never see thanks to The Order. It wasn't fair. Like Arin, Kirie deserved to have a future, one free of Shadowmen and fear.

Feeling reckless, a plan began to form in Luca's mind. This never-ending war between Light and Darkness, a war they hadn't even started, had stripped them of their future. Why not make the most of whatever time they had left? The Bilderberg Meeting was just days away, and their imposed banishment was about to come to an end. There may never be a better time to do something for themselves. Luca just needed a few days of preparation and a few favors to make it work.

Nora stepped into the Grand Hall. "There's a call for you in the ballroom." She sniffed.

"Yes, ma'am," Luca and Kirie said in unison.

Nora took Arabella to get ready for bed while Luca, Kirie, and Alena made their way to the faraday cage. The receiver lay on its side on the desk. Luca pressed the speaker button.

"Mr. Bellamy?" he began.

"Good evening, Mr. Durant. I assume Kirie is with you?"

"Yes. Alena, too."

Alena leaned toward the phone. "Thank you for arranging our transport, sir."

"Of course. I'm glad you made it safely," Finn said kindly. "Now, onto business. I've worked everything out on my end. You'll leave before dawn. I'll have a private jet waiting nearby to take you to Denmark. Pack only your tactical gear. You'll be in and out in under twenty-four hours."

Kirie turned to Luca, brows pinched, and anxious energy pressed against their connection. Luca put his hand on hers, transferring a bit of warm energy into her skin until her face relaxed. She smiled at him in gratitude.

"Will a tactical team meet us there?" Alena asked.

"Yes. A trusted agent will meet you at the airport and transport you to Frederiksborg Castle. The rest of the team will be waiting for you nearby."

"Thank you. We'll be ready," Luca assured him. He looked back at Kirie and Alena, and they nodded in agreement.

"Wonderful. Remember to keep a low profile and don't do anything stupid. I'd hate to lose another good agent."

The three of us let that harsh reminder hang in the air like poison.

Chapter 8

Kirie

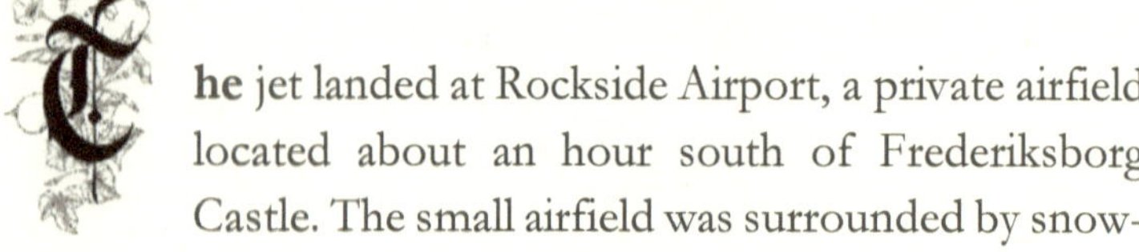

The jet landed at Rockside Airport, a private airfield located about an hour south of Frederiksborg Castle. The small airfield was surrounded by snow-capped mountains. Our pilot, a stoic middle-aged woman, assured us that we were safe to disembark. Though Finn's contacts had disabled the security cameras for our arrival, I couldn't help but feel exposed as we stepped off the plane, my eyes darting from hangar to hangar for hidden shadows.

A young woman dressed in a ninja turtle hoodie and oversized cargo pants met us on the empty runway. An old beanie covered her shoulder-length dark hair, and a chunk of blue peeked out of a tattered fabric. Was this the trusted agent

Finn was talking about? She looked more like a video gamer than a skilled agent who hunted Shadows for a living.

"I'm Zoeya. Tech specialist." She shook hands with each of us in turn with a strong, dry grip. Alena and Luca watched the girl closely, but Zoeya didn't seem to notice their tense postures and suspicious looks as she bounced happily ahead.

She led us to a beat-up 1970s Eurovan parked beside a metal hangar. "This is my van," she said, chest lifted in obvious pride. "Her name is Azizi."

The blue paint was rusty and peeling in places. If that were *my* van, I might keep that fact to myself. "That's an interesting name. What does it mean?" I asked, mostly for the sake of being polite.

"It's Arabic for 'my treasure'," she explained.

"Oh. Nice," I said, nodding. I hadn't known anyone to care enough about a vehicle to name it.

Zoeya threw open the back doors of the van with a flourish. "Welcome to my home," she announced, her face beaming with pride.

My jaw dropped. The interior of Zoeya's van was nothing like its faded exterior. The inner walls had been powder-coated black, and an L-shaped desk fitted with modern tech stretched along one wall. A long bench and a small kitchenette were built into the other side. The baby-blue velvet drapes covering the side and back windows were the only nod to the van's exterior. Everything else was new and state-of-the-art. I had to admit, the vintage facade was brilliant camouflage.

Alena leaned into the van, her nose wrinkling. "It's a bit cramped," she murmured.

Zoeya narrowed her eyes at Alena, her shoulders tensing. "Well, yeah, for a crowd, it is. But this is *my* space. I usually don't host visitors–especially the *rude* kind."

I hid a smile behind my hand and made a mental note not to insult Zoeya's van. The three of us climbed into the back. Luca put a hand on my lower back to help me in, and my skin heated at his touch. Zoeya drove an hour to the small town where Frederiksborg Castle was located. She parked "Azizi" in front of a small coffee shop and turned back to us with a wide smile. "Come on. The team's waiting inside."

We pulled our hoods over our heads before climbing out of the van. When we stepped into the warm shop, we were enveloped by the aroma of rich, nutty coffee and baked goods. My mouth watered. The flight from London had been long, and I was starving. Zoeya led us to a table where a group of strangers sat. They stood as we approached. A boy, slight and in his late teens, stepped forward and bowed low, his dark hair falling across his almond-shaped eyes. "Jomei," he said simply before stepping back.

"Sorry, Jo's not a talker." Zoeya sighed. "He's from Japan, and his job is to guard the east end of the perimeter—make sure the bad guys don't mess with my van."

Jomei swore in Japanese and pointed a finger at Zoeya. "I told you, my name's not 'Jo'. I'm not some Yankee boy. Use my real name!"

Zoeya reached over and ruffled his hair. He swung out at her, but she danced beyond his reach. "He's a bit prickly," she said with a cheeky grin.

Jomei's face turned red, and he sat back down, flashing her the middle finger.

An intimidating man with pierced ears and sleeve tattoos stepped forward next. "I'm Kiran," he said in a low, gravely voice. "I'm the trainer at The Center of Light in Mumbai." Kiran turned and pinned me with striking amber eyes set beneath a pair of thick, black brows. "You must be Kirie. Bert has told me all about you."

My eyes widened. "Oh dear. That can't be good." Embarrassment burned my cheeks at the thought of Bert complaining about me to his colleagues across the world. I could only imagine the things he said.

Kiran laughed. "All good things, I swear. It's an honor to finally meet you." Kiran shook my hand and stepped back.

An honor? He must be kidding. Bert did nothing but complain about my utter lack of skills every day for months. The idea that he said something *positive* about me was inconceivable.

"Kiran's on the southern perimeter. Anything goes wrong on the ground, he's our guy," Zoeya explained. I looked down at the long black duffle bag lying at his feet, likely full of long-range rifles–his way of dealing with problems on the ground, no doubt. Kiran caught me staring, and his mouth lifted in a confident grin.

A Middle Eastern man with a salt-and-pepper beard approached. "Name's Bodhi. I'm also on perimeter duty." His lips were set in a tight line. No smiles for that one. All three men were dressed in dark-wash jeans and black hoodies–the perfect outfit for blending in.

A tall woman in her mid-thirties joined the group, holding several pastries and a drink carrier with to-go cups. "This is Phoebe, our local agent," Zoeya explained.

Phoebe held out the food and drinks to the group with a smile. I grabbed a scone and cup of coffee, letting the warm liquid thaw my numb fingers. Despite her obvious kindness, the woman was physically imposing. She resembled a Viking with her high cheekbones, pale grey eyes, and braided ice-blonde hair.

"What do you do?" I asked.

"I'm in charge of comms," she explained with a thick Danish accent.

"Don't you monitor comms from your super van?" Alena asked Zoeya, motioning to the vehicle outside.

"Nope. We'll be using a closed circuit that I set up around the castle's perimeter. Come on, I'll show you." Zoeya nodded at the door, and we followed her out. She pointed to the tops of several businesses. Squinting, I spotted short metal antennas sticking up just past the rooflines. "Phoebe will make sure nothing disrupts our signal."

"My great opponents are usually squirrels and birds," Phoebe said with a wry grin.

Zoeya handed out tiny black earpieces to each member of the team. We slipped them into our ears as she did a sound check. Once we all confirmed they were working, Zoeya clapped her hands enthusiastically. "Great! Kirie, Alena, and Luca, you're with me in the van. Everyone else, to your posts. Let's get this show on the road!"

Kiran, Jomei, Phoebe, and Bodhi slipped away as we followed Zoeya to the back of her van. We parked several blocks from Frederiksborg Castle since security blocked off all streets leading to the stately building. Phoebe had set up long-range cameras and recorders just beyond their perimeter before we'd arrived, giving us a comprehensive view of the venue's exterior.

The four of us huddled in a van facing a line of high-definition monitors. The early spring air seeped into the van's interior, and I shivered. I burrowed deeper into my tactical jacket, noting that none of the others appeared to be affected by the chill.

"Security will be tighter than the devil's anus this year," Zoeya said, pointing to the screens. "And the guest list is—well, you'll see."

In the far left screen, a steady line of luxury sedans drove down the tree-lined lane at a leisurely pace. Early spring buds swayed in the cool breeze, and the soft white petals covered the gravel drive as if in ceremonial welcome to the esteemed guests. If I hadn't known better, I would have assumed we were watching the live feed of a royal wedding.

The lane opened to a sprawling lawn lined with manicured hedges. The palace had green framed windows set into white plaster walls and topped by a metal domed roof, patinated by age. It was serene, the gravel beneath the tires the only noise in the otherwise idyllic gardens.

"Did you know, Denmark's Frederiksborg Castle is known as the 'Palace of Peace.' Sounds like the perfect place to hold a secret meeting to end the world, am I right?" Zoeya laughed, amused by her own sarcasm. I shook my head. It *was* an ironic location for a doomsday meeting.

A brown rounded body crossed one of the screens, blocking the view of the palace lawn. An orange beak leaned down and began pecking the camera lens, the image vibrating wildly. Zoeya leaned forward and tapped the screen. "Move, you stupid duck!" she growled.

Alena folded her arms and snorted. "I don't think it can hear you," she quipped, her trademark mean-girl tone reemerging for the first time since Arin's death.

Zoeya turned and glared at her. "Hey! Be nice or get out of my van."

Unaccustomed to being called out for her rudeness, Alena's head jerked back, and her nostrils flared. She put her hands up in surrender. "I apologize." To my surprise, she sounded sincere. I refrained from giving Zoeya a high-five, but just barely.

The dignitaries and billionaires finally parked at the end of the long drive, and Zoeya clicked to the view of the front entrance. A contingent of uniformed footmen waited outside the front doors to greet the esteemed guests. Dozens of men and women spilled from their luxury sedans and SUVs into the courtyard. Luca turned to Zoeya. "Please tell me you have eyes on the inside."

She smirked and tapped a few buttons on her laptop. The far left screen flipped to a bird's-eye view of the gathering as if the camera were attached to the branch of a nearby tree. Zoeya then pulled out what looked like an Xbox controller from the front pocket or her hoodie. She moved the tiny joystick with her thumb, and the camera descended and zoomed through above the crowd. I turned to her, my brows raised in question.

"Microtech," she explained. "To the naked eye, it looks just like a fly. It's our ticket into that meeting."

"Cool," I said with a laugh.

I recognized several faces as a lineup of "who's who" filled the screens. Billionaire tech moguls and seasoned reporters mingled among high-ranking European and American leaders. Even a few celebrities were among the group. The most powerful and influential people in the world were present. Yet, for the first time in the meeting's history, not a single member of The Society of Light was attendance.

Zoeya's fly followed the illustrious crowd into the castle. The ushers led them through the opulent foyer and down a long hall decorated with gold-stamped portraits and crystal chandeliers. I wondered if the guards understood the significance of this meeting, or if they were just as clueless about the danger as the rest of the world. If they *were* aware, what was in it for them?

The guests walked single file into a grand hall like a line of ants. Zoeya's microtech landed on the edge of the crown molding, providing a wide-angle shot of the entire hall. A twenty-foot gold chandelier hung in the center of the long rectangular room that no doubt once hosted lords and kings for centuries. Dozens of antique chairs were set up in a semicircle with a single tall-backed seat sitting in the center of it all. Clearly, that was meant for someone in a position of power. The whole setup felt like a secret cult meeting. I wouldn't have been surprised if, at any minute, they began chanting or sipping blood from a chalice.

The guests' hushed conversation bounced about the space as they each found their seats. The atmosphere quickly turned somber as the last dignitary was settled. A middle-aged man in a finely tailored suit walked to the middle of the room and sat in the center seat. Behind him, a guard shut and locked the doors, sealing the dignitaries in and the world out.

"Can we get an ID on the man in the center?" Luca whispered.

"On it." Zoeya tapped away at her laptop. The camera zoomed in on his face, and tiny little points and lines mapped his features.

"Welcome to the annual Bilderberg Meeting," the host said in greeting. "As many of you may have already guessed, this year will be unlike those that came before it." The speaker turned to face the four men to his left. Each looked uneasy, their mouths pulled down at the edges.

"Well, this is interesting," Zoeya said with a frown. She zoomed in on the men's faces on a separate screen, and Alena gasped.

"Isn't that the General Secretary of China? And that"–she pointed to the tall blond man next to him–"the Prime Minister of Russia?"

Luca nodded grimly. "And next to them are the leaders of Iran and North Korea. If I'm not mistaken." He ran a hand across his downturned mouth. A sliver of dread seeped through our connection.

"I'm guessing those countries aren't usually invited," I said, though I already knew their presence at a meeting with European and American dignitaries was strange, at the very least.

"Yeaaaah," Zoeya said, drawing out the word. "Those particular nations haven't received invitations to a Bilderberg Meeting in the seventy years they've been held. They aren't exactly allies."

The speaker dipped his chin in minor deference to the tense guests. "I'd like to thank the representatives from China, Iran, Russia, and North Korea who are joining us for the first time. We welcome your willing collaboration in this great effort." His words sent a ripple of unease through the assembly. The guest representatives simply nodded curtly, their postures unbending.

"I have an ID on the speaker," Zoeya announced. She rotated a monitor toward us. On the screen was the NATO official webpage. The host smiled back at us, his name and title listed beneath the photo. Alexandar Koskinen, NATO Secretary General.

"Bloody hell." Luca leaning back in his seat and ran his hands through his hair.

Mr. Koskinen continued addressing the assembly. "We have long sought a solution to the unending conflicts between nations. It has been a difficult task, to say the least, in a world full of diversity and conflicting ideologies. Despite exhaustive negotiations, the assembly has decided that the modern societal construct cannot not be maintained."

Several heads in the assembly nodded in agreement, and a smattering of side conversations broke out. The guests' faces were strained and grim. Koskinen lifted a hand and waited for the murmurs to quiet.

"At our last meeting, it was established that the current world structure no longer serves mankind's best interests. Therefore, it must be destroyed so that it can be rebuilt under one government."

"Oh, my gosh." I put a hand over my mouth.

Koskinen locked eyes with each member of the assembly before continuing. "Our objective today is straightforward. Every country will stand and report. A timeline of events will then be reaffirmed, and final arrangements set. Once that's complete, each representative will be excused to make the final arrangements. Are there any questions or concerns?"

The speaker's eyes swept across the general assembly. The representatives squirmed uneasily in their seats, but no one spoke up. The tension was thick as smoke.

"Very good. We will proceed," the speaker said. He turned to the newcomers first. "The representative from China will now report."

An old man stood and offered the speaker a quick bow. "China is set to take control of Taiwan in the next twenty-four hours," he declared with a thick Mandarin accent. "Our ships are in place and ready to defend our position in the Pacific."

"Very good." Koskinen nodded and turned to the next in line. "The representative from Russia will now please report."

The Russian Prime Minister, a tall, thin man with a long face, stood and adjusted his suit jacket. "As you all know, Ukraine surrendered two days ago. Our troops will reach the Poland border by nightfall."

"Very good." Koskinen turned to the Iranian leader. "The

representative from Iran will now please report."

The man in question stood, a red and white keffiyeh atop his head. He shifted back and forth on his heels, and he spoke with a quavering voice. "Our troops are moving against Israel as we speak. Our allies have them surrounded and are preparing to meet the Americans in the Red Sea."

The NATO leader nodded. "My thanks to each of your nations. Your willing participation is invaluable to the success of our mission. Moving on." He clapped his hands, and several assembly members jumped in their seats, startled. The speaker then turned to the right side of the room. "The representative from the United States of America will now please report."

A short, blonde woman in her mid-fifties stood and adjusted her pantsuit. "Our warships stand ready in the Red Sea and the Pacific. We'll have boots on the ground in Russia within seventy-two hours."

The NATO speaker nodded and continued through the room in the same fashion. Each representative gave their reports, some with confidence, others with tremors in their voices. Though the emails Luca retrieved in D.C. proved many were unwilling participants in this New World Order scheme, there were just as many eager faces in the assembly. They *wanted* the world to burn.

Finally, Koskinen turned to the last representative. "Our esteemed technology representative, you will now please report."

Unlike the rest of the assembly, this man was dressed casually with a hoodie beneath his blazer. I instantly recognized him as the CEO of the largest tech company in the world. Nearly everyone on planet Earth would recognize him for his wealth and contributions to the tech industry. The man shifted in his sneakers and swallowed hard before answering. "All firewalls will be down at the agreed upon hour. System blackouts and network failures are set to roll out over the next few days."

The speaker nodded once. "Very good." The tech executive sank into his seat, his face pale and gaunt. I would bet good money he'd received his own threatening emails from "unknown."

Koskinen stood in the center of the room, facing the assembly with his hands behind his back. "All our preparations are made. The countdown for April 25th has begun," he said in an ominous tone. I shared a look with Luca and Alena. April 25th was just one week away. Just one week to stop the nations from going to war on a scale the world had never seen. Just one week to stop The Order from using those nuclear bombs created from the uranium stolen from that nightmarish Iranian mine. Tears stung my eyes. It was impossible.

"This meeting is adjourned. May God keep you and yours safe during the dark days to come," Koskinen said with a bow.

Zoeya snorted. "May God keep the harbingers of death safe," she said in a mocking tone.

We watched silently as the assembly filed out of the room with the energy of a funeral procession. Zoeya tapped on her laptop, switching to the outside cameras. The British representative, some high-level politician whose job it was to stoke the feud between England and Russia, appeared in the east exit frame. Gravel ground beneath his patent leather heels as he stepped out into the golden sunlight that shined off his grey hair like a halo. Birds sprang from their limbs, chirping excitedly as they disappeared into the sky. The man, dressed in a black polo and khaki pants, lifted his phone to his ear.

"We leave in the morning," he whispered. He paused for a beat before continuing. "Yes, of course I asked about our son.

They assured me that he is unharmed and will be waiting for us at the safehouse. Now, get packed," the man snapped. He slipped the phone back into his pocket and readjusted a pair of black-framed glasses before exiting the frame.

A security guard in a black suit stepped into view next. He looked down and paused. Bending over, the guard stared directly into the miniature camera. Squinting, he tapped the lens, and our view shook wildly. The agent leaned into the screen so close that I could see the pores on his face and the shadows clinging to his skin. My heart skipped a beat. *Shadowman.* He lifted a hand to his ear and murmured, "We have a security breach."

"Not good," Zoeya groaned. She put a finger to her earpiece. "Phoebe, they found camera number six."

Phoebe replied with a string of Danish expletives.

Donovan

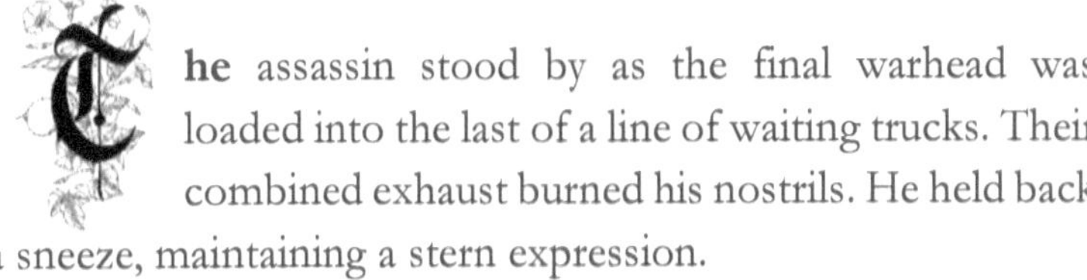

The assassin stood by as the final warhead was loaded into the last of a line of waiting trucks. Their combined exhaust burned his nostrils. He held back a sneeze, maintaining a stern expression.

Donovan was no genius. Not like Luca and his kind, with their superhuman mental capabilities. Regardless of his dimwittedness, he was just bright enough to know that hundreds of nukes were unhealthy for the planet.

Donovan was no tree-hugger, either. One couldn't accuse him of being a conscientious citizen who cared for the well-being of the earth or its inhabitants. He didn't fear melting ice caps, carbon emissions, or rising ocean levels. No. The assassin feared extinction. His own, to be exact.

For the first time since joining The Order, the assassin wondered who *exactly* he worked for. He'd never met the leader of The Order. No one had. It had never bothered him before. Donovan had always thought of his employer as a faceless overlord, the grantor of power and cruelty. The Order gave him a paid license to kill, a dream job for a man like Donovan who lacked a basic level of empathy. He happily took his bloated paycheck without question.

As the trucks carrying the world-ending nukes rumbled down the road to their destinations, doubts began to form in his mind.

The Order had constructed dozens of bunkers for the blackmailed dignitaries to ride out the apocalypse. They'd promised the fools positions of power after the dust had settled. The Order was to usher in a new world, one nation under Darkness. But Donovan knew the bunkers were lies. How could he not? He'd helped rig them with explosives.

The assassin shifted his stance, gravel crunching beneath his heels. The Shadowmen were also promised elevated positions in the new regime. The Order assured them that they'd live as kings in a world free of Bright Ones. For the first time in his long and bloody career, Donovan questioned his employer. Was The Order lying to them, too? He was beginning to suspect The New World Order made of Darkness was just as made up as the Christians' promised a Heaven made of Light.

As he watched the last truck fade from view, one thing was glaringly clear. They were all fucked.

Donovan could no longer go on believing everything would work out in his favor. The Void didn't intend for any of them to survive. The bombs would destroy every city across the planet. He knew enough about the dark side of humanity to imagine what would follow. Mankind would destroy itself in quick form, him included.

What the assassin couldn't wrap his mind around was the true nature of the leader of The Order, and what he could possibly want with a dead planet. The members of The Order had always lusted for power for power's sake. It didn't go deeper than that. But one couldn't rule over the dead. Donovan's brain hurt trying to suss it out.

He was surprised when his thoughts strayed to Luca. For the first time in his living memory, the assassin's stone-cold heart twisted in his chest. Luca would be dead soon, like the rest of them. But...so what? He was an Agent of Light. Donovan rejoiced in their demise. The knot in his stomach must have been indigestion, the assassin decided. The boy was insufferable, a Bright One who couldn't be completely darkened. His only failure. Well, other than the girl, the one who, against all odds, was still breathing.

Ciara approached and punched the assassin's shoulder, startling him from his uncharacteristic and disturbing thoughts.

"I have good news," she said with a sharp grin. Her voice was raspy from the fire Luca had started in the uranium mine. Unlike Donovan, she hadn't had the sense to hold her damned breath and therefore deserved what she got.

He grunted in reply, not in the mood to engage with the deranged shadow. Of all the apprentices Donovan had trained, she was by far the most bloodthirsty. Like him, she killed for the love of killing. Bright Ones, civilians, children, didn't matter. She killed anyone she could get her small pale hands on, and she did it with a maniacal glee. He should be proud of his young apprentice. Instead, her presence was beginning to grate on his frayed nerves.

Ciara tilted her head like a deranged bird, a strand of shocking red hair falling across her brow as she assessed him. "We have a lead on Luca and the girl." Donovan's heart twisted again, but he stubbornly ignored it. "Don't you want to know where we're headed?" she prodded.

Donovan pulled a crushed cigarette from his vest pocket. Patting his other pocket, he found his lighter and struck a flame. Donovan breathed in the sweet nicotine as he watched the line of trucks disappear into the distance. He hadn't smoked in years. The damage to his lungs and lingering smell affected his hunting abilities. But that didn't matter anymore, did it? Donovan took another hit. Soon, the hunt would be over for all of them, would it not?

Ciara sneered at him. "What's wrong with you?"

"Just thinking," Donovan replied with a shrug.

"That's new for you," she said, waving away a puff of smoke. "When you're done thinking, you might want to pack. We're headed to London–your old stomping grounds."

With one last glare, the girl faded into smoke. Donovan took another drag on the stale cigarette.

Well, wasn't that fitting? It would end where it began.

Chapter 9

Kitie

hey're on the move," Phoebe said through the comm. "Five black sedans. Shadowmen among them."

"Time to go." Zoeya wasted no time climbing over the center console into the driver's seat. As the engine roared to life, Alena slid into the seat beside her. The van jerked forward, throwing me into Luca's solid chest. He wrapped his arms around my waist, saving me from landing face-first into the van floor as Zoeya careened down the road.

"Luca, we need a location," Zoeya called over her shoulder.

"On it." Luca steadied me before sliding in front of the computer screens. He began typing furiously, and, in seconds, four red dots appeared on a digital map. I leaned forward to study it. Jomei, Kiran, Bodhi, and Phoebe were scattered across a two-mile radius.

Luca tapped his earpiece. "Bodhi. Jomei. Meet us at the corner of Slatgade and Bagerstræde." Their only response was their heavy breathing through the comms as they ran. "Zoeya, did you get that?"

"Got it."

"Kirie, be ready to let them in," Luca yelled, motioning to the back doors.

I slid across the metal floor to the back of the van. Two turns later, Zoeya squealed to a stop at the curb. I threw open the doors, and Bodhi and Jomei jumped in. Zoeya hit the gas as I pulled them shut again, nearly ripping my arms off with the opposing force. I latched the doors shut and shook out my stinging arms. As the van bounced and swerved down the narrow roads, I climbed back to the bench to brace myself against the wall.

"Where are Kiran and Phoebe?" Zoeya asked, her hands white knuckling the steering wheel.

"Head to the south side of town," Luca directed, tapping away at the keyboard.

She yanked the steering wheel to the right, sending us all reeling. Jomei fell into my lap, knocking the air out of me in a gush.

"Sorry," he said, his face aflame. He slid off my lap and onto the floor to brace his back against the bench. My stomach pitched as Zoeya took yet another corner at neck-break speed. Without warning, the van screeched to a halt. Bodhi opened the back doors this time, and Kiran jumped in. Phoebe slid in beside Alena up front, and we were moving again.

The interior of the van was crowded and smelled of sweat and leather. Luca had abandoned the computer and taken up watch at the back windows. In a crouched position, he pulled the velvet drapes aside, revealing a backward view of the narrow road. A black sedan turned the corner as we passed, following close behind.

"We've got a tail," Luca shouted up to Zoeya. She cursed and hit the gas, pushing the engine to its limit. Her eyes bounced between the side mirrors, a crease etched deep in her brow.

Kiran swore. "Can you shake them?" he questioned Zoeya.

Beside him, Bodhi snorted loudly. "Not in this piece of junk."

"Hey!" Zoeya yelled, twisting in her seat to glare at him. The van swerved wildly, and a chorus of cries rang out. "Be respectful! This is a *surveillance* van. If you wanted a getaway car, you should have ordered one."

The engine behind us revved, and their car shot forward, nearly kissing the van's bumper. The screens along the van wall blinked out one at a time, confirming they were Shadowmen.

Bodhi pulled out a dead cellphone from his back pocket and tapped the screen. "They're messing with our tech," he grumbled.

Zoeya switched lanes, throwing us into the side wall as she narrowly missed a slow-moving Passat. "Come on, Azizi. You can do it," she encouraged the van.

"We need to shake them," Phoebe said.

Kiran snorted. "And then what? It's just a matter of time before the other Shadowmen catch up with us." He pounded the van wall, the metal reverberating. "This damn vehicle is a problem; it's too recognizable. We need to dump it and make a run for it."

"No one is dumping anything," Zoeya protested. "What is wrong with you people?"

Luca turned away from the back window to face the group. "We need to split up. If we separate the Shadows into smaller groups, they'll be easier to defeat. Once we neutralize our tails, we meet up at the airport." My stomach tightened at his use of the word *neutralize*. We were going to have to engage in hand-to-hand combat with the Shadowmen. Again.

"We can't use our comms or cell phones as long as there are Shadowmen nearby. How will we communicate with each other?" I asked, bracing myself as the van bounced wildly.

"We'll be able to use our tech as soon as we eliminate the Shadows," Phoebe called over Alena's shoulder. Everyone nodded and began preparing their weapons of choice. Not one of them appeared worried or bothered by the prospect of "eliminating" someone. And why should they? If it were up to the Shadowmen, we'd all be dead. Not just us, but all mankind. I could no longer hold on to my natural aversion to killing. Ready or not, it was time to grow up.

Another engine revved behind us, and our attention was pulled back to the road. Two more black sedans with dark-tinted windows pulled up next to the van, flanking us on each side. Zoeya pressed harder on the gas, but they easily kept up.

Her hands whitened as she gripped the wheel. "Okay, I'm going to break away and drop you all off at a blind corner. Then, I'll lead as many of them away as I can. You're on your own at that point."

"I'm staying with the van," Alena told Zoeya.

Zoeya shot her a glare. "I don't need a sidekick."

Alena twisted fully in her seat and glared back. "Don't be stupid. They already saw me in the front seat. They'll know we split up if I'm no longer here, and the others will lose their lead. I'm going with you."

Luca and I looked at each other as they continued to bicker.

He raised a brow, and I shook my head, mystified by the explosive dynamic between the two women.

"Fine, stay!" Zoeya growled. She turned her head and called over her shoulder, "Everyone else, get ready to jump out."

Phoebe climbed awkwardly into the back, and we all moved toward the double doors. The stone-faced Agents of Light palmed their guns, and I followed suit. The metal was cold in my sweaty hands. I took a deep breath and reminded myself that I was an Agent of Light, too, trained by the most talented–and the grumpiest–trainer on Earth. I had this. Zoeya took a hard right without slowing, and we braced ourselves against one another as the van tipped onto two wheels. My heart rate spiked as our pursuers' brakes squealed in the background. The road curved sharply ahead, a tall building providing cover.

Zoeya hit the brakes. In one fluid moment, the other agents jumped lithely out of the van, and I awkwardly stumbled after them. A moment later, Alena pulled the doors shut behind us, and the van squealed away, leaving the smell of burnt rubber in its wake. We split into pairs–Kiran and Jomei, Phoebe and Bodhi, and Luca and me. We walked in opposite directions without saying a word.

Luca and I scanned our surroundings before tucking our guns back into their holsters. We pulled our hoods over our heads and speed-walked down the shop-lined road. Our movements were synchronized, having practiced traveling this way through much of Europe.

"Do you think they saw us?" I asked, risking a glance over my shoulder.

"Not yet. Let's move faster." Luca picked up his pace.

"Easy for you to say," I grumbled, pushing myself to a near run. "Your legs are twice as long as mine."

The afternoon sun was slowly setting on the quaint Danish

town, the buildings casting long shadows across the city streets. Thankfully, traffic was light. I watched as shoppers meandered in and out of stores. I envied the citizens' false sense of security and their uncomplicated lives. Little did they know they only had a week to live.

We'd covered several city blocks before we passed a pair of women standing on the edge of the sidewalk. Both were in their late thirties or early forties. As we passed, I made eye contact with one of them. I quickly looked away, but not before her pupils dilated unnaturally. The women promptly fell into step behind us, and I could feel their chilly black stares on my back.

"Behind us. Two females," I whispered to Luca.

Luca nodded once. "Follow my lead."

When we turned the next corner, he grabbed my hand and pulled me through the nearest doorway. We were standing in a run-down shop with rows of antique knick-knacks. Nodding to the kind-faced Danish man sitting behind the counter, we ducked behind one of the many cluttered shelves. We waited, holding our breaths. A moment later, the bell rang over the door. My already racing heart picked up its pace. I peeked between the colorful wares and saw the women from the street standing at the entrance, scanning the store. I squeezed Luca's hand, and we shared a grim look.

They split up, each taking opposite sides of the small shop. In moments, they would see us. I pulled my gun from my side holster and took a deep breath, praying that whatever happened next, the old man at the register would survive. I watched as one of the women casually began to walk our way. I'd always marveled at how ordinary the Shadowmen appeared. She could be anyone's mother with her short brown bob and average build. If it weren't for the chill in the air and darkness clinging to her form, I wouldn't have seen her coming. As she rounded the corner, Luca suddenly pulled me into his arms, and the air around us turned icy. "What are you…" I began, but the words were stolen from my mouth as our surroundings seemed to disappear into cold smoke. My breath caught in my throat. Whispers suddenly floated around me. Their words were menacing and desperate, their tone dark and desolate.

I opened my mouth to cry out, but Luca cupped his hand over it, making a little shushing sound in my ear. I shivered but held still. Through the mist, I could see the form of the woman pass by. I tensed, expecting the shadow to see through the darkness shrouding us. Couldn't Shadowmen see through darkness? The woman paused for a moment but quickly moved on.

My relief was temporary. Tendrils of smoke slithered across my skin, and a violent shiver rolled through me. There was something seductive about the malicious whispers in the shadows. Like The Void's presence, it was as enticing as it was frightening. My eyes slowly slid closed as I was drawn into the nothingness the shadows promised. *NO!* I forced my eyes open and shook my head to clear it of the poison swirling around our entwined forms.

Luca's body began to shake, and I could sense he was fighting a battle for control. The darkness wanted to consume him, chase away his light. The two sides of Luca warred with one another for domination, and sweat dripped down his temples as he fought to maintain control over his shadows.

"They're not here," a muted female voice said on the other side of the mist. The other woman swore, and two blurred figures rushed past us again, presumably to check the nearby buildings. Slowly, the shop came back into view as Luca's shadows dissipated.

"Did you just use…" I began.

"Come on," Luca cut me off, pulling me to the shop's back door. We rushed down a narrow alleyway that led to another busy street. A car zoomed by, nearly hitting us, whipping my hair around my face in a frenzy. I pulled a hairband from my wrist and tied it back.

I wanted to press Luca about what happened in the antique shop, but the firm set of his jaw stopped me. "How are we going to get to the airport?" I asked instead.

"We need to borrow a car," Luca ground out between clenched teeth. He seemed to be fighting some internal battle. I could see the inky emotions pouring off him in dark wisps.

I grabbed his hand and smiled, attempting to pull him out of the pit of self-loathing I could sense he was drowning in. "Good idea. Let's find an unlocked car. It'll be faster than breaking in." I led him by the hand, pulling on doors of parked cars as we raced down the street. Luca was slightly sluggish in his movements as he continued to battle his inner tempest. I pulled the handle of an old grey sedan, and the door popped open.

"I'll drive," I offered. Luca simply nodded.

I slid behind the wheel and placed my hand over the scratched ignition. Back in Rome, Bert taught a class on how to hotwire any car using our Light ability. At the time, I'd been shocked that my self-righteous, rule-following trainer would teach us how to commit grand theft auto, but he'd insisted it would come in handy one day. Like always, Bert was right.

Closing my eyes, I called forth my inner energy. I sent a bolt of electricity through the ignition coil, and the car's engine purred to life. I turned to Luca, and my self-satisfied grin melted. His jade green eyes—burning with both fire and smoke— bore into mine. A possessiveness radiated through our bond so fiercely, it stole my breath.

He pulled me to him and pressed his full lips to mine with punishing pressure. He moved back and growled, "That was bloody hot."

My skin flushed, head to toe, and I promptly forgot my name and where I was. His hands tangled in my hair as he devoured me with his gaze, our noses nearly touching. My own possessive desire, enhanced by the adrenaline singing through my veins, had me grabbing fistfuls of his shirt and pulling him into me.

The sound of another engine drew my eyes away from Luca's magnetic stare. I looked up at the rearview mirror and saw a car parked behind our stolen vehicle. Inside were shadowy figures. The heat promptly drained from my body. Luca followed my gaze and swore.

"Go, go, go!"

I grabbed the steering wheel and hit the gas. Our pursuers promptly gave chase. We wove in and out of slow-moving traffic, nearly hitting several bikers and pedestrians on their way home from work.

"Tell me where to go," I cried, pressing harder on the gas and throwing glances in the mirror. I swerved around a city bus, nearly hitting the bumper. The bus driver honked angrily.

Luca pulled his phone out of his pocket and tapped the screen, shaking his head. "They're still too close. I can't access my map app yet," he growled, tossing his cell into the sticky center console. "The airport is southwest of here, but we need to lose the Shadowmen first. We don't want to lead them to the jet."

Our tail stayed on us as we merged onto Highway 6, a two-lane road leading out of town. I pushed the gas pedal to the floor. The speedometer read 120 km/hr, then 140. Sweat trickled down my spine. The trees sped past us in a dark green blur as we raced through the countryside, weaving in and out of the occasional traffic. The shadows' sedan was a newer model than ours, and they were quickly gaining on us.

"Faster, my love!" Luca yelled. I pressed harder on the gas, but it was no use. The engine was giving us everything it had. I watched them gain on us in the rearview mirror, and I knew we couldn't outrun them. Up ahead, there was a fork in the road. One way curved gently to the left, and the other was a sharp right turn leading to a heavily wooded lane. A plan formed in my mind, one inspired by our earlier disappearing trick. "Hold on, I have an idea."

As we approached the fork, I flipped on my left blinker. The Shadowmen sped up, nearly hitting my bumper. At the last minute, I pulled the wheel sharply to the right. Luca braced his hands against the dashboard and door as we pitched to the side, two wheels momentarily leaving the pavement. When the car settled, I decelerated, pulling over onto the side of the road.

I parked in a shallow ditch and left the engine running.

Breathing heavily, Luca swung around in his seat. "What are you doing? They're just going to turn around and follow us."

I pushed the car door open, feet already on the ground. "I'm counting on it."

Luca followed me as I ran through the thick brush toward the tree line.

"What are you doing?"

"How far do you think we can project our power?" I called over my shoulder.

"Twenty feet or so," he replied, looking at me as though I'd lost my mind.

"If we combine our energy, maybe we can get twice that," I mused, searching for the perfect tree. A car engine revved in the distance, and I quickened my pace.

Luca's pace matched mine. "Kirie, what are you…" His brows shot up in realization. "Oh! I see. Eliminate them all at once. Brilliant!"

I nodded. "Exactly."

We quickly hid behind the largest tree we could find that was still in range of the road. We had a minute, maybe two, before they found us. I leaned against the rough bark and took a steadying breath of forest-scented air. My heart rate began to settle. Luca stood in front of me, hands braced on the trunk on either side of my head. A single ray of sunlight cut across Luca's brow, illuminating his jade eyes. His irises mirrored the forest surrounding us, so deep and full of life. Birds chirped happily, and bees buzzed busily around us. I almost smiled as I soaked in the solar energy filtering through the trees. If we weren't being hunted by psychopathic shadows, this moment would be perfectly peaceful.

"There!" Luca whispered, pointing up the street. The Shadowmen's car raced by, followed by brake lights and the squealing of wheels. *Good*, I thought. They saw the car. I straightened my shoulders it sped backwards.

"Aim for the gas tank," Luca whispered

I nodded. "On the count of three."

The Shadowmen quickly approached our parked car. Two hundred yards. One hundred yards. Fifty. We clasped hands, and the energy between us grew exponentially. Luca and I locked eyes and began the countdown together. "Three. Two. One."

We stepped out from behind the tree and raised our free hands. As the car passed us, we shot twin bolts of pure energy at its flank. Our aim was true, and the explosion sent us flying backward into the bushes. I landed with an umph. My ears began to ring, and my vision was fuzzy as I lay prone amidst the foliage.

Twigs dug into my scalp as I turned toward Luca. He was lying on the ground next to me, fighting to regain his breath. "I can't"–*gasp*–"believe"–*gasp*–"that worked."

I sat up and rubbed my blurry eyes until I could clearly see the macabre scene before me. In the center of the road, the shadow's car was upside down and fully engulfed in flames. Two dark figures dangled from their seats, unmoving. I looked away, pressing my hand to my mouth.

Luca sat up with a grunt and pulled his cellphone from his back pocket. He turned the screen toward me, and it lit up immediately.

"Thank goodness," I said with a sigh.

He climbed to his feet and extended a hand to me. "Come on, let's get to the airport."

We used Luca's phone to find our way back to the airfield. The ride there was surprisingly quick and uneventful, which meant the others were successful in "neutralizing" their targets also. A small group of black-clad agents was waiting on the tarmac for us when we pulled up. I stepped out of the car and quickly counted the heads. Kiran, Phoebe, and Jomei. I looked around. Where was everyone else?

A baby-blue Eurovan squealed to a stop next to us. A knot in my chest loosened, and an unexpected sigh of relief passed through my lips when Alena's grumpy face came into view. I laughed out loud at the strangeness of the moment.

Luca looked at me with pinched brows. "What's so funny?"

"I never thought I'd be relieved to see Alena," I said with another laugh.

Luca's mouth lifted into a heart-stopping grin, and he pulled me to him, pressing his lips to my sweaty forehead. I leaned into him and soaked in his heady energy.

Zoeya and Alena climbed out of the van and joined the group. I studied them, looking for injuries. Though both looked a bit disheveled, they seemed otherwise okay. We were nearly all present and accounted for.

"Jomei, you're covered in blood," Zoeya said, reaching up to touch the boy's cheek.

"It isn't mine." He shrugged off her hand.

Zoeya rolled her eyes and turned to Phoebe, who stood alone. "Where's Bodhi?"

Phoebe dropped her chin and stepped away from the group, her eyes empty and lifeless as she stared at the ground. "Bodhi didn't make it," she finally said, her voice lifeless.

Hot tears instantly burned my eyes. Kiran grabbed his hair and swung away from the group. "Fuck!" he screamed to the sky, his outburst making me jump. Jomei and Zoeya began openly crying. I turned away and covered my face, unable to watch their naked grief.

Behind us, the jet's engines roared to life, covering their cries. One by one, we climbed aboard. Kiran joined us several minutes later, stone-faced and stoic. The long flight to London was quiet, with few hushed words spoken between us. The team's loss was heavy in the air. Our individual battles with the Shadowmen had left us covered in dirt, sweat, and blood, and we each took turns showering in the jet's small bathroom.

Once everyone was settled, we called Finn on the plane's encrypted phone to let him know what we learned from the meeting.

Zoeya took the lead, informing the leader of The Society of Light that we had just one week to stop The Order from igniting a world war and blowing us all to hell.

"I want everyone to meet at the safe house," Finn ordered.

"Nora will pick you up from the airport. Do not contact anyone. This information doesn't leave this group. Understood?"

"Understood," we said in unison.

Luca leaned forward. "Sir, may I have a word in private?"

"Of course," he replied.

I watched in confusion as Luca took the phone off speaker and stepped away from the group. After a short, hushed conversation, Luca placed the phone back in its holder on the wall and sank into the leather chair next to mine.

"What was that about?" I asked.

A smile played on his lips. "Nothing, I just wanted to clear something up with your dad."

Yawning, I lay my head on his shoulder. The adrenaline had fully leached from my body, and fatigue had set in. My heavy eyes slipped closed, and I made a mental note to grill him on it later. The bounce of the landing gear hitting pavement woke me as the jet touched down at a private airport outside of London. Kiran, Jomei, Alena, Pheobe, and Zoeya filed out of the plane with the energy of a funeral procession. When I stood and moved toward the exit, Luca grabbed my hand and pulled me back to my seat.

I turned and raised a brow at him. "What's up?"

"Hang out with me for a while," he said with a grin.

Someone closed the hatch from the outside, and the roar of the jet engines crescendoed. The pilot was clearly preparing to take off again, and we were going to get stuck on the plane. I looked out the window, confused as everyone else piled into a black Range Rover with Nora at the wheel.

I turned to Luca again, brows tightly knit. "Luca, the pilot is about to leave. We need to get off."

His smile spread as he draped an arm over my stiff

shoulders. "We're not getting out here."

My heart rate quickened. "What do you mean?"

He pulled me close and pressed a quick kiss to my lips as the plane began taxiing down the runway. "We're going on an adventure."

"What the…we can't *go on an adventure*. We need to stop the Shadowmen from destroying the world."

"I already talked to Finn. He's on board with it."

"Are you crazy?" I tried again to pull from his embrace, but he held me fast. "We need to prepare for war. We only have one week, Luca." I couldn't believe he was doing this now, of all times. The world leaders were instigating a international conflict, and the Shadowmen were on their way to plant the bombs. We were in a race against the doomsday clock.

Luca took my face in his hands, fully aware of the panic and anger coursing through me. "And if things don't go our way, one week will be all we ever have. I want to spend those days giving you everything you deserve."

All the fight left me, and tears rolled down my cheeks as what he was saying hit me. "You don't think we're going to stop them in time, do you?"

He pressed a whisper of a kiss to my lips and pulled back to look into my eyes. "We'll only be gone for forty-eight hours," he said, dodging the question. "Let the others fight the bad guys for a while. Besides, The Society of Light has been battling Darkness for thousands of years without our help. They know what they're doing."

My shoulders fell in defeat. Luca was right. Finn and the other agents would do what they could to find the bombs. Neither Luca nor I specialized in intelligence, so until we had orders from Finn, we weren't really helpful. My muscles relaxed as the jet swiftly lifted off the ground. Up, up, and away, we flew. Away from the bombs. Away from the shadows. We were getting away from it all, if only for forty-eight hours. I let out a sigh and tucked myself into his side.

"Okay. Let's go on an adventure."

Chapter 10

Kirie

Again, I stood at the edge of the world with my feet in the sand. Only, instead of The Void's deserted coast, this beach was full of sound, color, and life.

The turquoise waves of the Mediterranean Sea crashed gently onto white sand with a *shush*. Feeling a sudden urge to touch the water, I rushed toward the surf. The sunbaked granules scraped the bottoms of my bare feet, and I quickened my pace. I finally reached wet sand, and it compacted under my weight. A wave crashed over my toes and up my bare legs, the salty sea spray stinging my exposed skin.

Seagulls screeched above, circling the beach in search of unguarded treasures. I lifted my head and watched their silly dance as I soaked in the unobscured sun. The energy in my core was so full I could light up the world. *So this was the ocean,* I thought in wonder. It was far grander than I could have ever imagined.

Before that moment, I'd only ever seen the sea on TV and online. When I was little, I begged Mom to take me to the beach, any beach, but after years of excuses, that dream died. Of course, I empathized with her need to keep me safe. She understood long before I did that the boogeyman was real, and scary things really did live in the shadows. Still, I grieved the childhood that could have been, the family trips we might have taken. Not only had she shielded me from the evil of the world, but she'd also shielded me from its beauty. Guilt churned my stomach, nearly souring the moment. My price for breaking free was her untimely and gruesome death. It was a crappy deal.

A white yacht bobbed just offshore. This, I assumed, would be our home away from home for the next forty-eight hours. When the jet touched down in Corsica, a French island in the Mediterranean, Luca announced he'd chartered a boat for two days. Like Finn's term "safe house," Luca's use of the word "boat" didn't adequately describe the vessel before me. Stately and long, the yacht was another thing I'd only seen in movies.

Laughing, Luca caught up with me and dropped our shopping bags in the sand. After leaving the small airport, we stopped to buy swimsuits and summer clothes, since we'd only brought our tactical gear to Finland. The moment the rental car pulled up to the beach, I jumped out, kicked off my shoes, and ran toward the water in breathless anticipation.

Luca stood behind me. His broad chest warmed my back, and I soaked in his energy. I could live a million years and never get enough of Luca's electrifying presence. I yearned for him to wrap his arms around my waist, to rest his head in the crook of my neck. Reading my intentions through our bond, he did just that. I smiled in satisfaction. I could get used to this kind of power.

"So, does it live up to the hype?" he asked. The vibrations from his deep voice traveled through me, and the hair on my arms rose.

"What? The yacht?"

"The ocean," he replied, burrowing deeper into my neck.

I took a steadying breath and turned back to the azure sea. "It's so big." It was such a ridiculous understatement that I laughed out loud. In theory, I'd known the ocean would be *large*, but the immensity of it had been inconceivable. The crystal-clear blues and greens reaching from land to horizon. The brine-scented breeze. The melodic crashing surf. It was all so breathtaking.

Luca chuckled in response. "Yeah, I guess it is."

I closed my eyes and lifted my face again to the golden sun. "I don't ever want to leave." I sighed. "Thank you for giving me this."

Luca stood upright, his mouth leaving my neck. I turned and caught him staring down at me.

"I just…" He paused, struggling to get the words out. "I just wanted you to experience this in case this war doesn't go our way."

My chest tightened at the sheen of tears in his eyes. I couldn't blame his lack of faith, as his fears mirrored my own. How many times had The Void shown me the destruction of our planet? How could I not question the possibility we might lose to the Darkness? We stared at one another, my own salty tears running down the back of my throat.

We were doomed, and we both knew it. It only took a hundred bombs to trigger a nuclear winter, and The Order likely had at least three times that. Even if we could stop half of the bombs, the remaining detonations would destroy the planet. Cities would fall. People would die in the tens of millions. The poisonous sun-deprived soil would fail to produce crops. Those unfortunate enough to have survived the initial blasts would soon perish from radiation-induced cancer, disease, or starvation. Like the cherry on top, The Order had made sure the nations were unable to work together to rebuild, having blackmailed them into yet another world war.

Luca pressed his forehead to mine. "It isn't fair. I want a life with you—*a million years with you.* Our time was stolen from us before we ever even had a chance." His voice broke on the last word.

Luca's anger and frustration pulsed through our bond, amplifying my own. Our lives had just begun. Luca was finally finding peace, and I was finally finding *myself.* I wanted to grow more, experience more, *love* more. Even if, by some miracle, we survived what was coming, the world would never be the same. My dream of becoming a scientist was all but smoke.

Would there be any universities left? Would there be labs? I looked back at the crashing waves, heart heavy in my chest. Would there be beaches left to sink my toes into, or would we be left with nothing but radioactive wastelands?

Together, we grieved what could have been. Our futures had been stolen by those who went before us, our lives lost to others' greed and lust for power. Luca's pain was a powerful thing, and it tore at me. I turned in his arms and cradled his face in my palms, desperate to ease his pain.

"Hey. We're here *now*. We're together *now*," I said, holding his gaze. If all I had were two days with Luca, I was going to make them count. "We finally get to be together without Nora lurking around every corner. Let's not waste this time worrying."

He let out a long sigh and nodded. "You're right. I'm sorry for being such a melancholy brat."

"You're forgiven. Now, come on!" With a laugh, I grabbed his hand and pulled him toward the dinghy at the water's edge, where a friendly French deckhand waited to ferry us to the "boat." A small crew greeted us when we climbed on board the palatial yacht and led us across the deck to our cabin below. I tried not to gawk at the sheer opulence of the leather seats, glossy wood floors, and bubbling hot tub.

Our suite was spacious and bright. A massive king bed sat in the middle of a modern room surrounded by end tables. The staff left us to settle in. Luca walked to the center of the room, and his shoulders relaxed for the first time in weeks. Soft morning light streamed through the windows, casting lines of golden light across his face. A dark lock of hair fell over his brow, and his green eyes shone like gems in the sunlight. He stared at me with such focus that my breath caught in my throat.

My heart beat a frantic rhythm in my ears. He was so beautiful, almost too painful to look at. Pulse racing, I closed the cabin door and pressed my back against it, excited, yet afraid to fully enter the room. In an instant, the peace I'd felt on the beach was replaced with self-doubt. I was embarrassingly unprepared for what came next. I'd had nearly zero experience with boys. What if I disappointed him? What if finally coming together was the thing that broke us?

"Come here, love," he whispered. His voice was smooth, amber honey–pure seduction. I would have melted into a puddle on the floor if my frayed nerves weren't keeping me upright. I took a steadying breath and walked toward him on sandy feet.

Luca spread his arms, and when I stepped into his embrace, my shaking eased. I let out a sigh of pure relief and contentment. Luca's light was a homecoming. My eyes slid closed. Deliciously warm energy settled around my sun-kissed skin, loosening every muscle. He held me with gentle strength, rocking me to the rhythm of the waves beneath us.

Luca lowered his head and nuzzled my neck, and I tilted my head further to the side. His warm lips brushed my collarbone, and liquid fire pooled in my lower belly.

He wrapped a lock of my hair around his hand. "You're covered in sand," he whispered. "Come. I'll run a shower."

I followed Luca into a luxurious bathroom where a massive glass surround shower dominated the space. Luca turned the faucet to hot, and we stood in awkward silence as the water came to temperature. I wanted to ask him to stay, but cowardice sealed my lips shut. I'd never undressed in front of a boy before.

"I'll–um–wait outside," he finally said, moving uncertainly through the door.

"No," I blurted, grabbing hold of his wrist. I cleared my throat and softened my tone. "Stay."

I tugged him back into the room. Grabbing the hem of his shirt, I pulled it over his head. My breath caught in my throat as his sculpted chest came into view. He was *magnificent*. Luca shivered as I ran a hand down the defined topography of his muscles, marveling at his utter perfection. He wove his hands beneath my shirt and tugged it roughly over my head. I stepped into him, our chests touching.

"Help me wash my hair," I whispered.

"At your service," he said, running a hand down my sandy tresses.

I froze. I'd heard those words before–no, not heard, *read*. Every time Parisxxxi8 and I ended our conversations, he'd sigh off with *At your service,* with a hat tip. Every. Single. Time. "What did you say?" I stared up at Luca, realization dawning. I was so *stupid*.

His dark brows pinched in confusion. "What do you mean?"

I took one step back and grabbed my shirt from the floor to cover my chest. "You said, 'At your service'."

Just like Parisxxxi8.

"Oh." Luca took his own step back, his face dipping in a guilty frown. "I see. I should explain."

The space between us cooled as we stared at one another.

I broke the silence first. "It's been you all this time, hasn't it?

"Yes," Luca began.

"Were you ever going to tell me?" The heat in my face rose, and I knew my cheeks must be beet-red.

Luca leaned back against the vanity and ran a hand through his hair. "Of course. I just–" He tilted his head back to study the ceiling as if the answer were written there. "I just never found a good time."

A pulse of anger shot through me. I shook my head at the weak excuse. "Uh huh. You had plenty of time. We've been together for weeks."

A frosty touch of fear and doubt seeped through our bond as he struggled to form a response. He was afraid of my reaction. *Good*, I thought. He should feel bad. All this time, he'd been lying to me about being my scientific pen pal. My face burned at the thought of all the messages I'd sent to what I thought was a friend overseas. All the while, he knew exactly who I was.

"Well, then I guess I was afraid of how you would react," he said with a sigh.

"Why did you reach out to me online in the first place?"

"It was a favor for Abbott. He wanted help determining if you were a Bright One. He thought you'd respond better to someone closer your age."

Of course, he had. I had foolishly assumed Abbott discovered and monitored my conversations with Parisxxxi8 on the chatboard. I never once considered that Paris was an Agent of Light himself. Our discussions had never felt like a fishing expedition, rather a conversation between friends.

"All this time..." I let my hair fall around my shoulders and sank back. I felt so exposed and betrayed. Parisxxxi8 had been nothing but supportive, never taking advantage of our friendship. Still knowing Luca had hidden his identity for so long felt like a violation. "Do you even care at all about biophotonics?" My voice was small and unsteady.

Luca took a hesitant step toward me, testing the waters. I watched his approach, but when I didn't protest, he slowly closed the distance between us.

"Of course, I care, my love. Biophotonics is my favorite subject." A small smile played on his lips.

I glared at him. "Liar."

"I swear, my intentions were pure," he declared, raising his right hand as if he were on the witness stand. "It *was* an assignment at first. But I felt drawn to you from the very first day. In fact, I had to send Arin to scout you out at the science fair because I was worried I wouldn't be able to hide my connection to you."

I narrowed my eyes at him, seeing the holes in his logic. "But that didn't stop you from coming to my hospital room."

I remembered thinking Luca was an angel when I first woke in that hospital bed after Donovan tried to strangle me to death. His light not only healed my neck, but it also restored my will to live.

"Well, I couldn't send Arin. He was shit at healing," he explained with a shrug.

I pressed him further. "Fine, but if you and Abbott already determined I was a Bright One, why come to my parents' funeral?" I began.

Luca placed a tentative hand on my left hip, and though I was mad at him, I didn't have the strength to pull away. "Your pain was so intense, and I swear I could *feel* your grief. I had to see you." Luca swallowed hard before continuing. "And there you were, the most beautiful girl I'd ever seen, even broken and bruised."

I rolled my eyes, refusing to be derailed by compliments. If Parisxxxi8 was simply a means to determine whether I was a Bright One, why the months of messages that followed? Why not stop the charade? "Fine, but why did you continue messaging me once we arrived safely in Paris?"

He placed his other hand on my right hip. "Because I'm a selfish prat, that's why. I should have left you alone. I should have given you space after we ended things at our apartment. But the connection between us continued to grow until it caused me physical pain to be parted from you. It was as though a piece of my skin had been ripped from me.

The pain was mutual. I felt his absence equally as strong. But Luca hadn't come back, even staying away from Arin and

Alena to avoid seeing me. "If it was so terrible, why did you stay away for so long?"

Luca's eyes dropped to the floor. "Because you were right when you said you deserved better."

I thought back on that horrible morning, standing at opposite ends of our apartment hallway. Hearing Ciara on the other end of that phone had played on all my insecurities. I already suspected that I was out of Luca's league. That call just confirmed it. I'd lashed out, not knowing how deeply my careless words would wound a man like Luca. He'd spent much of his life feeling like he was tainted and broken, and my words only seemed to confirm *his* insecurities. What a mess. What a waste of time.

I leaned into him and sent a stream of energy through our connection. "I didn't mean what I said. I was just hurt and confused."

He dropped his head until our foreheads met. "I'm going to kill Ciara for taking all those months from us," he whispered.

"Me first," I vowed. When the time came, Ciara was all mine.

As my anger turned to Ciara, my ire toward Luca cooled. True, he wasn't upfront with me about Parisxxxi8, but given the state of the world, it was a minor thing. We didn't have the time to sweat the small stuff.

"One last question. What does the name Parisxxxi8 mean?" The Paris part made sense since Luca had been living in that city at the time. But I'd always wondered about the meaning behind the strange combination of letters and numbers.

His brows rose, surprised by my question. "Oh. It refers to a verse in the War Scroll," he explained. "1QM, Column 1, line 8, to be exact."

"What does it say?" I asked, not doubting for a moment that he had it memorized. He was a Child of Light after all.

Luca didn't hesitate. "Then the Sons of Righteousness shall shine to all ends of the world, continuing to shine forth until the end of the appointed seasons of darkness. Then at the time appointed by God, his great excellence shall shine for all the times of eternity; for peace and blessing, glory and joy, and long life for all sons of Light."

He recited the verse like a sacred prayer, and a halo of light shone off his skin. The hair on my arms stood on end as the magic of the words hung in the air several moments after they were spoken.

It was a prophecy of war and pain. It was a prophecy of fate. But most of all, it was a prophecy of *victory* and *long life*.

I captured Luca's eyes and smiled. "See, there's a little hope left in you after all. Now come on, we're wasting the hot water." I dropped my shirt and pulled him beneath the shower's spray.

But, soft! what light through yonder window breaks?
It is the East, and Juliet is the sun.
Arise, fair sun, and kill the envious moon,
Who is already sick and pale with grief
That thou, her maid, art far more fair than she.
Be not her maid since she is envious.
Her vestal livery is but sick and green,
And none but fools do wear it. Cast it off.
It is my lady. O, it is my love!
O, that she knew she were!
She speaks, yet she says nothing. What of that?
Her eye discourses; I will answer it.

Romeo and Juliet by William Shakespeare

Chapter 11

Kirie

The sun woke me early the next day. Luca lay by my side, his breaths long and even. I gently laid my head on his chest and watched him sleep. He was both inhumanly handsome and darkly complex, an alluring combination. From the moment our eyes first met, I could sense there was *more* to Luca–like looking at a light at the end of a long and dark tunnel. More than our connection, it was his depth that appealed to me. That and his sexy British accent. With or without the bond, I would have fallen for him. I was still just a girl, after all.

He wasn't without his flaws, though. I finally had time to process everything I'd recently learned about the man lying beside me. After the initial shock, it made perfect sense that

Luca was Parisxxxi8. In fact, it was embarrassingly obvious. The sting of that minor betrayal had quickly worn off, and I wasn't going to waste my last days on Earth being mad about the fact that he didn't tell me he was my online pen pal.

My bigger concern was what happened in the antique shop in Denmark. The thought of it made my gut tighten with worry and confusion. Luca had wielded his inner shadows like a true Shadowman. But did that mean he was one of them? My head spun as I tried to separate the Luca I knew from his shadows. True, he'd done horrible things in his past. But he'd been a *child* and a victim himself. And, true, his time with Donovan had left a stain on his soul. But did that mean he was *bad?* Did that make Luca a Shadowman himself?

I drew patterns along Luca's chest with the tip of my finger, my mind chasing its tail as I worked to understand this complex creature next to me. If he hadn't used his ability to shield us from our attackers, we might be dead. I nearly laughed out loud at the absurdity of that fact. I'd spent my entire life fearing the dark. Who could blame me? Nearly every bad thing that happened to me happened in the dark. Not once had I considered that it might one day save me.

Perhaps darkness itself wasn't the enemy. Perhaps the real enemies were those who used the shadows to hide their abuses. We all had a little darkness within us, didn't we? Maybe it was good to acknowledge the shadowy parts of oneself—healthy even. I thought of the walks Luca took each morning at Mentmore Towers. He'd had the bravery to walk alongside his ghosts, accepting their presence without letting them destroy him. Who would Luca be without his perilous past? He was steel, forged by fire. Staring at his beautiful sleeping face, a fierce possessiveness settled over me. Dark one or not, this man was *mine*! Until my dying day. Which may just be exactly one week away. The thought filled me with a mixture of dread and longing.

Sensing my stare, Luca woke with a yawn. "Morning, Love." He rubbed a hand down my bare back and smiled, making my toes curl. "How long have you been up?"

"Promise me that whatever happens, we'll be together."

Luca blinked his eyes at me in confusion. "What are you on about?"

"If we don't make it, if we don't find the bombs in time—promise me we'll be together in the end."

His tired eyes cleared instantly as understanding dawned. He lifted onto one arm and hovered over me. "There's not even a question, my love. I'm not letting you out of my sight ever again. Come hell or high water, I'll be by your side," he vowed.

I extended my pinky between us. "Swear it."

He eyed my little finger with suspicion. "What's that?"

"It's a pinky promise."

"What the bloody hell is a pinky promise?" he asked, scrunching his nose.

"It's a sacred American tradition." Fighting a smile, I grabbed his hand and linked his pinky with mine. "A pinky promise can never be broken."

His little finger squeezed mine, and with focused determination, Luca swore, "On my word, we will be together to the end." He sealed his oath with a kiss.

We spent the remainder of the two days exploring the island and each other. We toured Bonifacio, a beautiful cliff-side city with white-stone buildings built nearly two centuries ago. I marveled at its rich history and strong resistance to time. As we walked hand-in-hand along the cobbled streets, I felt the ghosts of the long-gone villagers, their love for their island echoing through time. I placed a hand on one of the ancient walls and wondered if there would be anything left of this beautiful town for future generations to explore, or if it would soon be reduced to rubble.

We drove into the mountains and hiked to a breathtaking waterfall. I stood before it, letting the refreshing spray wash the sweat from my face. I felt like a kid, frolicking in nature with a cute boy at my side. For the first time since my parents' deaths, I wasn't looking over my shoulder for hidden assassins. We laughed often, relishing the little slice of freedom we'd carved out for ourselves. We were proving that light persisted even in the darkest of times.

A current of fear and grief flowed beneath my joy like an underground river. I knew this magical moment with the man I loved wouldn't last. We still had to return to the reality of our possible defeat. But I would do it with Luca at my side, his hand firmly grasped in mine.

Chapter 12

Luca

irie sat cuddled next to Luca as the plane touched down at the small airport near London. He held her tightly, a strange mixture of contentment and dread swirling in his gut. Luca could feel time slipping through his fingers like sand through an hourglass. He'd never been particularly interested in the construct of time until the moment he realized he was out of it. Now, time meant everything to him. Perhaps it was because he'd never had anything to look forward to before. Each day of his life was a painful struggle to hide his shadows and play the part of the perfect Agent of Light. The past few weeks changed all that, and he found himself craving more time. Thanks to Nora, Luca was finally confronting his past rather than hiding from it.

Then there was Kirie. He craved an infinite amount of minutes and hours with her.

Luca replayed the past two nights over again in his mind. She was like a riptide, her energy drawing him helplessly to her. Kirie hadn't been his first lover. Though he'd never been the philanderer everyone pegged him as, he hadn't been celibate either. No, Kirie hadn't been his first, but she would be his last.

He knew he was all wrong for her, but he didn't have the strength or moral character to care anymore. Luca drew circles on the smooth skin of her arm, basking in the light and love radiating through their connection. Kirie's love for him was as undeniable as it was undeserved. No, Luca didn't deserve her, but he'd kill to keep her anyway. Not that it would matter. On April 25th, all Agents of Light and nearly every civilian save The Order, and the greedy top one percent would likely be dead.

Reality came rushing back as they exited the plane. A sleek sedan waited for them on the runway, engine running. Finn had arranged for Nora to pick them up at the airport, and Luca was surprised that he was happy to see her. During his time at Mentmore Towers, he'd forged a sort of closeness with the old woman. True, she was a hard ass, but she'd also understood Luca's shadows in a way no one else had. Instead of handing him empty platitudes, Nore had given him the tools to save himself.

Luca held the back door open for Kirie. As he slid in beside her, Kirie gasped. A familiar derisive laugh drew his eyes to the front of the car. Donovan sat behind the wheel, not Nora. Luca swore and grabbed the door handle, but it was locked.

"Good 'ening, my boy." He smiled at them through the rearview mirror.

Luca raised a shining palm and pointed it at Donovan, still reeling from his sudden reappearance in his life. In the same moment, Kirie slipped a knife from God-knows-where and was pressing it against Donovan's neck from behind. Donovan put his hands up and laughed.

"What the fuck are you doing here?" she growled. Her hand shook as she pressed the blade into his neck. Luca's face heated. He'd never heard her swear before, nor had he seen her move with such speed. In any other circumstance, it would have been hot as hell.

Donovan turned his head to Luca, hands still raised. "Luca, call off your bird. I come in peace."

"Peace?" Kirie scoffed. "Do you even know the meaning of that word?"

A heady mixture of her red-hot anger and ice-blue fear shot through their bond, but Kirie held her composure. Luca put a steadying hand on her back, never lowering his own biological weapon. He would gladly let her exact her revenge on the odious man. It was poetic, even, being killed in the same way he'd killed Kirie's mother. Luca was tempted to sit back and enjoy the show. There was one little issue…

"What did you do with Nora?" Luca asked, knowing that the older woman—or her body—had to be nearby.

"Tell your little bird to lower her knife, or that old crone won't breathe another day."

Luca stared in confusion at Donovan's profile. It wasn't like his old tormentor to leave people alive. His general M.O. was get in, kill everyone, get out. As far as Luca knew, he and Kirie had been the only survivors of his attacks. Using someone as leverage was a new tactic for Donovan. A confusing one. Intrigued, Luca decided to play along.

"What are you doing here, Donovan?" Luca increased the

intensity of his light, a warning.

"Whoa," Donovan lifted his hands higher in faux surrender. Luca wasn't fooled. Donovan would die before he admitted defeat. "It's like I said, I come in peace. Now, tell the girl to lower her knife." Donovan's Adam's apple bobbed once. He may be The Order's number one assassin, but Luca knew Donovan's little tells. He was nervous. That was new, too.

Kirie tightened her grip on her knife's handle and leaned forward, pure hatred pulsing through their connection. "Tell her yourself, asshole. I'm sitting right here."

If Nora's life wasn't in the mix, Luca would've told Kirie to slide the knife across the bastard's throat. Hell, he would have applauded her for doing the world a favor. As it was, Luca said, "If we hear you out, will you guarantee Nora's safety?"

"The old bat is all yours, right as rain. I just need a moment of your time."

Kirie looked back at Luca, and he nodded. Reluctantly, she lifted the blade from Donovan's neck. Still, she held the knife tightly in her fist, her posture that of an asp ready to strike.

"You have one minute to tell us whatever you want to say," Luca warned.

Donovan lowered one hand and began pulling something from his back pocket. Luca's light intensified again, turning nearly blue in hue.

"Watch it," he warned in a low growl.

"Relax." Donovan held out a folded piece of paper.

Luca looked at it with suspicion. "What is this? You brought me a letter?"

"It's a *gift*." Donovan shook it like a treat in front of a dog.

"We don't want anything from you," Kirie snarled, brandishing the knife.

Donovan ignored Kirie, locking gazes with Luca instead.

"Go on. Take it. I promise you'll want to read what's inside." His black eyes were tight and insistent, and his voice had lost its usual sarcasm.

Something was different about the Donovan sitting in front of him; Luca could feel it. He dimmed his light slightly and carefully slipped the paper from the assassin's fingers, making sure not to touch his cold skin. Luca's light illuminated the page as he unfolded it. The creases in the paper were deep, as if they'd been folded and refolded many times. Luca could almost *feel* Donovan's anxiety etched into the page's grooves. His brow creased as he scanned its contents. The words "April 25th" were written at the top of the page, followed by a list of addresses. Luca's eyes scanned the locations several times before he finally made the connection. The cities matched those on the doomsday map found in the D.C. files. Donovan had given him the locations of the bombs!

Luca looked back at Donovan with wide eyes. He simply nodded in confirmation. Bile rose in his throat. It sickened Luca that, after all these years, they still understood one another without speaking. Kirie's head ping-ponged between the two men, suspicion and worry etched into her beautiful face.

"What? What is it?" Kirie asked, a slight tremor in her voice.

Luca held the paper out between them like an accusation. "What the hell are you playing at, Donovan?" he demanded. Donovan was the most self-serving, bloodthirsty bastard on the planet. He never did anything that didn't directly benefit himself. Why would he give them this information? Was this some sick game, some way to distract them?

Instead of offering a sardonic retort, as was his nature, the assassin simply stared down at the creased paper. A frown pulled at his thin chapped lips. Again, Luca sensed that something was off about this Donovan.

Finally, he spoke in a low, gravelly voice. "Because when the world dies, we all lose."

Luca barked out a disbelieving laugh. After all the evil he'd done, The Order's top assassin was suddenly worried about the state of the world? Impossible! He was chaos and death incarnate. Luca's light flared once more, and Kirie extended her blade, ready to strike.

"Now you care about the fate of the world after you helped set it aflame yourself? I call bullshit!" This was clearly a trap. Perhaps he wanted to lure Agents of Light to those locations so they could take them out one by one. It was a stupid plan. No one would trust intel freely given by a Shadowman, least of all this one.

Donovan swallowed hard again. "Believe what you like, my boy, but this *is* an accurate list. You need to put your self-righteous pride aside long enough to use it."

"If you're so worried about the fate of the world, why not take care of it yourself?" Luca asked. He squinted at the older man, trying to find the truth written somewhere in the lines of his face. There, in the tightness of his mouth, the crease between his brows, something he'd never seen on Donovan's face before…fear. It unsettled Luca to see him this way. Donovan didn't have emotions. What could possibly shake the unfeeling? Why would Donovan be worried? The Order's dark agents' ascent to power in the New World Order was all but assured. What, then, would prompt his old tormentor to betray the organization he'd sold his soul to serve?

Realization washed over him like a cold tide. "You don't think *anyone* will survive, do you?" he whispered. And there it was, written all over Donovan's face–the confirmation of the thing he feared but could not fully accept. "The Order means to kill everyone. Agents of Light, citizens, Shadowmen–The Order means to destroy us all."

Donovan's face hardened. Pushing his door open, he pointed again to the paper in Luca's hand. His finger shook a little, another thing Luca had never seen him do. "You won't get a chance like this again, boy. Don't let me down."

"What about Nora?" Kirie called after him.

"She's having a nice little nap in the trunk." He grinned, his sarcastic mask slipping back into place. With the flick of a wrist, he tossed the keys into the back seat and disappeared into smoke.

"Are you just going to let him go like that?" Kirie asked, pointing her blade at the open door.

"Kirie, look." Luca held the paper out to her.

She cringed away from the paper as though it had teeth. "We can't trust that man. You know that better than anyone. It has to be a trap."

"Just look at it. The addresses match the cities on the map we found. Exactly." Luca held it out to Kirie again. With an exasperated huff, she snatched it from his hands and scanned it. Her brows pinched. Her memory was as good as his. She'd recognize the locations.

"Why would he give us this?"

Luca stared out his dark window. "He knows The Void never intended to create a New World Order led by Shadowmen. He knows it's all a lie."

The truth had been there all along. How many times had The Void shown him scenes of absolute devastation? How many times had it revealed its true intent? The Void wanted to cloak the world in absolute darkness, to destroy all light and life. Like a jealous God, it would kill its own creations, converting their energy into dark matter. Like Noah's flood, it was a kind of benevolent genocide. The thought made Luca nauseous.

"He's right." Kirie sighed, lowering the paper. "When I was in the mines, The Void's visions revealed that it intended to destroy all light and energy in the universe."

Luca sighed and ran a hand through his hair. "Donovan must have discovered The Void's game and hatched a plan that didn't endanger his own life."

"Yeah! Using *us* to do the dirty work," she scoffed. "He's such a loser."

Luca laughed at her pouty face. "He *is* a loser. But he's also a survivor through and through. Helping us deactivate these bombs before they can be used works in his best interest."

"No. Nope. No," Kirie said, shaking her head. She tossed the paper onto the seat. "Donovan is a psychotic Shadowman. He killed my parents and tortured you for *years!* You, of all people know what kind of man he is. We can't trust a word he says." Kirie's pale cheeks turned bright pink like strawberries and cream. She blushed like that the first time they'd met at her mother's funeral. Like then, Luca wanted to kiss every inch of those pink cheeks.

Luca cleared his throat and shrugged his shoulders, trying to regain his focus. "We don't really have a choice, do we? This is the only lead we have. It's either chase down these bombs or lie down and die."

Kire threw her hands up. "Fine. Let's trust the psycho that ruined our lives. Whatever."

Luca couldn't stop the laugh that burst out of him.

Kirie folded her arms over her chest and glared at him. "What's so funny, Luca Durant?"

"Nothing. I'm just enjoying this new spicy side of you. It's hot." Luca pulled her to him and kissed the tip of her nose, slightly dousing Kirie's fire. "The world must be upside down if Donovan is our brightest hope for winning this hopeless war."

She snorted, and damn if it wasn't the cutest thing Luca had ever heard. This girl was turning him into a lovesick idiot. It was just his luck that he'd found happiness just to have it torn away by a global nuclear war.

Maybe it didn't have to be the end. Maybe he could begin a new life as a whole person, being loved by Kirie. Luca looked at the paper lying on the leather seat between them, and a dangerous feeling crept through his veins. *Hope.*

Luca tucked the list into his pocket and climbed out of the car, pulling Kirie out after him. "Come on, let's get Nora out of the trunk. We have work to do."

Chapter 13

Kirie

Nora was not happy. We'd made it to the manor in record time with Luca behind the wheel, but it was still well after midnight when we arrived. Alena helped me guide an unsteady and irate Nora to bed. Once she was settled, Luca and I made our way down to the Faraday cage and emailed Finn an encrypted image of the list. The phone rang immediately as if he'd been actively watching his emails. Luca and I shared a look before picking up.

"Where did you get this list?" Finn asked by way of greeting.

"What, no 'Hello' or 'Good job in Denmark. I'm glad the Shadowmen didn't kill you?'" I shot back. My mood was shadow black. Donovan's reappearance had deeply unsettled me.

"My apologies," Finn replied with a laugh. "I thought vacations were supposed to be relaxing."

His joking tone only stoked my anger, and I glared at the phone. "Nothing like being confronted by your mother's murderer to ruin a good time."

Finn's laughter abruptly cut off. "Wait. Hold on. Let's back up."

I sat back in the metal chair and let Luca tell Finn what happened at the airfield. His words faded into the background as I began to imagine an alternate reality where I'd found the guts to slide the knife across Donovan's throat, finishing his reign of terror on our lives once and for all. I could all but feel the warm, sticky blood flow over my hand as he gasped for air like my mother had done when he'd killed her. Had that only been months ago? Finn raised his voice, pulling me sharply from my bloody daydream. I blinked and sat up straighter.

"Let me get this straight. Some shadow assassin drugged Nora, stuffed her in the trunk, locked you in the car, all so that he could just hand you a list of The Order's secret nuclear bomb sites." Finn summarized hotly. "Tell me you're not taking this intel seriously."

Luca ran a hand roughly through his hair, pulling several brown strands free from their roots. "I can't believe I'm saying this, but yes, I believe the intel is good." I felt how much those words cost him through our bond. It was killing Luca to trust Donovan.

"And you, Kirie? What are your impressions?"

"As much as I hate to admit it, I think he's telling the truth. I suspect The Order secretly intends to kill every living thing on Earth, including the Shadowmen." I held off telling Finn exactly how I knew this. It wasn't the time to explain The Void and his ugly visions of death and destruction. I still couldn't wrap my mind around the planet graveyard it had shown me for fear of speaking it into existence. "Donovan must have come to the same conclusion. Giving us the locations is self-serving."

I chewed on my bottom lip as Finn considered this for a moment. "Fine. Let's assume for now that this was given in good faith. According to this list, the bombs will be delivered to these locations in five days. That should give us a good head start. Give me a few hours to do some research and cross-referencing before we move forward. I want to make absolutely sure the intel is good before we go chasing after phantom bombs."

Luca frowned. "Then what? There are close to two hundred locations on that list, sir. April 25th is just two days away. How can we deactivate each bomb in time?" Although his words conveyed frustration, I could sense renewed hope through our connection. Luca believed this could work.

"Fortunately for us, Mr. Daiko hasn't been seen or heard from him in over thirty-six hours. He appears to have gone dark. I believe we no longer need to worry about him leaking intel to the enemy."

"Are you certain of that?" Luca challenged.

"Mr. Durant, please remember to whom you speak," Finn

chided. "I have access to all communications going in and out of every network across the planet. If Daiko were communicating with our agents or infiltrating our system, I would know about it."

"Really? You missed it the first time," Luca shot back. "Diako has been leaking information to The Order for months."

"I wasn't in the habit of spying on my colleagues before now, so yes, I missed it the first time."

"You guys. Focus!" I yelled over them. Their bickering was starting to irritate me. "There are two hundred bombs in two hundred locations and just three days before they're delivered. Finn, can you mobilize a force big enough and quickly enough to stop them from detonating or not?"

Finn let out a heavy sigh. "It will be tight, but it can be done. Let me worry about that for now. Get some sleep, and I'll call you in the morning." Just before Finn hung up the phone, he added, "Oh, and tell Nora to prepare for company."

"Good night," I said sarcastically to the dead dial tone.

The house was silent when Luca and I headed to bed. We walked hand in hand through the sleepy mansion. The ticking of the grandfather clock in the grand hall echoed loudly in the silence. I chased sleep for hours as I lay wrapped in Luca's arms. Normally, I found his scent and warmth comforting, but my entire body was too tightly coiled. My head pounded in my ears, punctuating each passing second. I turned to the digital clock on the nightstand. It read four a.m.

I turned to look at Luca. For the first time since coming to

Mentmore, he slept peacefully, snuggled into my back. While our encounter with Donovan had left me on edge, the list had given him hope. I could sense a lightness through our connection. I wished I shared that hope, but our run-in with Donovan had dredged up an inky well of anger and grief. It was as though all those months of healing hadn't happened, and I was right back at my parents' funeral.

Taking anything from Donovan, even a simple piece of paper that may or may not help us save the world, felt like a betrayal of my parents. He murdered my mother in front of me, stalked me for months, tortured the man I loved for a decade, only to show up one day to ask for a favor. I almost wished the bombs *would* go off just so he could *finally* die. My stomach soured at the cruelty of my own thoughts. No. What I really wanted was justice—something of which there was little left in the world. Perhaps part of growing up was realizing true justice and happily-ever-afters were just fairytales. Perhaps the good guys didn't win in the end.

Giving up on sleep, I lifted the covers gently and slipped out of bed. I let out a sigh of relief when Luca stirred slightly but didn't wake. The estate was dark and silent when I slipped into the downstairs study and turned on the TV. Sitting on the antique couch, I flipped through the four channels this drafty old house afforded. My legs itched from an uncomfortable mixture of boredom and anxiety. I settled on a twenty-four-hour news station, chewing on my bottom lip as the local reporter delivered the early morning news.

"Tensions between Israel and Iran have escalated as one hundred Iranian drones entered Israeli airspace overnight. Though minor damage was reported, the president of Israel has vowed swift retribution," the reported said.

I pinched the bridge of my nose and squeezed my eyes shut, as my head began to pound. Things had already been set in motion. It shouldn't surprise me; I knew the timeline. The dignitaries were carrying out their marching orders, and this seemingly minor escalation was all a part of the bigger plan.

For most of the Western world, this attack, though alarming, would feel distant and non-threatening. My chest tightened thinking of the tens of millions of civilians who would see the same news in the false security of their own homes, unable to see the forest for the trees. How many stories of foreign conflicts had I ignored because they didn't affect my daily life? If I hadn't been a literal fly on the wall at the Bilderberg Meeting, I might not have seen the pattern either. The safety of my youth had only ever been an illusion.

Bang, bang, bang

I jumped to my feet, heart in my throat. Someone was knocking at the front door. Nora, wrapped in a housecoat, stood at the top of the grand staircase as I passed through the Grand Hall. Her white hair stood on end, and a frown tugged at her sagging cheeks. Luca followed closely behind.

"Who on earth is at the door?" the old woman groused.

"Oh, right. Finn said to expect company," Luca said with a yawn.

Nora rounded on Luca and pointed a finger at him accusingly. "You should have told me," she chided. "I'm not at all prepared for company!"

Luca put his hands up in surrender. "Sorry. I didn't want

to wake you."

Nora waved him off with a look of disgust and rushed down the staircase to the grand entry.

An older man in a black bulletproof vest stood in the doorway. He shook off the light raindrops dotting his shoulders. My face lit up. "Abbott!"

I ran down the short staircase and threw my arms around Abbott's middle. Luca quickly joined, wrapping his arms around us both. His joy at being reunited with his mentor shone brightly through our bond, warming my core.

Abbott stepped back and patted Luca's cheek affectionately. Then he smiled at me. "It's good to see you, Kirie."

My chest filled with happiness at seeing my old high school teacher. We'd left Rome in such a hurry, and I didn't know what had happened to him. "It's good to see you, too. What are you doing here?"

"I was kidnapped and forced to come," he said, hitching a thumb to the front drive.

I stepped around Abbott and saw Finn climbing out of a black sedan that likely cost more than my parents' house back in Colorado. Instead of the casual business attire I was used to seeing him in, Finn was dressed in full tactical gear usually reserved for active-duty Agents. Behind him, six agents in matching black gear stood in front of an identical car, staring up at Mentmore Towers' massive exterior with a mixture of awe and exasperation.

Abbott turned to Nora and bowed. "I hope you don't mind

company, Ms. Nora," he said with a smile. "You're about to be flooded with guests. The rest should arrive tonight."

Nora lifted her chin. "Would it matter if I did mind? You never listened to me before."

My brows shot up in surprise. "Do you guys know each other?"

Abbott nodded. "We went on a few missions together back when I was an agent," he explained, a fond smile on his lips.

"That was a million years ago. I hardly remember it," Nora said with a sniff.

"Still as sweet as ever, I see," Abbott whispered to me on his way into the house.

Nora met Finn in the entryway. She folded her hands in front of her and bowed. "Mr. Bellamy, it's nice to see you again. Nice weather we're having, are we not?"

Finn stepped forward and wrapped her in a hug. "Nora, my dear, it's wonderful to see you in person again," he said warmly. "Now, why don't you show me around? I'd love to see the progress you've made on my house."

Finn looped Nora's hand through the crook of his arm and led her into The Grand Hall. Nora's face turned pink, and she stammered, "Y-yes, sir. It would be my honor."

Finn winked at me as he passed, and I rolled my eyes. Nora adored him, and he damn well knew it.

Chapter 14

Daiko

e Daiko, co-leader of The Society of Light, had always been a pragmatic man. It was his ability to think without emotion that allowed him to climb to the top of the most powerful secret organization in the world so early in life. Daiko always came out on top because he'd learned to hedge his bets. That was what he was doing as he handed his luggage to the man in the suit and slid into the black SUV.

Everything was set. The Society would fall within the week, followed by civilization as a whole, all while he watched from a secure location. Recently, it had become abundantly clear that The Order would be the victors in the end. They'd infiltrated every level of government in every country across the globe.

Despite The Society of Light's influence and power, The Order still managed to gain control over world leaders and secured enough uranium to create hundreds of nuclear bombs. It was a done deal.

The Shadow that cornered Daiko several weeks ago had attempted to blackmail him working as a double agent for The Order. However, once he'd presented The Order's position of power, Daiko instantly became a willing participant. He'd laughed at the assassin's disappointed face, knowing the Shadow had been looking forward to torturing him.

Daiko's first test had been to deliver Kirie Sorenson to the Shadowmen, a task he was happy to complete. The moment he'd felt her power in his Paris office, he'd known that Kirie was a threat to his authority. She, along with the Durant boy, had the power to take over The Society—the whole world if they wanted. Daiko couldn't risk losing his position. Besides, the girl was so naive, planting the tracker in her jacket had been easy.

Though Ms. Sorenson had survived the Shadowmen's attack in Rome, Daiko held up his side of the bargain, and The Order responded in kind. Their proposition was as simple as it was enticing: aid in the fall of The Society of Light and earn a seat of power in the new world order. They detailed their plan, showed their cards, and Daiko knew: The Society would lose the battle for Earth whether he stayed loyal or not. He didn't hesitate.

Daiko had nothing to lose and everything to gain. He had few family members—no wife, no children. His mistress was the authority The Society of Light had afforded him. He cared only for his own survival and the guarantee of future power.

Once he arrived safely at the bunker, the list of every Center of Light across the globe would be delivered to The Order via the dark web. It was all set.

His dark sedan pulled up to a nondescript home on the outskirts of town. Daiko's lip curled in disgust as he took in the run-down porch and sagging roof. Normally, he'd have no reason to step inside such squalor, but he supposed that was what made it the perfect hiding spot. His driver led him into the basement to a metal door flanked by two men in tailored black suits. Daiko could feel the shadows pouring off their cold skin, and he suppressed a shiver.

"Sir." They dipped their heads as Daiko passed. Their deference was intoxicating. Even the enemy bowed to him now. He briefly wondered if these dark agents would be spared by The Order in the end, or if they'd collateral damage. He didn't wonder for long. Once the thick metal door was sealed shut behind him, he'd forgotten all about the men.

He took a tour of the bunker, evaluating what was to be his home for the next several months. Marble floors and a state-of-the-art kitchen. Antique Chinese furniture dating back to the Qing Dynasty. A king-sized bed covered with high-quality sheets. A pantry full of his favorite foods. They'd followed his list of requests to perfection. He nodded in satisfaction. This would be an acceptable space to wait out the apocalypse.

According to the plan presented to him by his shadow liaison, Daiko would emerge from the bunker only after The Order had successfully eradicated the Children of Light and set up a stable, central government. At that point, he would then take his place in the highest levels of the New World Order—and everyone would bow to him.

Daiko pulled his laptop from his suitcase and placed it on the table. The Order had held up their end of the bargain. It was time for him to uphold his. He logged onto the dark web and downloaded the list of every Center of Light and safe house across the globe, along with a detailed inventory of their arsenal, compiling them into an email to "Unknown." He'd been able to locate Luca and the girl just outside London that morning, so he added their coordinates as well. He'd been disappointed to learn his close colleague had set up a secret safe house without his knowledge. After all their years serving together, Finn Bellamy hadn't trusted him. He was right not to, of course, but that was beside the point. *It wouldn't matter soon, anyway,* he thought with satisfaction. Finn would burn with the rest.

His finger hovered over the trackpad for a moment before he hit *send.* He sat back in his chair and sighed. It was done. He'd sealed the world's fate in one click. The Society of Light would fall within hours. Adrenalin shot through his veins at the sheer power he'd just wielded. Power was a drug to Daiko, an addiction he treasured above all else.

Feeling like a god, Diako walked to the bar and poured himself a drink. A moment like this should be celebrated. Leaning against the countertop, he faced the flat-screen TV attached to the concrete wall and turned on the news. He looked forward to spending the next few months sipping on brandy and watching the old world fall from the safety of his underground bunker. He swirled the amber liquid in the crystal decanter and smiled to himself. No more hiding in the shadows. No more directing from behind a curtain. He would be a king in the new world, and everyone would finally know his name. They would both love and fear him.

Hours later, Daiko slipped on a pair of red silk pajamas and turned in for the night. As he flipped the light switch off, a series of clicks filled the cavernous bunker. The last thing the leader of The Society of Light saw was a flash of brilliant white light.

Chapter 15

Luca

The other agents arrived just after dark. Luca watched from the front door as a line of late-model military Jeeps, tanks, and trucks rolled up the drive. They approached, lights off and slow-moving, so as not to garner attention from the sleepy neighbors. Two dozen male and female agents dressed in black tactical gear climbed out and immediately unloaded metal crates and gun cases.

A man with a thick beard and even thicker Scottish accent stepped forward and greeted Luca with a firm handshake. "Guid eenin, Durrant. Hou ar ye?"

Luca's chest warmed. "Doing well, Ailbert, all things considered. I see you've brought the calvary." Luca gestured to the agents hauling equipment into the estate.

Ailbert puffed up his chest comically. "Aye, that I did. Cannae let those shadow bastards win, now can we?"

"No, sir, we cannot." Luca slapped Ailbert's massive arm. "I'm happy to fight by your side."

His old friend smiled, his crooked teeth flashing behind his bushy beard. "It's eh fine day in 'ell when a Scott fights alongside a bloody Englishman."

Luca laughed. "That it is."

Kirie joined Luca on the front drive as her classmates pulled up in the back of a 1950s soft skin army truck, chaperoned by Bert and Aonani's mother, Leilani. The deep lines in the trainer's face said it had been a long trip. Luca helped them unload from the tall vehicle. A young girl of maybe thirteen took his hand and smiled at him.

"Well, hello there," she said with an Australian accent, batting her eyes. Luca bit back a laugh. This must be Eden, the difficult classmate Kirie told him about. She hadn't exaggerated; the pre-teen *was* trouble. Luca quickly handed her off to Nora, thankful she wasn't *his* trouble. A pair of unruly boys hopped out next. They pushed and shoved each other, laughing like a pair of hyenas. He was beginning to understand the cause of Bert's obvious exhaustion. A tall girl with midnight skin and a shaved head climbed out next. Her energy was calm and still, like a placid lake. Luca's muscles relaxed unconsciously, and he knew this must be Dawn.

Kirie rushed forward, swinging a tiny fireball with a mess of curly black hair into her arms. Aonani, Luca guessed.

"Hey! Put me down right now. I'm not a doll!" the girl protested. Kirie set her on the ground, her face flushed with happiness. Luca couldn't help but smile, too, as Kirie's joy saturated their bond.

"I just missed you, little stinker." She ruffled the girl's hair. Aonani swatted her hand away and gaped up at the manor.

"Mom! I get to live in a castle like a princess. This is so *awesome!*" Then she was off, presumably claiming dominion over her kingdom. Her mother, a middle-aged woman in a flowy green dress that swished around her ankles, gave Kirie a tired smile before chasing after her tiny tyrant.

They spent the next hour searching for extra bedding for the newcomers, but their search only yielded a couple of cots and several old mattresses. They were shabby and smelled slightly of mold, but at the end of the world, a bed was a bed. The antique furniture was promptly repurposed, and Luca felt sympathy for the agents who would end up sleeping on the torture devices the previous owners called sofas.

The stately estate quickly transformed, taking on a wartime atmosphere. Nora conducted operations like a general, pointing fingers, barking orders, and making lists. Tables were used for cleaning and assembling artillery, and the stink of sweaty bodies and gunpowder soon overrode the manor's usual moth-eaten cloth and lacquered mahogany scent. The presence of so many Agents of Light was electrifying. Their combined energy was enough to light up Piccadilly Circus.

The troops convened in the ballroom at midnight to strategize. A small army of Agents of Light stood facing their leader, their moods somber. The older agents held glasses of whiskey to steel their nerves. Luca, Kirie, Alena, and Abbott stood shoulder-to-shoulder in a tight line. Surprisingly, Zoeya walked up in another Teenage Mutant Ninja Turtle sweater and stood next to Alena. The two seemed to gravitate to one another despite their ongoing bickering.

Mr. Bellamy called everyone to attention, and all eyes turned to him. The leader of the oldest organization in the world stood in the center of the gathering with his feet slightly apart and his hands folded behind his back. Luca marveled at the man's ability to control a room. He could handle Mr. Bellamy when he was acting as Kirie's father, challenge him even. But when he slipped into leadership mode, power rippled off him, and his command over a crowd was absolute. Luca felt truly cowed.

"As you all know, Mr. Daiko has been colluding with The Order," he began in an authoritative tone. An angry murmur rippled through the assembly. Finn held up a hand, and the agents fell silent. "We can reasonably assume that he's provided the enemy with highly classified information. Our centers of Light as well as personnel are no longer secure."

"Where is he now?" Kiran called out. Vengeance was written all over his rigid stance. Clearly, he wanted blood for Bodhi's death. Luca hadn't known the two men long, but he imagined their bond was something akin to his and Arin's. Luca knew better than anyone the pain Kiran must be feeling over the loss of his fallen brother.

"Unfortunately, Mr. Daiko has gone dark, both tactically and metaphorically. Given what we know about The Order's plans, it is likely that he's made a deal with the Shadowmen and is now hiding in a bunker somewhere. On the bright side, we no longer need to worry about him monitoring us or relaying information to the enemy."

"The man was an arse. I say let 'em rot in his wee hidey-hole!" Ailbert yelled, throwing back his whisky.

"Here, here!" several agents yelled in agreement.

Mr. Bellamy waited patiently for the cries to die down once more. "As you know, The Order has acquired an arsenal of nuclear weapons they plan to detonate across the globe. Their goal is nothing short of total annihilation. Thankfully, we were able to acquire a list of the bombs' locations."

"Where did you get this list, and how do we know it's reliable data?" Kiran challenged. His arms were folded tightly over his chest, his veins clearly visible.

"It's enough to say that I've confirmed the intel is good," Finn said in a firm tone. The two men stared each other down. The air crackled with their warring energies, and the hair on Luca's arms stood on end. Kirie leaned into him, and he put a reassuring hand on her lower back. Luca wondered if the staring contest would come to blows, but after several tense moments, Kiran finally backed down. Satisfied, Mr. Bellamy nodded and continued.

"Each package will arrive at its designated location on the morning of April 25th, which is"–he looked down at his watch–"approximately thirty-six hours from now. Your assignments are simple. You will each be given a drop location.

You will intercept and deactivate the bombs before the shadows can use them against the public. You will then reconvene at the nearest safe house. The addresses are listed on your assignment sheets. Each safe house is outfitted with provisions and a satellite phone. You will check in once your mission is complete and you are safe. Any questions?"

Phoebe stepped forward. Her ice-blonde hair was slicked back in a high bun, giving her face a tight look. "There are two hundred locations," she said in a thick Danish accent. She pointed her sharp chin at the dozens in assembly. "We can't possibly be everywhere at once."

"Of course, you're right. About a thousand agents worldwide have already been activated, and Mrs. Delgado is working with us to coordinate efforts," Mr. Bellamy explained.

Luca's brows shot up in surprise. They'd given him the list just a day ago. The man worked fast.

"Any other questions?" Mr. Bellamy made eye contact with each agent across the ballroom, but no one else stepped forward. He clapped once and pointed at Nora, who was waiting in the wings. "Wonderful. Nora has your assignments."

The older woman walked to the center of the gathering and called out teams of four, handing each a sheet of paper. Nora ordered Luca to step forward along with Alena, Zoeya, and Kirie. He sighed in relief, thankful he wouldn't have to beg Mr. Bellamy to put them on the same team. He and Kirie had pinky promised to stay together to the end, and he intended to keep that promise. Nora handed Luca their assignment, and the girls leaned over his shoulder to read the details of their mission. There were only three lines of text printed on the otherwise empty sheet: the names of the group members, the location of the bomb, and the address of their assigned safe house.

Alena pointed to the address at the top of the paper. "Does anyone know where this is?"

Luca nodded. He'd recognized the street from his childhood living in London. Mr. Bellamy likely assigned London to him, knowing he was familiar with its streets. "That's near downtown London, a city municipal building, I believe. We'll need to leave early to avoid morning traffic."

Kirie, Alena, and Zoeya formed a circle and began making plans. They would be leaving early on the morning of April 25th. That gave them one more day at Mentmore to prepare. Luca sensed someone shift uncomfortably behind them, and he turned to see Abbott standing alone. He studied his mentor. There were deep grooves in his mature face, and his lips were thin and tight. Something was bothering Abbott.

Luca turned, opening the circle to him. "What's your assignment?"

The older man put his hands in his trouser pockets and shrugged. "I'm going to stay here to help Nora secure the safe house and keep an eye on the juvenile agents."

Luca walked over and nudged Abbott playfully with his elbow, trying to shake him from his melancholy. "What's wrong? Not looking forward to babysitting?"

Ignoring Luca's ribbing, Abbott let out a heavy sigh. "No, it's not that. I'm happy to help where I'm needed."

Luca turned to the others. "I'll catch up with you all in a moment. Abbott and I need a word."

Seeming to sense Luca's worry through their bond, Kirie led the others away. "Come on, guys. Let's grab some weapons before the other agents claim the best ones. Zoeya, do you prefer guns or sharp objects?"

The young woman threw her palms up, her face twisting in disgust. "Oh, no! I work with *tech*. It's my job to deactivate the bomb. I'll leave the cutting to the rest of you," she said, pointing to Alena and Kirie. Alena rolled her caramel eyes and began lecturing Zoeya on the need for each Agent of Light to be able to defend herself.

Once they were out of hearing range, Luca turned to Abbott and placed a hand on his forearm. "Tell me what's on your mind, my old friend."

His eyes lowered to the glass of whiskey in his hands, absentmindedly swirling the amber liquid. "It's just…I've been a part of The Society of Light since I was a child. I've devoted my life to its edict of bringing light, peace, and freedom to the world." He paused, seeming to struggle with his words.

Luca considered his mentor closely, realizing with a start that his light had dimmed slightly. Abbott had always been the most optimistic and unbothered man he'd ever known. In all the months he'd trained Luca to master his shadows, he'd never once lost faith in him, even when Luca lost faith in himself. Seeing him now, diminished and defeated, saddened Luca. It was as if the ground beneath his feet was no longer steady.

"No one has been more devoted to The Society of Light than you," Luca said, trying to reassure him.

"Thank you." Abbott nodded and swallowed hard before continuing. "It's just…I question my discernment. I wasn't able to identify the enemies standing right before me. I trusted Mr. Daiko, worked with him for years. And I *loved* Arin. To me, they were both essential members of The Society of Light. They were *Bright Ones,* defenders of goodness and light. Their betrayal has shaken my faith in mankind. It has made me question my very existence."

Luca's heart twisted in his chest. He, too, had questioned his ability to read people after Arin's defection. He'd missed all the warning signs, relying on his devotion to his brother rather than his critical brain. If he'd only been awake, he might have saved Arin from the Shadowmen's tactics. He might even be standing next to him at that very moment. But Abbott's disillusionment went deeper than his own personal failure. Abbott had lost faith in his belief system. Luca hadn't experienced a loss of faith after Arin's death because he'd never bought into the illusion that The Society of Light was perfect. When Abbott had brought him in, Luca had been exposed to the darker side of the organization. Despite their claim to hold the higher ground, many agents and leaders treated him like a second-class agent, someone who couldn't be trusted. He was only ten years old at the time—a *child.* If it hadn't been for Abbott's influence, they might have tossed him right back onto the streets for the Shadowmen to devour. Still, Abbott had been steadfast in his faith in The Society and its ideology. Until now, it seemed.

Luca draped an arm around his mentor's shoulder. "*You* are the light and hope in this organization. Think of all the countless children you rescued from the Shadowmen who hunted them. And if it weren't for you, I'd be either a serial killer or six feet underground. Arin's and Daiko's actions do not negate the good you've done."

"Perhaps you're right." Tears filled Abbott's eyes. "But it's more than a faith crisis. Arin was like a son to me. I just…I miss him," he confessed, his voice thick with emotion.

Luca's own eyes burned, and his throat tightened. "I do, too," he whispered. He and Abbott hadn't had the chance to fully process what happened in the Iranian mine. Abbott had led the mission that night, and Luca knew he'd carry the guilt of its failure, whether it was *his* fault or not. In the wake of Mr. Daiko's betrayal, Abbott clearly hadn't had the chance to fully acknowledge Arin's betrayal or his death.

Luca wrapped his arms tightly around his mentor as he sobbed. It broke something inside Luca to see Abbott fall apart. He'd always been his rock, his steady ground. Alena, somehow alerted by their pain, separated from the others and joined them. She and Luca wrapped Abbott into a tight hug, and they mourned their fallen brother together.

Chapter 16

Kirie

The agents retired to their makeshift beds, and their excited whispers echoed from the Grand Hall like we were at one big sleepover. Their hushed voices mingled with my spinning thoughts, chasing away sleep. In just two days, a world that had been here for millions of years would either end or it wouldn't. Most of the agents were leaving the next day, and then it was up to Luca, Alena, Zoeya, and me to save our little corner of England. Giving up the pretense of sleep, I decided to make use of the bathroom before the other agents awoke. It was still dark beyond the window, and the sun wouldn't be up for another half hour. I lifted the blankets slowly, trying not to wake Luca, but his arm flexed around my hip before I could make it out of bed.

"Where are you going?" Luca grumbled, eyes still closed.

"Bathroom. Let me up." I slapped his arm playfully, and Luca released me with a groan. I tiptoed down the dark hallway, peering over the railing to the agents below. It was nearly dawn, and some were beginning to stir. They looked as though they'd had a rough night. I felt guilty for sleeping on a plush queen-sized bed, but not enough to want to give it up.

As I exited the bathroom, I ran headlong into a mess of caramel hair.

"Oh, I'm sorry!" I squeaked. Alena stood in the doorway. I put my hands up in surrender out of habit, but she simply yawned and elbowed me out of the way.

"Mi scusi," she said before shutting the door in my face. I sighed in relief and turned back to my room.

BOOM

An explosion rent the air, rattling the windows and vibrating the walls. It slammed into me like a punch to the chest, knocking the breath from my lungs. Alena darted out of the bathroom, and we stared at one another with wide eyes. Behind her, the bathroom light blinked off.

"W-what the hell was that?" I stammered.

She shook her head and turned back to her room. "I need to find Arabella."

Bedroom doors flew open one by one as the rooms belched their residents. The agents below ran upstairs, and within seconds, the dark hallway was full of pajama-clad Agents of Light on high alert, each holding weapons of varying kinds. Even my classmates had sprung from bed. Leilani held a sleepy Aonani in her arms, and Dawn and Eden were pressed against the walls. Liang stood in front of a red-eyed Dayton, with a long sword at his side. The boys' stern expressions mimicked Bert's signature glare, as if they were ready to take on a million Shadowmen. I would have laughed at the pair of them if I weren't so unsettled.

Luca was by my side in an instant, hands alight. "Are you okay?" I simply shrugged, not sure what had happened.

Bert appeared at the end of the hallway and flipped a light switch along the wood-paneled wall. Nothing happened. "Il y a une coupe de courant," he called in French. *The power is out.*

Zoeya ran up the stairs wearing Teenage Mutant Ninja Turtles pjs and fuzzy slippers. She halted at the top step, panting heavily. "Come on, everybody," she called out, face grim as she waved for us to follow her. "That sound came from the sky."

We followed Zoeya in a single-file line down the grand staircase, through the vestibule, and out onto the front drive. Dozens of feet crunched in the gravel as agents, young and old, searched for the cause of the explosion. I gasped as an orange ball of fire came into view in the southern sky. The air was charged with electricity, sending my hair on end.

A commercial passenger plane roared overhead, pulling our gazes from the fireball. It was flying entirely too low and was losing altitude by the second. Suddenly, it disappeared from view, and a flare of light exploded across the pre-dawn horizon. A breath later, the ground shook so fiercely, my teeth chattered. I grabbed Luca's arm to steady myself.

"My god," Dawn whispered.

We stood in stunned silence as we processed what we were seeing. Something had exploded above just minutes before we lost power and the plane fell to the Earth. Clearly the explosion was the cause. My stomach rolled thinking of the many people aboard that aircraft. How many poor souls had just crashed to their deaths? One hundred? Two hundred? Three? I clapped a hand over my mouth and leaned over, fighting nausea. Luca placed a warm hand on my back.

Zoeya stood in the center of the drive, studying the orange orb. "Looks like a low-altitude EMP," she said.

Aonani lifted her head from her mother's shoulders, her tiny face scrunched in confusion.

Dayton turned to her. "EMP stands for *electron magnetic pulse*," he began to explain like an older brother.

Her curly black hair bounced wildly as she climbed down and glared up at the boy, fists tightly balled at her side. "I know what an EMP is, you dummy!"

Dayton folded his arms and looked down his nose at Aonani. "Oh yeah? Then explain it to me if you're so smart," he challenged.

"It's when a bad guy detonates a nuclear bomb in the sky, and the electromagnetic surge blows up all the electronics. Stuff like phones, cars, and planes stop working. That's why that big plane fell from the sky, you idiot. EMPs are bad news." The little girl stuck her tongue out at him.

Zoeya nodded. "The scary little girl is correct. This is really bad news."

I straightened and gazed back up at the orange sky. This was more than *bad news*. EMPs had the power to cripple entire cities in a single moment. Our whole modern society relied on our use of electronics, and destroying the grid destroyed a city's ability to access heat, water, and energy. It wouldn't be long before that whole area would devolve into complete chaos.

"If all the vehicles are fried, does that mean you can't complete your missions?" Eden asked.

Zoeya shook her head and pointed to the line of late-model military vehicles the agents rode in on the night before. "No. Those vehicles were built in the 1960s and 70s, so they don't have computer chips." Her brows lifted, and she pursed her lips. "We're lucky Mr. Bellamy has a thing for antique military vehicles, or our mission would be over before we got started."

I stared at the late-model Jeeps and SUVs. Finn did love old things; that was true. But this was too much of a coincidence. I turned back to the manor, thinking of the Faraday cage sitting smack dab in the center of the ballroom. He must have known this would happen. He clearly prepared for it. I ground my teeth together. A little warning would have been nice. I searched the crowd for the man in question, but he was nowhere to be seen.

Arabella pulled on Alena's hand, eyes wild and lip trembling. "What's happening?" she asked, lip trembling. "What's going on?"

Alena bent down until she was face-to-face with the ten-year-old. She took her hands in hers and leveled her with a sober look. "The final battle between Darkness and Light has begun. It's time to be brave, mi bambina. Can you do that for me?" Tears began to roll down Arabella's cheeks, but she squared her shoulders and nodded with grim determination. I couldn't help but admire the strange girl. Out of all of us, besides Luca, she was most acquainted with the dark, and she was prepared to meet it head-on.

"Come inside, all of you, and get dressed," Nora called from the front door. "Mr. Bellamy wants everyone in the ballroom in ten minutes. We've got a mission to complete, and the clock is ticking." With the stature of a general, she stood at the entryway, ready to usher the troops inside.

The agents sprang to action. Luca and I ran to our room and were dressed in our black tactical gear within three minutes. We filed into the ballroom alongside a contingent of uniformed agents in under five minutes. Finn was in the Faraday Cage when we arrived, hunched over the telephone speaking quietly to someone on the other end. He hung up and walked out to meet us.

We gathered in a semi-circle around our leader. I nervously ran a hand over my weapon vest, ensuring my throwing knives were secure as Finn confirmed that The Order had indeed deployed an EMP over London. All unprotected electronics were dead—planes were falling from the sky and utility systems were offline—in other words, it was the beginning of the apocalypse.

The Shadowmen had detonated a freaking nuclear bomb in the atmosphere above a major city! My whole body shook from fear and shock at their sheer audacity. Logically, I knew they were planning to do much worse, but witnessing such a brazen attack sent shockwaves through my system.

"Unfortunately, it doesn't end there," Finn continued. "As I feared, Mr. Daiko leaked the location of our centers. As we slept, The Order executed a coordinated attack on every Center of Light across the globe. I just got off the phone with Mrs. Delgado, and she confirmed that none of our centers still stand."

My body felt numb as the reality of the situation sank in.

"Were there any survivors?" Phoebe asked. Somehow, her face was even paler than usual.

Finn offered her a reassuring smile. "Thankfully, our casualties were few. After Mr. Daiko went dark, we felt it prudent to evacuate our centers. However, that does mean our ability to communicate is severely limited. Many other cities were hit with EMPs, further complicating our ability to coordinate a defense. We will have to rely on satellite phones and landlines going forward."

"What about the mission?" Kiran questioned. "Didn't you say all transportation is down? How will we get to our locations in time if we can't fly?"

Kiran's team was assigned to Mumbai, India, and they were set to leave for the airport that afternoon. Without working airplanes, intercepting their assigned nuke by tomorrow would be impossible. I chewed on my bottom lip as the agents argued over the logistics of a nonviable mission.

Nora clapped her hands three times and yelled, "Quiet!" The room fell silent.

"Thank you, Nora." Finn bowed to the older woman, who nodded in return. "Do not fear. We've prepared for scenarios such as these. We are not without resources. Each vehicle has a satellite phone in EMP-proof bags tucked beneath the back seat, so we will still be able to communicate over long distances. As for transportation, I own several hangars at Northolt Airport, which are stocked with enough late-model Learjets to get each team where it needs to go. But they're old and slow, so you'll need to leave within the hour to hit your marks in time. You must stay vigilant. The civilians will be desperate and afraid, so stay off the main roads."

The agents began to break ranks, but Finn stalled them with a raised hand. "One more moment." He waited until the room fell still and all eyes were on him, making eye contact with each agent. "I do not need to remind you of the gravity of our situation. This is the moment you have trained for all your lives. For thousands of years, the Children of Light have battled against Darkness. Like a mighty dam, we have kept the forces of evil at bay. It may seem as though the cards are stacked against us, that Darkness has the upper hand. But all is not lost. As long as we live and breathe, there is hope. We will not go gently into the night. We will hold onto the light." Finn's voice rang with righteous authority, his rallying words echoing off the ballroom walls. "In this, our darkest moment, our power *will* break through the Darkness. We will not fail mankind in this, our final hour."

Each agent raised a shining fist in the air with a cry, and a blinding light filled the room. Tears pricked my eyes as I joined them, my own skin shining with exhilaration. My chest felt as though it might explode with pride and conviction. I had to admit that dear old dad knew how to deliver a speech. I was beginning to understand why he was chosen to co-lead The Society of Light.

Finn nodded his approval. "You are dismissed. God speed!"

The Agents of Light gathered with their teams and prepared to leave. Their nervous energy sent chills skittering across my skin, and I could almost taste the adrenaline in the air. This was it, just like The War Scroll had prophesied. The seventh and final battle for Earth had begun. A familiar pressure grew in my core as panic threatened to take over my body. I took a deep breath, trying to suppress my fear. Everything was moving too fast. We weren't ready. I watched the agents work together like a practiced dance as they packed their weapons and gear, and I realized that perhaps it was just *I* who wasn't ready. Just seven months ago, I was a sheltered high school senior. Now I was going to war against an ancient force too vast to comprehend. True, I had grown since my mother's death, but was I strong enough to go against The Void?

Luca grabbed my hand, sending a bolt of warmth and calm through our bond. "Come on, let's get out of the way." He called over to Alena, who was still holding Arabella's hand. "Collect Zoeya and meet us in the kitchen. We need to make a new plan."

Donovan

Donovan sat in the driver's seat of a nondescript SUV, hidden deep within a copse of trees. Just up that hill sat a stately English manor. Its towers reached high in the air, ostentatious and imposing, just like the agents hiding within. Donovan and Ciara waited in silence for the signal from fellow shadows that it was go time.

In the quiet of the cabin, he heard the cock of a pistol. He turned to look at his apprentice. His eyes widened in surprise. Ciara held a firearm aimed directly at his face. Her colorless lips lifted in a cruel smile.

"What the fuck are you doing?" he said, swiping at the gun. She leaned back, dodging his efforts to disarm her.

"We know about the list," she rasped. She offered no further explanation. None was needed. Donovan's stomach sank. They knew what he'd given the boy. Of course they did.

"You don't understand. This war…everything we've been fighting for, it was never just about killing the Bright Ones. The Order means to destroy us all." He knew appealing to the psychotic girl was useless, but Donovan couldn't just lie down and die.

"You know, I've always looked up to you. The Order's finest assassin. Now look at you." Ciara cocked her head to the side and frowned.

Donovan swiped at the gun again, unsuccessfully. "Listen to me, you bloody twat!" He roared, heat rising in his pot-marked cheeks. "The Order doesn't intend for any of us to survive. We're leading ourselves to our own slaughter."

Ciara tightened her grip on the gun, her face twisting into a hateful mask. "You've lost your mind, old man. The Society of Light has fallen. The nations are under our control. All we have to do now is to destroy the existing structure, and this world is all ours. That's all we have to do, and you nearly fucked it up!"

Ciara pulled the trigger, and blood suddenly coated the driver's side window. Donovan slumped over the wheel, a gaping hole in his forehead.

Ciara wiped a drop of blood from her cheek and climbed out of the car, where a small battalion of Shadowmen waited. "Come on. Let's go bag some Society scum."

Chapter 17

Kirie

**he** four of us sat around the kitchen table, each holding a cup of hot tea. The warmth did little to ease my trembling fingers.

"How bad is it out there?" Alena asked.

Zoeya set her mug down and sighed. "EMPs are designed to destroy a city's entire grid. That means medical facilities, police stations, businesses, shipping yards, everything will have come to a halt instantly. Ninety percent of the world's population will die within a year if we don't find a way to get the grids back online."

Luca pinched the bridge of his nose and scrunched his eyes closed. "That's only half of the equation. If we don't deactivate the bloody bombs in time, not only will they wipe out a huge portion of the world's population, but the radiation will also trigger a nuclear winter that will finish us off for good." He let his hand drop to the table with a thud. "Either way, it's the perfect plan of extinction."

Zoeya pointed a finger at Luca. "Exactly. Even if we were able to find and neutralize enough of the bombs to save some semblance of humanity, which will now be more difficult without the use of technology, it would still take years to rebuild the infrastructure destroyed by these EMPs. By then, most of us will have starved to death." She shook her head. "We're officially the walking dead."

"I don't accept that!" Alena slammed a fist on the table, spilling her tea. I jumped in my seat, startled by her outburst. "I refuse just to lie down and let Darkness annihilate us without a fight." Her skin began to glow, illuminating her beautifully fierce face.

Luca raised his teacup. "Here, here! We'll fight until the end."

We all raised our cups in solidarity. There was a tightness in my chest, a mix of pride and fear. No, we would not go quietly into the night. We were Children of Light. What were we if not beacons? Dead men walking or not, we would shine.

My classmates tromped into the kitchen like a herd of elephants.

"Ms. Nora said we could have a snack," Dayton announced, heading straight for the pantry, the others close on his heels.

Eden grabbed a fruit tray from the fridge, and she, Dawn, and Aonani sat at the end of the table to share their bounty. Zoeya reached over Eden's shoulder and snagged a strawberry.

"Hey!" Eden cried "Get your own food!"

"Eden, be kind," Dawn chided the girl. She smiled at Zoeya and pushed the tray a few inches her way.

"Well, thank you, Dawn. That's very kind of *you*." Zoeya grabbed another strawberry and stuck her tongue out at Eden who leveled her with a glare.

Finn walked into the kitchen next, and the crowded room fell silent. My rowdy classmates froze, their eyes widened and mouths pinched as the all-powerful Mr. Bellamy graced us with his presence. I knew he was a powerful man, one of the most powerful men in the world, but I still couldn't understand why everyone seemed so nervous around him. To me, he'd always just been, well, *Finn*, light instructor and birth dad. Bert was one hundred times scarier.

"The other agents are just about ready to leave," Finn announced.

Aonani slumped in her seat and pouted. "We have to stay behind and hide in a bomb shelter like babies!" she grouched.

I perked up. "We have a bomb shelter?" In the many days I'd spent at Mentmore Towers, I'd never once run across one. It certainly wasn't part of Nora's initial tour.

Finn walked over to the fridge and took out a water bottle. "Indeed, we do. The Rothschilds had one installed beneath the garden during World War Two. The children will stay there until the coast is clear." He uncapped the water bottle, pressed it to his mouth, and tipped it back.

"But we want to help." Aonani stuck out her sticky bottom lip as far as it would go.

Finn set his bottle down and tried to smother a laugh at Aonani's dramatic pouty face. "Someday, my little warrior. But not today." He turned to our team. "What's your plan for reaching your drop location tomorrow?"

Luca leaned his elbows on the table and let out a tired breath. "Obviously, things have changed in the past few hours. Normally, it takes about an hour and thirty minutes to reach London using the M1. However, we'll need to assume major roads will be littered with dead vehicles and desperate citizens, making them impassible. Our best bet is to take country roads, which…"

"Which will take much longer," Alena finished for him.

"We'll need to leave before dawn to ensure we don't miss the drop off," Zoeya said around a mouthful of strawberry.

Finn focused his attention on Luca. "Mr. Durrant, how well do you know the English countryside?"

Luca shrugged. "Not well, I admit. I spent most of my youth in London."

Finn nodded and pushed off the kitchen counter. "Well, I guess you'll need to get there the old-fashioned way–using *paper maps.*"

Zoeya snorted loudly. "Where are we going to find old maps of London?"

"I believe I saw a stack of them in the basement last time I was down there." Finn turned to me. "Kirie, why don't you go see if there's anything current enough to be helpful?"

My eyes widened. "The basement?" I squeaked. It wasn't that I didn't want to go on a search for early 20th-century maps. I'd never seen one outside of the movies, and I was curious. It was the thought of going down to the *basement* that caused dread to pool in my belly. I'd rather go into an abandoned attic than some creepy old basement any day of the week.

Finn pointed to Eden, who was chomping on a handful of blueberries and staring longingly at Luca. "Eden."

She jumped in her seat with a squeak. "Yes, sir?"

I covered my mouth to suppress a smile. Her growing infatuation with my boyfriend was becoming more obvious every minute. The poor girl had no poker face.

"Why don't you go with her?" Finn asked, a smile playing on his own lips.

"You got it, mate," she said with a cheeky salute.

I reluctantly stood and headed toward the exit. Eden followed me out, smiling shamelessly at Luca as we passed. We made our way through the servants' quarters to an old wooden door that led to a stone staircase. My heart rate sped up as we descended into the daylight basement. I gazed longingly at the light switch on the wall, wishing desperately that we had electricity.

Two rows of concrete pillars lined the room, creating a kind of hallway down its center. It smelled of mold and wet stone. Weak light filtered in through the high, narrow windows lining the outside wall, casting deep shadows in the corners. A shiver passed through me. There was never enough sun in England for my liking.

"I hate basements," I said, kicking aside a box of brass fixtures. The clanking echoed off the concrete walls.

"Are you scared?" Eden taunted.

I shrugged. "Maybe."

We had an unfinished basement in Colorado that my mom used strictly for storage. Anytime I was forced to go down there, I'd turn on all the lights and leave the door at the top of the stairs wide open. It never helped ease my fears. The concrete floor was cracked, damp, and cold even during summer. "I used to think the devil lived in my basement back home."

Eden snorted. "That's just dumb. The devil doesn't exist."

I thought of Donovan holding a knife to my mother's throat and frowned. "Doesn't he?"

We split up to look for the maps. The low ceilings were covered in spiderwebs, and a low-hanging strand caught in my hair. I swatted at it violently, imagining an eight-legged monster crawling all over me. I nearly gagged as I wiped the sticky threads from my fingers. The only thing I hated more than basements and darkness was spiders. They creeped me out with their too many eyes and their too many legs.

"Hey, I think I found something," Eden called. I followed her voice to the basement's east corner. She stood next to an antique table covered in boxes and heaps of folded maps. Bingo. I picked one up and blew off the thick layer of dust. A white cloud billowed around us.

"Watch it!" Eden waved her hand across her face and coughed dramatically.

"You're fine," I replied, rolling my eyes just as dramatically. I never had a little sister, but I imagined it would be something like this.

I picked up the nearest map and unrolled it. It was one of Kent, England, from the early 1990s. Interesting, but too old to be helpful. I set it down and rifled through the boxes someone had haphazardly dumped on the antique table. There were dozens of rolls and books of paper maps, some yellowed with age and curling around the edges. I picked up another map, about four feet in length, and spread it across the tops of the boxes.

Eden leaned over my shoulder and pointed to a date stamped into the corner. "This one's from 1902. That's cool."

I ran my fingers over the outdated streets and landmarks. It would be great in a frame, but totally useless for our mission. "Cool, but too old."

A rustling like dried leaves echoed down the concrete hallway behind us. My back straightened. "Did you hear that?" I asked.

I walked into the center of the basement, straining my eyes and ears for a gust of wind or footsteps–anything to explain the rusting noise. Nothing. "The back door must have been left ajar," I murmured.

Eden snorted behind me. "Maybe it's the *devil*."

I shook my head. The girl had an endless supply of sass. "You're such a brat. You know that, right?"

"Well, yeah," she said with a laugh. "That's part of my charm."

There was a rustling sound again. This time, Eden's smirk slipped from her mouth, and she slowly joined me in the middle of the long, basement hallway.

The hair on my arms stood up as the air became heavy and cold. My hand began to tremble. I quickly made for the exit, but when I reached the stairs, I noticed Eden wasn't behind me. Turning, I saw her standing motionless in the center of the hallway, seemingly stunned. "What?" I asked.

She held up a hand and blew out a puff of white air that curled around her fingers.

"Oh, crap," I breathed. My own breath came out in a puff of white.

Eden rubbed her exposed arms, her skin covered in goose flesh. "Know what? I think I hate basements, too."

We turned and ran up the stairs two at a time. Just before we reached the top, the door to the upper floor slammed shut. I lunged forward and turned the handle. Locked. I didn't even know the door had a lock.

Icy dread spread through my veins. "This is bad."

Eden let out a tremulous laugh. "Stop being gutless, Kirie. It's just Aonani playing tricks again." She pushed me aside and pounded on the door. "Hey, dipstick! This isn't funny. Let us out, or you'll regret it," she yelled.

I tuned Eden out as she continued her assault on the door and crept down the stairs, squinting as I searched the dim room for moving shadows. Just as my foot touched the last step, a high-pitched laugh echoed against the stone walls, and pure panic stole my breath at the sound. I would know that one-of-a-kind psychotic laugh in a crowded room.

Ciara.

The Order found us.

"What was that?" Eden crept down the stairs and moved to pass me, but I elbowed her back behind me. Ignoring her cry of protest, I positioned myself between her and the looming threat.

"Stay behind me," I commanded. For once, the foolish girl didn't argue.

Standing in a defensive position, I pulled my energy into my core and then down my arms. My glowing hands cast the shadows into the far corners of the underground room. I turned and whispered to Eden. "Remember what Bert taught us." Her eyes widened as understanding dawned.

Several human-shaped shadows rushed from the darkness. I shot bolts of energy in quick succession, scattering them before they collided with us. Eden ducked and covered her head, her high-pitched scream nearly shattering my concentration. I shot bolts of light at each advancing shadow, hitting none. They disappeared into the dark corners again.

I swung on the younger girl. "Eden! Stop screaming. On your feet! *Now!*"

She threw a hand over her mouth and nodded, her wide eyes glassy with fear. Eden stood, her knees visibly shaking.

"Remember what Bert taught us," I said again. Eden whimpered but did as I said. She set her feet hip-width apart, and her hands began to glow. "Good. Whatever happens, don't let them touch you."

The shadows rushed us again, swirling around us like a tornado. Eden and I shot bolts of light at the moving targets, doing minimal damage. I growled in frustration as I shot faster, depleting my energy source.

Through the maelstrom, a girl with blood-red hair and black orb eyes emerged. My blood began to boil as Ciara strolled forward as if she hadn't a care in the world. Her fellow shadows stopped circling us and reverted to their human forms. They lined up on either side of her, three black-eyed men and two women, each wearing nondescript dark clothes. It was clear by their smug smiles that they believed they had already won. Two young girls cornered underground. Easy. Didn't they know it hadn't turned out in Ciara's favor the last time she had me trapped underground? Didn't they know by now I wasn't so easily killed?

I bared my teeth at the demon, my body flushing hot with fury. The last time I'd seen Ciara, she'd forced me to watch Arin die in that hellish mine. Killing Arin had been nothing but a sick game to her and her fellow Shadowmen—a way to break

Luca and me so that we'd hand over The Society's secrets. They'd *fed* off our grief and pain like sick vultures. Ciara was a monster wearing a human face, and I hated her with every fiber of my being.

"Long time no see, little doll," she rasped. I startled at the strange sound. Gone was the high, child-like voice that had haunted my nightmares. Something must have happened to her throat in the fire. I inspected her as she strode closer. Her pale white skin—once as youthful as her voice—was now red and rippled in places. So she hadn't escaped the fire completely. A smile rose on my own face at the thought. Good. I hoped that it had hurt.

"Who the hell are you?" Eden said, leaning around me. I elbowed her back.

"Ooh, delightful," Ciara purred. "Fresh meat. This is going to be so much fun!"

"You will not touch her," I said through clenched teeth. I would die before I let her harm another one of *my* people.

I raised my palms and shot bolts of energy at Ciara's chest. Dipping and weaving, she rushed forward, successfully dodging my assault. She slammed into me, and we tumbled into a mass of flailing arms and legs, nearly missing Eden, who screamed and fell back. My back hit the cement floor with a thud, and pain shot up my spine. Ciara placed her icy palms on either side of my face, preferring to fight with her hands like always. Familiar feelings of defeat and depression slammed into me at her touch, but this was familiar ground for me. I'd endured worse for longer. I was no longer afraid of her darkness. Gritting my teeth, I forced her dark energy from my body, refusing to let her venom undo me this time. Using a maneuver Bert had taught me, I hooked my leg beneath hers and flipped her onto her back. Straddling her chest, I punched her in the face over and over. She laughed with each blow as if I were hitting her with feathers.

Another Shadowman wrapped an arm around my throat, yanking me up and off Ciara. I clawed at the shadow's arm as Ciara lazily stood to face me, blood dripping from the corner of her slit lip. Behind me were the unmistakable sounds of Eden and another shadow scuffling. Adrenaline pumped heavily in my veins. I had to get Eden to safety. I had to warn the others.

Pulling every spark of energy left into my core, I directed it into the man's skin. He cried out, releasing his arm from my neck. I dropped into a crouch and swept his legs out from beneath him. He fell hard onto the cement with an umph. I shot a bolt of light at his chest–right where his black heart lay. He jerked once and lay still. Dead. Ciara hung back, seemingly enjoying the show.

Ignoring her, I jumped over the shadow's prone body. Eden lay ten feet away, whimpering as the female shadow held her hands to her skin. My pulse quickened. I knew the torture she was enduring. Within minutes, Eden might be lost. I pulled the shadow off my friend by her hair. Ciara laughed as she watched me attack her fellow shadows, completely unconcerned about their welfare. I wasn't surprised at her lack of empathy. Ciara's soul was as black as The Void.

Reaching down, I pulled Eden up from the floor. She blinked as she woke from the shadow's nightmare. "Go! Run!"

I yelled, pushing her toward the basement door. She stumbled up the stairs, and I turned back to face Ciara.

"You're truly sick," I spat. Her only answer was a sharp, predatory smile just before she dissolved into smoke.

I heard a splintering crack behind me, and I spun around. Eden stood at the top of the gaping doorway, panting. I nearly cried in relief when I saw she'd blown the basement door off its hinges. "Kirie, let's go!" she yelled, waving me forward.

Several more Shadowmen poured in through the basement windows, filling the space with a cold fog. One by one, they materialized. At least a dozen black-eyed monsters stared back at me.

Time to go. Shooting a volley of bolts at the mass, I turned and raced up the stairs.

Chapter 18

Kirie

y heart pounded in my ears as the shadows chased us up the basement steps. I nearly ran into Eden as I burst through the doorway.

"Hurry," I gasped, grasping her hand.

We ran through the labyrinthine, door-lined halls, the shadows not far behind. The passageways were narrow in the servants' quarters, and the dingy windows let in little light. Turning a sharp corner, I pulled Eden into an empty room and locked the door. It was small and the air was musty, as if it no one had entered the room for ages. In the corner, I saw a tall antique wardrobe. I dragged Eden into it, and quietly shut the doors. We huddled together in the darkness. The of the cabinet smelled of mothballs and dust, threatening to make me sneeze. Eden's body vibrated with fear and nerves. I sent a small stream of energy through our joined hands for comfort. Her shaking eased, but only slightly.

We held our breaths as a wave of ice and malice entered the room. Eden clung to me with shaking arms. Our hearts beat so loudly that I worried the Shadowman would hear them. But the shadow, whoever it was, must have been in too big a hurry to be thorough, because it quickly moved on, taking its chill with it. I let out a cautious breath of relief as the temperature returned to normal. I knew our luck wouldn't hold. Our energy was a beacon for the Shadowmen that couldn't be hidden for long. Fresh dread dripped through my veins when I realized that the further from us the shadows moved, the closer they got to the others. Aonani and the boys, Luca and Finn...they'd all be caught off guard.

I leaned into Eden and whispered, "I'm going to cause a diversion while you run and warn the others."

She shook her head. "No way. I'm staying with you," she whispered back.

"We can't fight all those shadows on our own. We need backup."

Eden lifted her chin defiantly. Still, I could see the trembling of her chin in the dim light. "I'm no coward. I want to stay and fight with you."

I admired the girl's bravery, even if I suspected it was mostly bluster. "Eden, they're headed straight for Aonani,

Dayton, Dawn, and Liang. You need to warn them before it's too late."

Eden's face paled at the sound of their names. Though she was cranky and mean at training, I had no doubt Eden loved our classmates. They were the closest thing she hard to family since her own had virtually abandoned her. Eden chewed her bottom lip, obviously debating whether to stay and fight or run to warn the others.

Finally, she nodded. "Okay, I'll go. Tell me what to do."

I let out a breath and began quickly formulating a plan. Nora had taken Luca and me on a tour on our first day at Mentmore. I remembered a large, square courtyard located in the center of the servants' wing. If I could lead at least some of the Shadowmen into the sunlight, I would have a slight tactical advantage. I prayed that the British sky would be clear for once. "I'm going to draw the shadows deeper into the servants' quarters while you head back to the Grand Hall."

She gripped my hand tighter. "I'm scared," she whispered. Her bright eyes filled with tears.

I leveled her with a steely stare. "We are the Children of Light. Be brave and remember what Bert taught us." His lessons hadn't failed me yet.

We crept out of the cabinet, and I peeked out of the doorway, Eden close at my back. Somewhere at the end of the long hallway, I could sense a dark presence, though the Shadowman was not in its corporeal form. We had mere moments to act.

"Wait a ten seconds after I leave, then run as fast as you can. Don't stop until you reach the others," I whispered.

Eden nodded. "O-Okay." Tears trailed down her freckled cheeks. "We got this, right?"

I nodded resolutely. "We got this."

I took a steadying breath and stepped into the hallway. Several Shadowmen instantly materialized and began their pursuit. I ran straight at him, and just before we collided, I darted into a short hallway to my right that led to the courtyard. Tugging on the antique, twin doors, my stomach dropped as they stuck on rusty hinges. I pulled harder, forcing the weather-worn doors open just enough to squeeze through. Behind me, the shadows yelled for their cronies to join them.

I ran into the center of the courtyard. Crawling vines covered the stone walls, and overgrown bushes obscured the cobblestone floor. It was obvious that no one had set foot in the courtyard in decades. I looked up and cursed under my breath when I saw the wispy grey clouds covering the sun. Fast footsteps approached the courtyard doors. I pulled as much energy from the filtered light as I could, knowing I'd need more to take on multiple shadows.

A dark cloud suddenly blew the doors nearly off their hinges, and six shadows swept through the opening. One by one, they materialized. Ciara strolled into the courtyard behind them. For better or worse, my plan to lead them away from the residential wing had worked. I prayed Eden was already somewhere safe, warning the others.

They stopped about a dozen feet from me. Ciara dipped her head low like a predator ready to pounce. "Time's up, little doll," she said in her raspy voice. "No more running. No more hiding. This ends here."

A strange sense of calm washed over me, and my back straightened. Ciara was right. We couldn't continue this game of cat and mouse forever. Nor did I want to. I was sick of looking over my shoulder, sick of being hunted by this girl with her black eyes and even blacker soul. Full sun or not, this ended today.

I ran a hand down the hilts of my daggers in my vest. Thankfully I was already dressed in my tactical gear. The Shadowmen had made a mistake that morning in that their initial attack had prepared us for battle. If it hadn't been for the EMP, I might be facing Ciara in my pajamas.

"This is my kill. No one intervenes," Ciara warned the others. She stared me down, her head cocked to the side like a bird of prey watching a mouse. But I watched her, too. For the first time since meeting the psychotic girl, I realized that Ciara wasn't much taller than my five-foot-two inches. In fact, from afar, she looked like…just a girl.

We squared up in the dim space. And just like that, I was back to that awful night in Paris, standing in a courtyard, battling with Ciara to the death. Only this time, I wasn't timid or afraid.

I only needed was a bit more sunlight. As if the heavens heard me, the clouds suddenly parted and sunlight filled the courtyard. A smile spread across my face as I spread my arms wide, soaking in the unfiltered solar energy until my chest filled to near bursting. Ciara and the other shadows flinched and shrank back toward the shadows along the wall.

"What's wrong, Ciara? Can't stand a little sun?" I taunted.

Ciara's small hands curled into fists as she squinted against the sunlight. "I'm not a vampire, you stupid girl," she rasped. "I can stand the light." She scratched one of her exposed arms, the lie written all over her burned skin. I smiled, knowing Luca and I did that to her.

"I would've thought Shadowmen were better liars than that." I was feeling bold and reckless. True, I was outnumbered. And true, Ciara was a formidable opponent. But when there were hundreds of nuclear weapons headed our way, what did I have to lose? Everyone on the planet might be dead within thirty-six hours anyway. If I wanted to defeat Ciara once and for all, it was now or never.

Schooling her features into a mask of indifference, Ciara stepped forward. "I received good news recently. The Order finally gave me the green light to kill you. I guess they don't need you and your boyfriend's help to end The Society of Light after all. Someone else did it for you. The Society of Light has finally fallen, and I get to watch the life drain from your eyes. Isn't that exciting?"

We already knew who had taken The Void's offer to betray us to The Order. But Ciara did have reason to feel victorious. Thanks to Daiko, they had us backed into a corner. The Order controlled every nation and its weapons, so Ciara no longer had reason to hold back. But then again, neither did I.

I continued to soak in solar energy until my skin began to glow. My hair lifted from my shoulders, and my feet threatened to rise from the ground as they had that night in Paris when I'd lost control of my powers. But I'd grown up since Ciara and her cronies ambushed Luca and me all those months ago. With Finn's help, I'd learned to command the energy surging within me, and my feet remained firmly on the ground.

I shifted into a fighting position and raised my glowing hands. "I'm not a little doll anymore, Ciara." I shot a quick bolt of light at her feet, and she jumped back like a cat on tin foil. "And you're not as scary as you think you are."

A male shadow began creeping around the side of the courtyard, likely planning to attack me from behind while I was distracted. Without turning in his direction, I pulled a dagger from my vest and sent it flying. He dropped where he stood. He made little gasping noises, but I didn't break eye contact with Ciara to see if my aim was true. In my periphery, another shadow crept toward me. I sent another blade flying, and a female shadow gasped as she fell to the courtyard floor. From the corner of my eye, I saw my knife's hilt protruding from her right eye.

Ciara bared her sharp teeth and stalked slowly forward. Her black irises spread until her eyes were shark-like, and her pale skin turned ashen grey. Shadows from the corners of the courtyard gathered around Ciara, drawn to her as if she were a black hole. My skin chilled, and a familiar dread pooled in my belly. Their thoughts crowded my mind, threatening to pull me into a dark hole from which there was no return. My shoulders hunched forward, and I gritted my teeth, pulling more light from the sun and using it to push Ciara's poison from my body. With a grunt, I straightened my back and lifted my chin. I was no longer afraid of her dark tricks. Because that was all they were. Tricks.

Shadowmen invaded your mind and preyed on your insecurities and fears. Ciara and her kind could make you want to die, to lay down your guard and let darkness in, but it was all in the mind. Beyond their weapons and cruelty, they had no power that wasn't given to them by their victims. The Shadowmen were all smoke and mirrors.

Unlike our shadowy counterparts, Children of Light had the power to harness and wield the very substance of life—energy. Our power was substantive and real. We could not only take life, but we could also give it, heal it, enrich it. I stared at the small, cruel girl with new eyes, finally seeing her for what she really was—a bully and a liar. I'd been stronger than her all along. I wondered how I hadn't seen it before. I outshone her in every way.

Light beat darkness. Every time.

Conviction pulsated through my veins, and the sunlight in my core grew until it felt as though I would burst from the pressure. Ciara sprang forward, but I easily dodged her attack, the energy in my cells giving me unnatural speed. I shot a bolt at her exposed back, and she cried out. I'd hit her shoulder, leaving a small smoking black hole in her upper chest, just below her collarbone.

"You bitch!" Her strangled scream echoed off the courtyard walls. The surrounding Shadowmen moved forward to intervene, but Ciara raised a hand. "Stay back. She's mine!"

Ciara dissipated into smoke and surged toward me again. The black mass enveloped me, blocking out the sun. In the darkness of her embrace, I was surrounded by the most intense grief and pain I'd ever experienced. In her shadow form, Ciara was able to channel unfiltered Darkness into my very soul. I fell onto my side and pulled my legs to my chest, my body shaking from the internal turmoil. My mother's lifeless body, blood flowing freely from her neck, filled my mind. Then Barry's form came into view, bent and broken on the kitchen floor. Jaques and Arin were next. Then The Void's voice surrounded me. A thousand whispers circled inside my skull, urging me to submit to the Darkness.

For the first time in months, I let myself cry. I cried for my mother. I cried for Arin. I cried for our broken world. Intense grief crashed over me like a tidal wave, but instead of letting the pain break me, I embraced it. My mother was never coming back—Arin was never coming back. Nothing would ever change that. I finally realized grief didn't have to be a curse. It could be a blessing—a way to memorialize those I'd lost—a way to prove they'd existed and that I'd loved them.

Somehow, I'd let my grief make me forget all my beautiful memories of them, like clouds blocking out the sun. I pushed aside my sadness and let the warmth of the good times shine through. My mother waking me on my birthday with a hug and chocolate chip pancakes. My stepdad taking me on summer hikes. Arin lying next to me in my Paris bedroom, making me laugh through the tears.

The Void's dark whisperings fled from my mind as if burned by my happy memories. I pushed myself to my knees, and I soaked in the solar energy, channeling it into every cell of my body. As my light increased, Ciara's poison was quickly purged from my cells, and little zaps of energy singed Ciara's shadow form, forcing her to retreat. She materialized on her knees several feet away. Once again, sunlight warmed my shoulders, and I greedily bathed in its solar rays.

"Is that all you've got?" I growled.

Struggling to my feet, I stepped forward. Ciara remained on her knees, chest heaving. Blood seeped from her shoulder wound, but her face betrayed no pain or fear. I doubted there was enough humanity left in her to feel anything besides hate. Knowing she was hardly human made what I had to do next slightly easier.

As the five Shadowmen rushed toward me on all sides, I thought of my last Christmas with Mom. She'd made my favorite holiday breakfast, elf pancakes. I let the warmth of that perfect memory expand through my core. Just like Finn taught me, I let the joy inside me spread. This time, instead of focusing the energy into my palms, I let it flow to every cell of my body.

I threw my arms out to my sides and let go.

The courtyard exploded in light. Energy poured from my limbs, my skin, my eyes. My hair whipped around my shoulders, and wind roared in my ears as if I stood in the center of an energy hurricane. Ivy vines and bushes caught fire, quickly burning to nothing. The approaching shadows cried out and fell to the red-hot cobblestone floor. They writhed in pain as their skin began to melt from their bones. With a final cry, Ciara leaped toward me, fingers curled like talons. I forced a concentrated stream of light in her direction, and she was thrown back by a wave of pure energy. As the last of my energy rushed from my limbs, black crowded my vision. I gritted my teeth and held onto consciousness. Once my last cell was finally depleted, I dropped my hands with a sigh. When my vision cleared, I was surrounded by piles bones of ash.

195

Chapter 19

Luca

**he** Grand Hall smelled strongly of gun powder and bitter coffee as the departing agents packed their weapons and downed one last cuppa. Mr. Bellamy retreated into the Faraday cage, acting as mission central via satellite phone and landline. Luca kept an eye on the doorway as he helped load guns with Kiran and Ailbert. It had been over twenty minutes since Kirie left with Eden to look for maps, and there was a strange itch at the back of Luca's neck. She should've been back by now.

He set the handgun down on the side table, placing a hand on Alibert's shoulder as he passed. "I'll be back, mate.

Just need check on something." The old Scot simply grunted in reply.

Luca made for the library, figuring Kirie had gone with the obnoxious Australian girl to wait with the other unhappy children. They'd spent much of the morning trying to convince any adult who would listen that they were ready to fight, to no avail. When he last saw them, the young trainees, including Arabella, had gone from sulking in the kitchen to sulking in the library. Luca understood their outrage. He remembered being their age, chomping at the bit, wanting to prove he had what it took to defeat Darkness.

Luca wrinkled his nose as he entered the stuffy library. It smelled like kid sweat and the onion-flavored crisps someone had left open on the couch. The room was pure chaos. Liang and Dayton were hiding behind armchairs on either side of the room, shooting rubber band bullets at one another. Aonani was playing on the library ladder, riding it back and forth like a jungle vine, while her mother chided her for disrespecting other people's things. Arabella sat at one end of the couch, watching the news, volume turned up, likely to drown out the noise. And in the eye of the storm, Dawn sat peacefully reading a leather-bound book on philosophy. Unfortunately, neither Eden nor Kirie was anywhere in sight.

"Hey!" Luca hollered over the din. The savages stopped what they were doing and faced him. "Any of you nippers seen Kirie or Eden?"

"Nope. Haven't seen them," Aonani said with a shrug. Then, the wild thing went right back to her ladder acrobatics.

Panic, not his own, slammed into Luca with the force of a freight train. Kirie. Something was wrong. His heart rate jumped into full gear as he ran from the library into the short hallway beyond. Eden careened around the corner. She barreled into Luca without slowing, nearly knocking him over. He caught her by the shoulders, steadying her before they both fell to the floor. Eden's body shook violently beneath Luca's hands, and her pupils were wide in terror.

He squeezed her small shoulders. "What's wrong?"

"They're here!" she gasped. Her eyes darted left and right. "Shadowmen are in the manor!"

In an instant, day had turned to night, and the hall was filled with undulating shadows. His hair stood on end as the temperature dropped. He could already feel the chill creeping up his spine and see the shadows in the corners growing long. The Order had found their hiding place. He had no doubt Mr. Daiko was the source of the leak; though, how he'd found Finn's off-record safe house, Luca couldn't guess.

Luca cupped his hands around his mouth and yelled toward the agents in the Grand Hall. "Shadowmen!" Then, he pulled Eden behind him and dropped into a defensive stance, hands alight. Shadows morphed into men and women, black-eyed and armed. "Stay behind me," Luca commanded.

Just then, Dayton ran out of the library barefoot and smiling. "What are you guys yelling about?"

Luca turned to the boy just as a bang split the air. Dayton gasped and stared down at his chest. His eyes widened. Blood bloomed like a rose across his shirt. With a grunt, the young boy fell onto his knees and coughed, spraying blood down his chin.

His young mate, Liang, rushed from the library. "What's going on, Day?" His eyes landed on his friend, and his face drained of color. "Dayton!" Liang rushed forward and caught him he slumped to the ground. Dayton's eyes rolled back into his head. "No! Help me!" Liang cried, struggling to hold the limp boy upright.

Another bullet lodged into the wall next to Eden's head, and all hell broke loose. Shots and shouts surrounded them from all sides. A battle had begun in Mentmore Towers.

"Take cover," Luca yelled. He dragged both boys back into the room, and Eden shut the door behind them. As he laid Dayton flat on the ground, Luca's body shook with the need to find Kirie. He looked down at the bleeding wound in the center of Dayton's chest and growled in frustration. The boy needed to be healed without delay.

Leilani rushed forward, her long, flowery nightdress swishing around her legs. "What's happening?"

"We're under attack! Quick! Barricade the door."

Eden, Dawn, and Leilani sprang into action, flipping the couch onto its side and pushing it up against the library door. They continued to add random furniture to the pile as Luca dragged Dayton behind the shelter of an armchair. He ripped away Dayton's shirt, exposing the bullet wound. Sliding his hand beneath the boy's back, Luca probed for an exit wound but found none.

"Shit!" he roared. Things were going from bad to worse in a hurry. "I need something to stop the bleeding!" he cried out. Dawn grabbed a throw blanket from the floor and tossed it to him. Luca balled the fabric and pressed it firmly onto the wound.

Shadowmen slammed into the door, shaking the frame. A barrage of bullets tore through the thick wooden door, narrowly missing their targets. The children screamed in fear. Luca would have to work quickly.

"Everyone, back up!" he commanded. His blood-soaked hands shook as more bullets zipped around them, lodging in the paneled walls and floor. They were sitting ducks. Luca looked around for an exit. They could break the windows, but there were hundreds of yards of flat lawn between them and cover. Out in the open, the Shadowmen would pick them off one by one.

Arabella poked her head around the legs of an overturned end table, her strange eyes wide with fear. "T-there's a secret room on the other side of that bookcase," she said, pointing to the bookshelves.

"Show me!" Luca insisted.

Nodding solemnly, Arabella crawled on her stomach to the center shelf along the inner wall. She pressed on the shelf's frame, and it swung open, revealing a small, windowless room.

"Great. Everyone in!" Luca yelled.

Liang and Eden helped him drag Dayton's body into the hidden space. He turned to the tall, peaceful one. "Dawn, isn't it?" The girl nodded. "I can't heal him with the bullet still in his chest. I need to remove it. Find something sharp for me. Quick," he ordered. Luca expected the young girl to balk at the command, but Dawn simply nodded and got to work.

She crawled across to the library desk and searched its drawers with quick fingers. Eden and Liang covered her, shooting bolts of light at the shadows who had begun to pry the door open. Black-tipped fingers reached around the edge of the doorframe.

"Here," Dawn cried, holding aloft a letter opener. She tossed it back into the hidden room, and Luca caught it mid-air. She army-crawled back inside and sat beside Dayton, holding his bloody hand.

Luca took a deep breath and pressed the sharp edge of the letter opener to the wound. Dayton's eyes sprang open with a gasp. He frantically pushed Luca's hands away, crying uncontrollably.

"Dawn, I need you to hold him down."

She pressed Dayton's shoulders to the ground and leaned over him. Dawn's hands began to glow, and she whispered calming words in her native tongue. Dayton's muscles loosened, and his eyes slid shut once more. Luca nodded at her with respect. He recognized a fellow healer when he saw one.

"Good. Keep that up."

Luca gritted his teeth and probed deeper. When the opening was wide enough for him to see into, he put a finger inside the hole to search for the bullet. The tip of his finger brushed across metal deep within the wound. "I've almost got it." Fresh blood pooled around the bullet, making it slippery and hard to grasp. He finally curled his finger around the offending piece and, with a prayer, pulled. The bullet came out with a sucking sound and landed with a thud on the wooden floor.

Luca called forth his power and pressed an energy-lit palm over the wound. Closing his eyes, he envisioned the skin closing, the muscles and tissues restitching, and within seconds, the wound was healed beneath his palm. Luca lifted his hand and inspected his work. It was rough and ready at best. The boy would have a scar, and there would still be pain. If only he'd had more time…

The library door beyond crashed open. Luca sprang to his feet and ushered Eden and Liang into the hidden room as Leilani attempted to wrangle Aonani in after them. Two semi-corporeal shadows swept through the door and materialized in the center of the library. Luca's heart dropped as three more followed.

Behind him, a young boy roared. Liang sprang from the hidden room, holding a long sword, blood and vengeance on his face. He twisted and twirled like a graceful dancer, cutting and dismembering the closest Shadowman with the edge of his blade. The shadow's screams were cut short as Liang brought his sword down on his neck, severing his head from his body. It rolled beneath his least favorite couch.

Luca gaped at the boy. He should have known better than to underestimate one of Bert's trainees. Clearly, the man was an expert coach. Luca raised his hands and shot bolts of energy at the remaining shadows, forcing them back into the hallway. Behind him, Aonani continued to struggle against her mother's pull.

"Let me go, Mom. There's a battle out there, and I want to fight!"

Just then, a shadow leaned into the library, aiming his pistol at the screaming girl. Leilani's eyes widened in alarm. "Look out!" She pushed Aonani out to the side just as the shadow pulled the trigger.

Blood splattered across Aonani's front. The little girl looked down at her soiled shirt and then back at her mother, her face scrunched tight in confusion. "Mommy?" She cried.

Leilani grunted and pitched forward. Aonani held out her hands to catch her. Together, they fell onto the floor with a thump.

Another shot rang out, this time from the hallway. The offending shadow cried out and fell to the floor, a gaping hole in his head. Alena rushed into the library, twin smoking pistols in her hands. Zoeya followed close behind, hands alight. Luca rushed back to Aonani, who lay trapped beneath her mother's prone body. She screamed her mother's name, pushing at her shoulders, whether to wake her or push her off, Luca couldn't tell. He reached down and lifted Leilani, allowing Aonani to wiggle from beneath her mother's weight.

She promptly threw herself over her mother's body, sobbing. "No! No! NO!"

Luca pressed two fingers to Leilani's neck. Her pulse was weak, but she was alive.

"Incoming," Alena yelled.

Another shadowy figure entered the library. Liang lifted his long sword, ready to dismember yet another enemy, but Luca held up a hand. "No! Go back to the room and guard Dayton and the others. They're injured and defenseless."

Liang nodded and rushed back through the hidden doorway. He turned back to his sobbing classmate. "Aonani, get in here," he cried, holding out a hand.

Ignoring him, Aonani released her hold on her mother and stood to face the shadow. She bared her blood-stained teeth, and a halo of light surrounded her angry form. She let out a feral, high-pitched scream, layered with all her rage and grief. She raised her tiny red palms and shot bolts of light in quick succession at the Shadowman. Her aim was a mess, but Aonani didn't seem to notice. She was a tiny nightmare to behold.

The Shadowman lifted his gun, and a bullet zipped past Aonani, missing her by inches. The little girl let out another unhinged scream, shooting sporadic bolts of energy at the dodging enemy. Luca launched forward. Dropping and skidding on his knees, he wrapped the little girl in his arms and pulled her away as another bullet whizzed by.

"Alena, take her!"

Alena lifted her pistols and shot the Shadowman in the chest. Then, she handed Zoeya her weapons and pulled a squirming Aonani into her arms, holding her tightly to her chest.

"Mommy!" Aonani screamed. Still crazy with grief, she fought against Alena's hold, scratching her arms in an attempt to return to her mother's side.

Alena gritted her teeth and held on tighter. "Hold on, little viper. Your momma's going to be okay."

"Over here!" Liang called, holding open the secret door.

Alena deposited Aonani in the saferoom. The minute Alena's arms were free, Arabella launched forward, wrapping her arms around Alena's legs with a sob. "It's okay, bambina. I'm okay." She patted Arabella's back reassuringly.

Luca turned to Zoeya. "Help me with this." He gestured to the Leilani's prone form. With a nod, Zoeya tucked the pistols into the front pocket of her hoodie and helped and Luca drag the unconscious mother into the crowded saferoom.

Footsteps pounded from beyond the library door once more. Luca, Alena, and Zoeya shared a steely look. Zoeya pulled the guns from her pocket, and with a nod, they rushed back into the library, kicking the hidden door closed behind them. But instead of another shadow, Bert appeared in the demolished doorway, holding a blood-soaked machete at his side. "Où sont les enfants?" he demanded.

"In here." Luca led Bert to the children's hiding place. "They're safe, but Dayton and Leilani are injured."

Bert nodded. "Je m'en occuperai." *I'll take care of it.* He slid into the hidden room, Alena close at his heels.

Relief flooded Luca's chest. With Bert and Alena there, the children would be safe, more or less. It was finally time to find Kirie. Luca leaned back into the room where Eden sat huddled close to Dawn's side. "Eden, where is Kirie? Why didn't she come back with you?"

The girl's face paled. "They cornered us in the servants' quarters. Last time I saw her, she was leading some psycho redhead away from the Grand Hall."

Dread pooled deep in Luca's belly. There was only one person he knew who fit that description. Ciara was there. Eden must have seen the realization on his face, because she nodded. "Yeah. They seemed to know each other." She gave him an apologetic look

"I'll stay here and help with the little ones." Alena nodded to the exit. "Go find your girl."

Luca nodded to his sister, feeling overwhelming gratitude for her strength. Bert grunted in impatience, shooing Luca away as he shut and locked the saferoom door.

Zoeya and Luca stood alone in the library, debris, blood, and severed body parts scattered all around them. Luca swallowed down the bile rising in his throat and turned to Zoeya. "I'm going to find Kirie. Will you be alright here?"

"Oh don't worry about little ol' me," Zoeya said with a smirk. Guns in hand, she walked over to the library door and positioned herself squarely inside the splintered, bloody doorframe. "I'll just stand here and shoot anyone who walks through this door." She shrugged nonchalantly.

Luca snorted. "I thought you didn't fight, tech girl." He distinctly remembered her stating that she was not that kind of Agent of Light.

Zoeya rolled her eyes. "Whatever. Just go find Kirie."

Luca saluted Zoeya and rushed out of the library and past the entrance to the Grand Hall. Beyond, he could smell the blood and gunpowder and hear the cries of battle. But he couldn't join his fellow agents in the fight, not when Kirie needed him.

Kiran stumbled through the doorway as he passed, shooting bolts of light at the enemies just beyond Luca's view. Ignoring his fellow agent, Luca turned toward the servants' wing. "Hey!" Kiran cried after him. "Where are you going? The fight's this way." He hitched a thumb toward the Grand Hall.

"I need to find Kirie," Luca called over his shoulder. "She's somewhere in the servants' quarters with Ciara."

Kiran's brow formed a tight line. He swung the rifle hanging from his back to his front and hefted it upright. "That bitch is here?" Despite her youth, Ciara was well known by the Agents of Light as she was an especially talented agent of Darkness and was responsible for many deaths. "I'm coming with you."

Luca nodded gratefully. "I won't say no to help."

Entering the servants' wing, a thick, dark mass greeted them at the end of the long passageway. Human forms materialized one by one. Their black eyes zeroed in on the two agents. Kiran fired his gun at the nearest shadow, but the demon dissolved into mist, and the bullet passed straight through to the wall beyond.

Luca growled in frustration. He didn't have time for this nonsense. He had to find Kirie now! Standing in the center of the hallway, Luca lifted his arms. Fury, like a cold flame, rose in his chest. His internal shadows awakened, attracted to his anger. Instead of tempering them, as he would normally do, Luca embraced them. He'd finally made peace with his darkness, and he no longer feared the ghosts from his past. A large Shadowman rushed him, and Luca dissolved into smoke. The man ran through him, causing a strange pressure in Luca's body, as if hit by a gust of wind. He rematerialized and swung on the stumbling shadow.

"What the hell?" Kiran yelled as he shot rounds at the other shadows. He looked at Luca with a mixture of revulsion and interest.

Ignoring him, Luca raised his palm and summoned his light. His power reacted immediately, no longer at war with his inner shadows. Luca wasted no time wondering at the opposing energies' sudden willingness to coexist as he shot a bolt of energy at the hulking shadow. The man dissolved, but not in time to miss Luca's shot.

The disembodied Shadowman screamed, and as he reformed, an angry welt appeared on his upper body. Burnt fabric had peeled away, revealing boils on his exposed chest. The man howled in rage and rushed forward. Luca dropped low, catching him by the middle and lifting him off the ground. He slammed the shadow into the wall. Plaster rained down on them.

Luca put a hand on the odious man's face and shot a stream of energy into him. The man screamed for a single moment before his skin turned to coal. Luca stepped back and let his charred remains crumble to the floor. Offering him no respite, the remaining shadows charged him on all sides.

Luca fell into a dance-like rhythm as he morphed in and out of his shadow and light forms, destroying the Shadowmen one by one. As his two energies synced, Luca felt a sense of rightness settle over him. He had never felt more at home in his own skin as he exacted justice on the dark ones in his true form. Years of self-hatred burned away. All this time, Luca's greatest weapon had not been his light ability alone, but the damaged, ugly parts of him as well. Donovan may have broken Luca as a child, but the man that emerged from the wreckage was stronger than the boy he had stolen.

Behind him, Kiran picked off the few trying to escape Luca's lethal fury. Once they were all dead, the older Agent of Light swung on Luca. Luca raised a shining palm in defense, readying himself for the attack. No Agent of Light had ever used shadow power before, and he knew how it made him look. This would only confirm what many in the Society of Light always believed about him. That he was too soiled, too dark to be an Agent of Light

"Look, I don't know what I saw back there," Kiran said, pointing to the charred bodies. "But that was bad ass!" He let out a surprised laugh and slapped Luca on the shoulder hard enough to knock him back a few inches. "You have some explaining to do, brother."

Luca lowered his hand and let out a breath. Perhaps not all Agents of Light were closed-minded arses after all. "We'll talk about it later, shall we? We still need to find Kirie."

"Lead on, brother," Kiran said, hoisting his rifle in ready position.

They followed the smell of burnt flesh all the way to the courtyard located off the kitchen. Luca and Kiran stood in front of the twin doors.

"On the count of three?" Kiran asked, rifle at the ready. Luca nodded, and he began the countdown. "One, two, three!"

The two agents rushed into the courtyard, ready to battle a host of Shadowmen. Instead, they found only one person standing in a halo of light. Luca stared at his love in awe. Kirie's body was aflame, blue in the center and reddish purple around the edges. Her eyes glowed pure white; no pupils showed. The courtyard was as bright as noonday. He'd never seen anything so luminous, or so terrifying. She was pure energy.

"Holy Gods." Kiran dropped to his knees and pressed his hands together in prayer.

Luca slowly approached her. People-shaped piles of ash were scattered across the cobblestone ground. Only one shadow remained semi-intact. Luca instantly recognized the body lying at Kirie's feet. In death, Ciara's familiar face was a frozen mask of hatred, her red hair spilling across the cobblestones like a pool of blood. She lay spread-eagled, having been thrown back by some incredible force. In the center of her chest was a four-inch hole, the edges singed black.

Luca reached for Kirie, not completely convinced that touching her wouldn't set him ablaze. She turned her glowing gaze upon him and raised a hand for him to stop. "I need a minute." Her voice was low and resonant.

By increments, her light faded. When her breathing had slowed, and her eyes were Caribbean blue once again, she looked upon Luca and Kiran with a somber gaze. "Have the other shadows been neutralized?"

Luca was stunned silent. Her voice carried new weight and her very essence exuded authority and strength. Somehow, in the past hour, Kirie had grown into a woman. Suddenly, Luca had a clear vision of future Kirie leading The Society of Light with precision and confidence. He wanted to bend his knee and swear loyalty to her on the spot. Instead, he stepped toward her.

"Are you all right, my love?" he asked.

"I'm fine. I just did what needed to be done." There was no panic in her voice, but Luca still wanted, no, needed to go to her.

Luca raised his arms, but Kirie just sighed. "I'm fine, really." She looked down at a still praying Kiran. "What's he doing?"

"Praying, I think," Luca responded stupidly. "You make a man believe in God."

Kirie sighed and put a hand on Kiran's shoulder. He looked up, and his large shoulders dropped. He let out a breath of relief when he saw Kirie's blue, not white, eyes.

"Kiran, did you neutralize the other shadows?" she asked again.

Kiran cleared his throat and nodded. "Yes, ma'am. Every last one of them."

"Wonderful. What do we do next?"

Kiran stood and turned in a circle, taking in the mess surrounding them. "First, we need to heal the wounded. Then, we take care of the bodies."

Kirie nodded. "Great. Let's get to work. The clock is ticking."

Chapter 20

Kirie

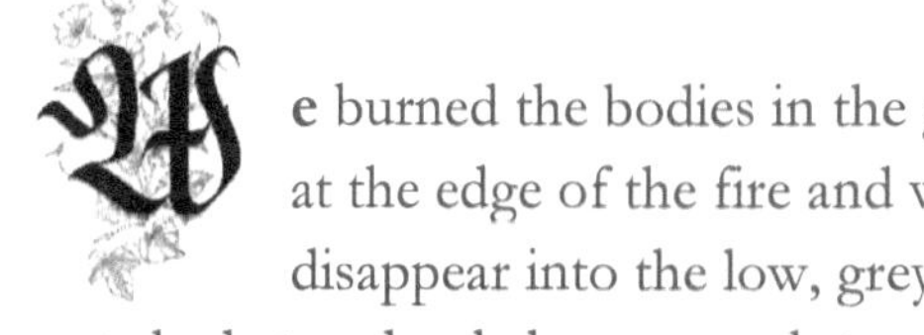

e burned the bodies in the garden. I stood alone at the edge of the fire and watched the smoke disappear into the low, grey clouds. The other agents had stayed only long enough to ensure the Shadowmen caught fire before heading back to the manor, but my feet remained rooted to the ground. The sickly-sweet scent of burning flesh singed my throat, and the flames warmed my cheeks as I watched our enemies turn to ash.

A memory from what felt like a million years ago floated to the surface of my mind. The kids from my Colorado high school often had bonfires in the nature reserve between my house and the school. I'd go with Rylie from time to time, drawn not to the other teens, but by the energy the fire would create. Ironically, that was also the exact location Cole had tried to kill me.

Bonfires and shadows.

I didn't recognize the girl I was before The Society of Light. That girl was ignorant and small. I wished I could go back in time and shake that naive version of myself, wake her up before it was too late. I would tell her that her intuition was right, that there was more out there for her. I'd tell her she didn't have to make herself small for the benefit of others.

I was no longer that timid rabbit who hid in the bushes from the boogie man. I no longer felt the same fear and revulsion of death. Defeating Ciara had been necessary—gratifying even. As long as she lived, innocents would die. I felt a sense of pride for being the one to stop her reign of terror.

I looked out past the pyre to the small English town visible just beyond the estate grounds. No doubt the citizens were terrified in the wake of the EMP. They likely had no idea what was happening to them, no clue of what was to come. That was another thing that had changed. I no longer envied their ignorance. It was better to face what was coming head-on rather than be sideswiped by it. Ignorance was not bliss when it took away your autonomy.

I finally turned from the macabre scene and walked up the long stone staircase to the manor. It was time to get back to work.

Mentmore Towers was a beehive of military activity. Teams traveling further distances left as soon as the fight was over to find and board the few airplanes that survived the EMP. The rest of us were set to roll out before dawn. We spent the remainder of the day cleaning up the blood and debris. Thanks to Bert's ministrations, Leilani had survived the attack, though she and Dayton were sent to bed for the day to continue healing and regain their energy. No one dared bother Aonani, who lay curled up next to her mother, sucking her thumb like a much younger child.

That night, Luca and I slept wrapped in the warmth of each other's arms. He held me like a drowning man to a lifeboat. We both knew, though neither of us was willing to acknowledge, that it might very well be our last night together. I memorized the texture of his skin, his hair, his lips, hoping that somehow, I'd retain those memories in whatever existence came after this life should things not go our way.

Two hours before sunup, Nora walked down the long residential wing, knocking on doors–a general rousing her troops.

In the predawn dark, Luca pulled me into his chest one last time and whispered, "I love you," into my hair.

"I love you, too." I turned in his arms and linked my pinky with his. "Remember, no matter what happens, we stay together to the end."

Luca's lips found mine. "Until the end."

We met in the ballroom. Finn was still in the Faraday cage, typing away at his computer and directing troops across the globe via landline and satellite phone. It was where he'd been when the battle broke out. Apparently, Finn had only gotten as far as the Grand Hall before it was all over, missing most of the action. I was a little sorry that I hadn't been able to see the great Finn Bellamy, leader of The Society of Light, in action before the fate of the world was finally decided.

The ballroom was eerily quiet as we armed ourselves with the leftover weapons. Finn left the cage to help me secure my weapons vest.

"Ready for this?" he asked, pulling my shoulder strap tight.

I snorted a laugh. "Would it make a difference if I wasn't? It's not like The Order is going to wait for me to grow up and finish training." Ready or not, The Void was coming.

"I suppose not." He leaned down until our eyes met. "Be careful out there. Don't try to be a hero. Get in, disable the bomb, and get right back here. Understood?"

"Understood," I agreed. Finn had nothing to worry about. I wasn't the daring, death-seeking kind of hero. I had no intention of putting mine or Luca's lives at unnecessary risk.

"Good." Finn stood back as if to inspect my armor. A frown tugged at the corners of his lips. I looked down at my tactical gear, searching for whatever Finn found amiss. "What's wrong? Do I have my vest on backward?"

He shook his head. "No. It's just…It's just that you look so much like your mother." Finn's eyes turned glassy. He looked down and cleared his throat. "I, uh, think she'd be really proud of the woman you've become."

My heart twisted. I took hold of this hand and squeezed. "I think so, too."

It was a lie, of course. My mother would've had a heart attack and died again if she saw me now. Following in my father's footsteps was the last thing she wanted me to do. But I couldn't spoil Finn's moment of wistful grief. It was clear he truly loved my mother, or at least the young woman she once was before fear and paranoia took over, and it was strangely comforting to grieve with someone who knew her.

Finn returned my squeeze with a sad smile. "I love you," he said, eyes bright with unshed tears.

I didn't know what to say in return. Did I love my father? I didn't know. Though we'd only been reunited for a short time, the familial connection was undeniable. But love?

Not waiting for a reply, Finn dropped my hand and went back to the makeshift command central in the cage. I took a deep breath and joined Luca and the others at the weapons table to add the finishing touches to my gear. Thankfully, the other agents had left me a replacement set of throwing knives. I slid each into the sheaves built into my vest, still speckled by the blood of the Shadwomen I'd killed. I gazed down at one of the knife's razor-thin edges—a tool made for killing—and waited for that familiar terror to set in. Instead, all I felt was confidence that I knew how to use it. Endless hours of training with Bert had forced me to confront my biggest fears and most terrifying memories, and it had paid off in my battle with Ciara. A small smile tilted my lips. It was finally time for the Darkness to fear *my* light.

I slid the final knife into place with a satisfying *snick* and wondered if this was how Donovan felt when he packed his black bag before a mission.

A hand touched my shoulder, making me jump. "Time to go," Luca said.

I shook off my morbid thoughts and nodded. "I'm ready."

Alena and Zoeya joined us, each dressed head to toe in black tactical gear. Zoeya's dark hair was pulled in a tight bun, and without her Teenage Mutant Ninja Turtle sweaters, she looked like a true Agent of Light. She pulled at the high collar of her shirt and shifted uncomfortably in her black boots.

"Hey! You look like a real field agent in that," I observed.

"I hate this," she grumbled, pulling again at her starched collar.

Alena rolled her eyes and sighed dramatically. "Stop whining. You look good." I watched with interest as Zoeya's face turned bright red at Alena's compliment. "Come on; we need to recharge our energy before we go," Alena said, tossing her high ponytail with her trademark sass.

Luca looked at the black sky outside the tall ballroom windows with pinched brows. "The sun hasn't risen yet, and the power grid is out. We're a bit short on power, wouldn't you say?"

"Come on, Luca. You just need to see the bright side," Alena quipped sarcastically. She tried to punch his arm playfully, but he ducked out of range. The two threw insults and fake blows like a pair of kids. I felt a spark of joy as I watched them play, wondering how I ever worried they were anything more than siblings.

The generator in the cage roared to life, startling me. I turned and stared at the noisy thing, biting my bottom lip in thought. The sun and electric grid might be down, but we weren't completely out of options. Normally, Children of Light absorbed ambient energy second-hand. In a world full of electricity and sunlight, there was a constant flow to pull from. But I'd been low in dark times before. Finn turned in his seat as I entered the cage and knelt in front of the generator. I placed my hand over the machine's black and orange shiny paint. Energy pulsed beneath my palm. It gave off very little ambient power, but if we could access the energy directly…

I pulled a blade from my vest and lifted the thick black cord. Luca and Alena stopped playing, following me into the Faraday cage as I peeled back the black casing.

"Hold on, Kirie. That's our only energy source," Finn cried, jumping from his chair.

I held up a hand. "It's okay. I'm not cutting it, just exposing it." Like in Rome, I placed my palm over the exposed wire. My skin began to glow as pure electricity poured into me. The rush was so unexpected that nausea assaulted my stomach. I dropped the wire with a gasp.

"Let me try that." Luca grabbed the wire and gasped as unfiltered electricity flooded his system. Beads of sweat ran down his spine as it quickly filled his depleted energy stores. His eyes were no longer green, but miniature suns, bright and gold.

I pulled the wire from his hands before he could explode. "That's enough," I cautioned, remembering the consequences of overdoing it.

"My turn," Alena said, pushing us to the side. A cautious Zoeya was next.

Full of energy and nerves, we were finally ready to head out. My classmates waited in the Grand Hall to say goodbye. Abbott, Nora, and Bert stood by, armed and ready to usher the children out to the bomb shelter upon our departure. I was relieved to see Dayton and Leilani standing, though they were pale and a bit unsteady on their feet. Aonani held her mother's hand tightly, eyes constantly moving about the hall, presumably searching for hidden shadows. My heart hurt at her loss of innocence. She was too young to experience such trauma.

Eden stepped forward and pulled me into a hug. Stunned, I was slow to return the embrace.

"Kick some Shadowman butt for me," she said fiercely.

"If all goes right, we won't need to kick anyone's butt," I teased, squeezing her tightly.

Finn entered the room, and all eyes turned to him. "It's time to take the children to the shelter."

Under Bert's stern glare, they made their way to the front door in silent protest. It was clear they didn't want to stay behind. My heart hurt to see Liang so quiet. During training, he and Dayton would spend hours sending each other silly memes and videos, always acting as young boys should. It appeared that yesterday's events had dimmed that spark. As the group gathered before the front door in the grand foyer, I realized Liang wasn't just sad about his friend's near-death; he was angry. I could feel the heat of it from where I stood.

Nora waited at the open door. "Alright, off you go."

Ling planted his feet firmly to the ground and lifted his chin defiantly. "But we don't want to hide in the ground. We want to fight!" he exclaimed.

"Yeah! We want to fight," Aonani yelled, stomping her foot.

"Silence!" Bert ordered, but for the first time, his students ignored his command and continued to argue.

"Enough!" Finn yelled, and they finally quieted. He stood before the children with his hands behind his back and a stern expression on his face. "I understand your frustration, and I appreciate your dedication to our cause; however, if things don't go our way today, if the rest of us fail in our missions, you will be the next leaders of The Society of Light. We must ensure that the next generation of Bright Ones survives. Understood?"

"Understood," they replied in unison.

Cowed, the children followed their leaders to the front drive, their shoulders bowed under the weight of Finn's words and the expectations attached to them.

A late-model army green soft-top Jeep was waiting for us on the gravel drive. As we loaded into the car, Arabella let out a cry and rushed forward. "I'm going with you," she cried, holding onto Alena's waist with a white-knuckled grip.

Alena put a hand on the crown of her blonde head. "You can't come with me, amore mio. It's too dangerous." Alena turned to Abbott, her brows knit in concern. "Take care of her?"

"Of course." Abbott gently pulled Arabella from Alena's legs. "We'll protect them with our lives."

Arabella fought against Abbott's pull. "But what if you don't come back? What if the shadows find me again?"

Nora rested a rifle over her forearm. "Then I'll blow them to hell. No one gets past me, child."

Heaven help anyone who tried, I thought. The old woman was terrifying. From what I heard, Nora killed her fair share of shadows the day before.

Alena stood before Arabella and held her tear-stained face in her palms. They began to glow slightly. "I'll be back in no time. I promise."

The little girl's shoulders dropped, and the fight drained out of her as Alena's light eased her fear. Arabella nodded and let Abbott lead her by the hand as they walked the other children down the hill to the bomb shelter located beneath the garden. A lone tear rolled down Alena's cheek as she slid into the backseat beside Zoeya. I took the front seat, sad to be parted from my classmates.

Luca drove fast. Zoeya and Alena spread a paper map we managed to uncover across their laps, directing Luca as we made our way through the English countryside toward London. As expected, dead cars littered the road. Thankfully, the EMP was deployed in the early hours of the day, so not many people had been out. The closer we got to London; however, the more difficult travel became. Luca swerved in and out of stalled cars, using the shoulder and driving over curbs when necessary. As we hoped, our early departure ensured that most people were still in bed; though, the occasional burning building suggested that riots had broken out overnight.

Country lanes gave way to city streets. The sun began poking over the horizon, and people started leaving their homes, disheveled and bleary-eyed. Most simply stared absently at us as we passed. Some called out and began chasing the Jeep until they got tired and gave up. The houses were close in this part of town, and the roads were quickly filling with the fearful and the desperate. Luca's hands tightened on the wheel and pressed harder on the gas.

"We're ten miles out," Zoeya called from the backseat. I chewed nervously on my bottom lip, anxious to get to our location, disable the bomb, and get back out of town. The citizens' hungry stares made me uneasy.

Luca slowed as he entered a neighborhood roundabout, avoiding the few cars that had stalled mid-turn. In the center was the statue of a knight on horseback slaying a dragon. I stared up at it in interest. The gory scene stood in stark contrast to the vibrant flower bed beneath it.

Zoeya leaned over Luca's seat and pointed straight ahead. "Take your next right."

As Luca turned the wheel, the ground shook beneath us so fiercely, the tires left the pavement. My head hit the top of the Jeep, and my breath was knocked from my lungs.

Luca hit the brakes, and we opened the Jeep doors, standing on the running boards for a better view. Dozens of citizens spilled out of their homes. They stood in the center of the road and looked up at the sky. I turned to Luca over the hood of the Jeep, opening my mouth to say something, but a bright light blinded me, cutting off my words. The world was silent for one beat, then two. Then a roaring, and I was thrown backward. My head collided with something hard, and it all went black.

Chapter 21

Kirie

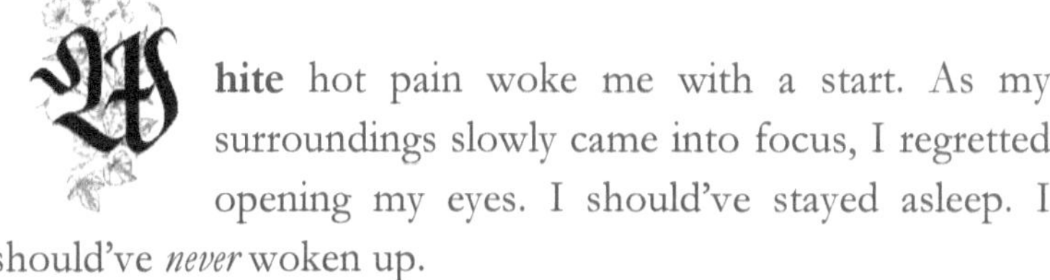

hite hot pain woke me with a start. As my surroundings slowly came into focus, I regretted opening my eyes. I should've stayed asleep. I should've *never* woken up.

The world was on fire and so was I. The acrid air stung my lungs, and my skin burned viciously. I took in what was once a thriving city with scorched eyes. Bodies lay heaped in the gutters and alleyways. Some moved, crying out in agony. Others lay deadly still. Burning flesh and a strange, earthy, metallic scent choked the air. I doubled over and heaved the contents of my stomach.

Wiping the bile and ash from my lips, I pushed to my feet, the hot pavement burning my hands. An ugly symphony of screams surrounded me. I pressed my palms to my ringing ears, but I couldn't drown out the hellish cacophony. Hungry flames raged on all sides, intent on devouring everything they touched. Heat singed my hair and seared my skin. I stared numbly at the blisters forming on the backs of my hands and trailed fingers over the sores forming on my face. Tears ran down my cheeks, stinging the open wounds. Somehow, my brain failed to register the pain.

Something on the horizon drew my attention. A mushroom-shaped plume rose in the sky above London. I stared stupidly at it, not fully comprehending. My body remained numb as my thoughts slowly cleared. The bomb…they must have detonated it early. But that didn't make any sense. We should have been able to intercept the delivery. We should have had more time.

I let out a strangled cry as reality settled over me. I hunched forward, grabbed my aching chest, and screamed. The sound was animalistic and unrecognizable to my own ears.

This was it. It was over. It was done.

After everything we'd done to stop them—after thousands of years of battle between The Children of Light and The Children of Darkness—Darkness had won in the end. I didn't realize how much hope I'd been holding onto until all hope was lost. There was no going back from here. This damage could not be undone.

I feared scenes like this were playing out across the globe, just as The Void had foretold. Though it was impossible to know how many of the other agents had managed to deactivate their targets, if even half of the bombs had detonated early, the planet would never recover. Anyone who hadn't been killed in the blasts would be dead within a matter of months.

I searched for Luca amid the carnage but saw only unfamiliar faces. I choked on the thickening smoke from the fires and moved blindly forward, tripping over random arms and legs lying strewn in the streets. My stomach seized, and I heaved again. Only bile came up.

I attempted to call out Luca's name, but my voice was weak, and the sound didn't carry over the screaming. Stumbling forward, I searched the burned faces, both hoping and fearing I'd find him.

I was surrounded by strangers, all living their own personal hells. Their blackened skin and horror-filled expressions tore at me, threatening to slice my chest in two. But no Luca. No Alena. No Zoeya.

Wrapping my arms around my middle, I coughed and continued numbly forward. The smoke grew thick and black, and a sharp pain spread in my throat. Breathing felt impossible. Somewhere in the corner of my consciousness, an alarm blared, warning that something inside me was broken–something vital, but I'd lost communication with my body. It was as if I were floating above it, watching the horror play out below. Nothing felt real.

I pushed forward several more feet before my sore-covered legs finally gave out. My knees hit the blackened street, and I collapsed onto my side. My face pressed to the broken ground. A foot lay inches from my face. The owner's shoe was burned away in spots, exposing the blackened flesh beneath.

In a distant part of my brain, that siren was still blaring, warning me that something was wrong. Whether from radiation poisoning, blunt-force trauma, or something else, I sensed my body was shutting down.

"No," I groaned, trying and failing to push myself up off the ground. This was wrong. Luca wasn't with me. I'd taken my eyes off him for only a moment. In the space of a breath, I'd lost him, maybe forever.

A sense of urgency stole my labored breath. I *needed* to be with Luca. We were supposed to go together in the end. We'd promised each other. Pinky promised. This couldn't be how our story ended, fading away in a sea of strangers. After all we'd endured, we couldn't be apart. I *had* to find him.

I squeezed my eyes shut and tried to clear my thoughts. He'd been standing on the other side of the Jeep when the bomb detonated, hadn't he? I remembered the shock and horror on his face, only a split second before the bomb detonated and my world went black. Luca *had* to be nearby.

A small flame flared to life inside me, telling me it wasn't too late. I could still find him, and we could still keep our promise. Summoning the last of my energy, I pushed to my feet. But as I renewed my search for Luca amid the rubble, the orange sky began to darken. I lifted my head and saw a black mass of rolling clouds quickly approaching. Only, they weren't emerging from the horizon; they were descending from above. Within moments, they blanketed the burning city. The roaring fires that seemed intent on devouring everything in sight shrank until they were nothing but puffs of black smoke.

The gathering storm was unlike any I'd ever felt. It was utterly silent, lacking in natural pressure or energy. The clouds absorbed all light and sound. My chest tightened and my body began to shake. Something terrifyingly familiar was coming.

Out of the clouds emerged a creature, tall, spindly, and dark as a starless sky. It stepped lightly down on the cracked, bleeding earth without even stirring the air as though its massive body weighed nothing. Several stories tall, it walked with unnatural grace. Gravity and drag had no power over it. Its eyes were pits, deep and endlessly black. The temperature plummeted, and I began to shiver. It bent over me, it wiry arms creating a cage around me. Emptiness settled over me like a frozen cloak. I knew this feeling. I knew this presence.

The Void, dark energy personified, had come down to Earth.

The Void towered over me, and I could sense that it was ancient, much older than the earth itself. Standing before it was like standing at the edge of a bottomless chasm. I was smaller than an atom in its shadow.

Bow, Bright One, and return to me, it said in a terrifyingly soft voice.

Involuntarily, my knees hit the ground, and my back bowed so low my forehead nearly touched the street. It spoke to my mind once more.

Light to Darkness. Dawn to dusk. All will reside within my eternal embrace once more. This is the day of my retribution.

I strained against the creature's hold in vain, but my aching heart and dying body were all too easily controlled. Satisfied by my apparent submission, The Void straightened and extended its vine-like arms. Its presence grew like a thunder cloud, covering the land. The radiation-filled clouds quickly blocked out the sun from horizon to horizon, reaching every corner of the earth. The city was plunged into an artificial night. Even the heavens ceased to shine. Survivors screamed and cried out for their loved ones.

We always knew the major killer wouldn't be the bombs themselves, but the nuclear winter that followed. The lack of sun would choke out our crops, starving everyone and everything on Earth. The deadly process was supposed to take months, but it appeared The Void was darkening the skies prematurely. For an eternal being, it had little patience for our deaths.

The Void's heavy presence pressed down on me. Despair seeped into my mind with a power far more potent than anything Ciara could produce. My dying body trembled, and my will to live diminished. I sensed The Void move through the crowd. One by one, the survivors fell silent as Darkness infected their minds.

My eyes dilated painfully as they searched for even a speck of light, but the darkness was complete. I lifted a hand in front of my face. The breath that bounced back at me was the only indication it still existed. Shivering, I lay down on my side again and pulled my knees to my chest, wrapping my arms around them. Shards of debris cut into my skin, but the pain barely registered.

My mind wandered through time and space. The streets of London faded, and I was in a cave high up in the Colorado mountains. Mom was standing next to me, young, beautiful, and so alive. A park ranger, dressed in brown shorts and hiking boots, motioned us forward, and we followed her deep into the labyrinth of the cave's tunnels. A string of lights drilled into the stone walls guided our path. Stalagmites and stalactites decorated the caverns with their otherworldly shapes. I drank in every word as the guide explained that they were thousands of years old, formed by water, drip by slow drip.

I could sense we were deep inside the mountain when the guide stopped at a large, grey electrical box with connecting wires that led to the string of lights. The guide explained that we were in a section of the cave where no sunlight could reach. Then, she pulled the lever, and all the lights turned off, plunging us into utter darkness. I grabbed Mom's hand, my chest full of fear and awe at the depth of that darkness. It was as if it went on with no end.

Sensing my anxiety, Mom pulled me close. I leaned into her grounding presence. "It's okay, Kir-bear. It's only darkness."

The warmth of my mother's hand dissolved, and I was back in London. I gagged on the overwhelming stench of death and ash.

Memory. It had only been a memory—one of a trip Mom and I had taken years ago—that was all. Yet unlike that moment in the cave, there was no comforting mother or capable guide, no cave walls echoing our breaths. No, *this* darkness really had no end. I waited for a tightening in my chest, a skittering across my skin, some physical manifestation of the terror I knew I must feel. Instead, all I felt was cold emptiness. The Void's shadows were working their way into my mind, numbing my senses and paralyzing my body.

All thoughts of finding Luca ceased. He was likely dead, anyway. Zoeya, Alena, all of them were most assuredly destroyed. I would be dead soon, too. My body already knew it; my broken mind was just playing catch-up. Death suddenly sounded like a respite rather than a penalty. In the end, darkness was a haven from the pain, a gift from The Void.

My breathing slowed as acceptance settled in. This was always going to be the outcome of this god-awful war. Deep down, I'd known it all along. I was a scientist, after all, and I knew the theory of eternal recurrence. All things reverted to their original state. It was inevitable. The Void had been telling me this from the beginning, I just didn't want to hear it. It had been prophesied since the inception of life. The Void, in its eternal wisdom, *knew* the universe and all things in it would return to a state of Darkness. I felt the rightness of this fact deep within my chest–in the exact spot where my light once flourished.

Like a dying flame, my remaining energy diminished by degrees, suffocating beneath The Void's choking shadow. I didn't fight it, for what power was there to pull from in such a dark place?

My shivering slowed and my arms and legs grew numb. Soon, I would feel neither cold nor fear. I would never again suffer the sting of grief. With a sigh, I raised my face to the unseen sky. Tiny flakes peppered my cheeks, fallout, no doubt, from the nuclear explosion. I let my aching eyes close and dreamt I was standing outside my home in Colorado. Snow was falling on my upturned face, my breath a puff of white smoke. Mom was there, too, holding a hand out to catch the falling flakes. We turned and smiled at each other, and I had the sense that we'd be together in the Darkness soon. My mouth curved into a peaceful smile.

Someone stepped on my arm, and I cried out. The pain pulled me back to Earth, shattering my peace, and it all came rushing back. My body still lay amid the devastation caused by the bomb we failed to neutralize. Shaking my head, I tried to shut it all out. I longed to return to the quiet bliss of oblivion.

"Kirie," said a voice said so faint I almost didn't hear it. My breath caught in my throat. I strained my ears and heard my name again. "Kirie." It sounded like Luca!

My heart thumped with renewed energy, and I uncoiled from my huddled position. Feeling my way forward on hands and knees, I searched the rubble and bodies for the voice calling my name. My hands ran over something squishy. I jerked back, my fingers coming away wet and sticky. My stomach clenched at the thought of what it might be.

"Kirie," the voice called again to my left. I reached out, and my hands landed on something warm and firm. I instantly recognized Luca's broad shoulder. Sight or no sight, I would know his body anywhere. I collapsed next to his familiar form. Grabbing fistfuls of Luca's shirt, I pulled him to me. I expected him to wrap his arms around me like so many times before, yet they lay still at his sides.

"Luca. Are you okay?" I whimpered. He didn't respond.

I searched for the connection that bound us together, but it was barely detectable. I ran a trembling hand over his hair, and it came away wet. He didn't react to my touch, though he had to be in immense pain. Something was wrong. I rested my cheek on his chest. Luca's slow, uneven heart rate was fading fast.

Clutching him to me, I cried out. "Don't go. Please, I need you. Stay with me!" Luca didn't so much as stir. I lifted my head, searching the darkness in vain. I needed a doctor, an ER, a defibrillator, anything. Luca was dying, and I was helpless to stop it!

I held him tightly and screamed until my voice gave out. Salty tears pooled in the holes in my cheeks. I poured my grief and anger into the atmosphere, much like I'd once released my energy. The air around our entwined bodies crackled as if in reply. Sniveling, I lifted my face again to the black sky. As the tiny particles landed on my cheeks, I sensed…something. I opened my palm and caught the falling flakes, and the dying ember inside me suddenly sprang to life. There was power in the air. The Void's shadows had veiled the energy inside the radioactive fallout before. Now free from their numbing effects, I could feel the *massive* store of it within each flake, making the hair on my arms stand on end. With a gasp, I opened myself to the energy, and it flooded into me, creating sparks in the darkness.

My insides began to warm, and a tingling sensation spread through my limbs. A halo of light surrounded me. I pushed it out into the sky, partially illuminating The Void that stood several feet away. Its spindly black form hovered over the mass of dying bodies, its soulless eyes watching as many took their last breaths. The Void turned toward my light, anger twisting its otherworldly features.

What is this? Its voice shook the battlefield like an earthquake.

I stood and faced The Void, pulling from the nuclear energy until my light fully exposed the eternal monster. Screams of the dying rose in crescendo as The Void roared his disapproval. Its tar-like shadows pushed against my light, but I gritted my teeth and pushed back.

Extinguish your light, Bright One. Again, the voice shook the ground, nearly toppling me.

"I will not!" I roared. The urge to comply was nearly overwhelming, but I did not back down. Though the pain of my injuries was acute, and the peace of Darkness called to me, begging me to return to its cool embrace, Luca lay dying in a pool of blood at my feet. For his sake, I would not give in.

I locked my shaky knees and stood firm. Fists at my side, I squared up with The Void as its presence overshadowed me. "I will *not*," I repeated.

The towering tyrant lunged for me, inky talons outstretched. I absorbed more nuclear power and raised my hands, shooting a beam of light at The Void. Energy leapt from my palms like a streak of lightning, missing the dark master by mere inches. With an unearthly shriek, The Void jumped back into the dark sky, fleeing from the force of my light.

A hole remained in the thick clouds where my light shot through, and a single ray of sunlight cast a macabre spotlight on a child's body lying in its mother's arms. Both were still and gray.

Without prompting, the nuclear energy continued to flow into me, feeding my energy stores. Light radiated from my pores, illuminating dozens of feet in every direction. My skin began to itch. I held them out and stared in awe as the sores on the back of my hands stitched themselves back together. Just as quickly, new lesions appeared. The radioactive fallout was feeding me energy and killing me at the same time.

I stared down at my glowing skin, and it dawned on me. I was a Bright One. One of the many Children of Light prophesied of in the Dead Sea Scrolls. We were warriors. We were teachers. And above all, we were *healers.*

I knelt next to Luca's crumpled form and ran my hands over him, assessing his injuries. The hope in my chest deflated when it became clear Luca was in worse shape than I'd imagined. Blood slowly seeped through cuts on his exposed arms and head, and his face was ashen white. He stared up at the sky, his eyes glassy and vacant. I suddenly couldn't breathe.

Shaking his shoulders, I cried, "Luca, talk to me!" With trembling fingers, I checked for a pulse and searched for our connected but found neither. His body was nothing but an empty husk.

"NO!"

I dropped my head and sobbed into his chest, loud and ugly. It was too late. *I* was too late! A crowd began to form around me, whether attracted to my naked grief or the light radiating from my skin, I didn't know. Their personal pain and suffering pressed in on me, stealing the little air left in my lungs. The crowd grew, desperate to stand in my glow.

Alena and Zoeya stumbled their way through the mob, both covered in ash and blood. Alena rushed toward Luca, her beautiful face shattering as she took in her fallen brother. Dropping to her knees next to me, she pressed her fingers to the inside of his wrist. A few seconds later, she sat back on her heels, her head dropping to her chest. She knew, as I did, that it was too late.

But I couldn't accept Luca's death. I wouldn't! I had been within death's reach myself, yet the nuclear energy I siphoned from the air had pulled me from its clutches. Why, then, couldn't it bring back Luca? I had to believe it could. I placed my glowing hands over Luca's heart and released a blast of energy. His back bowed violently. I waited. Nothing. I hit him again. And again. I sent bolt after bolt of energy into his heart. His back rose and fell with each hit, but it wasn't working.

Alena placed a hand on my back. "Kirie," she said softly. "He's gone."

I shook her off with a glare. Her gentleness enraged me. She was acting as though it was over, as though Luca was gone for good. But she was wrong. There was still hope. As long as there was energy running in my veins, I knew I could heal him.

I'd practiced healing for a short while with Finn back in Rome. Though I'd only worked on small injuries then, I hadn't been full of nuclear energy, nor had Luca's life been on the line. I pulled more power from the sky until my light illuminated the entire square.

The crowd surged forward. Zoeya raised two dimly lit hands and yelled, "Stay back!" They retreated in terror and confusion, but only a few feet.

I ignored the rabid mob and sent another powerful shot of energy into Luca's heart. His chest lifted off the ground and back again. I waited for him to breathe, open his eyes, do *something*, but he lay still.

"Come on," I cried. "Come back to me," I begged. Hot tears ran down my cheeks as I continued to pour energy into his chest. Nothing. I slumped forward, spent.

Alena studied me with pinched brows. "Kirie, where are you getting this energy?"

I raised a limp hand and pointed to the sky, unable to form the words.

Alena raised her face and closed her eyes. "Ah, yes. I feel it." Seconds later, her skin lit up and her eyes sprang open, her amber irises ablaze. With a feverish look, Alena grabbed my hand and an additional current rushed through me. Our skin brightened exponentially, creating a halo around our bodies. Cries of fear and surprise surrounded us. We were the only visible things left on Earth. Like moths to a flame, people began dragging their dying bodies across the broken earth to reach us.

Alena turned and held out a hand to Zoeya, who took it without hesitation. "Take from the nuclear energy in the air," Alena instructed her. Soon, Zoeya's light joined ours. We shone as brightly as the sun. The desperate crowd fell back, screaming and shielding their eyes from the brilliance of our light.

"Try again," Alena said, nodding to Luca. Through our joined hands, I felt her trust and conviction in my ability to bring him back.

I placed my free hand back onto Luca's cold chest. Instead of a jolt of power, I sent a steady flow into his core. At first, nothing changed, but slowly his skin warmed and brightened slightly. Still, no breath, no heartbeat. A single sob left my lips as doubt took over. Luca couldn't bring Arin back from the brink of death, and he was The Society's best healer. What made me think *I* could bring someone back to life?

Zoeya knelt between Alena and me and wrapped her arms around our waists. We huddled closely together, and our energies merged until we shone a brilliant blue. Visible threads of light linked our bodies as we formed a perfect circuit. Zoeya pressed her cheek to mine and whispered. "Don't give up." I took a deep breath and directed a single strand of pure energy into Luca one last time.

Luca sucked in a breath. We sprang back in shock. His eyes shone bright white and the veins beneath his pale skin glowed like bolts of lightning. Luca let out a strangled cough and sat up. Crying in relief, I pressed my face to his neck. There, I could feel a steady heartbeat. Alena and Zoeya turned to each other, hugging and crying together.

Color slowly returned to Luca's face, but he remained unsteady, swaying in my arms. "I feel like shite," he groaned, his British accent abnormally thick.

I tightened my hold in him. "Well, I guess dying does that to a person." My half-hearted laugh ended in a sob.

Luca raised a bloody hand to my face. His brows furrowed as he studied me. "Is that where I was?" he asked. I nodded, unable to say the words a second time. His hand wrapped around the back of my neck and pulled my forehead to his. "I'm sorry, my love."

"Don't do that again, okay?" I sobbed.

"Okay." Luca's lips pressed to mine, and his kiss tasted like blood and ash.

Chapter 22

Kirie

Our surge of light dispersed the heavy shroud that covered the sky, leaving behind wispy, orange-tinted clouds, turning our sick world jaundiced. Black smoke billowed from the surrounding buildings as the fires rekindled in The Void's absence, further polluting the toxic air. I pulled my shirt collar over my nose, but it did little to block the fumes.

Luca let out another strangled cough. His face remained pale, and his breathing was labored as his body and mind struggled to recover from dying. Holding Luca upright, I felt gazes upon me, prickling the back of my neck. Looking up, dozens of citizens' wet, red-rimmed eyes were trained on us.

Many in the crowd were clearly near death, their skin covered in sores, and pieces of flesh hung from their limbs, exposing white bone. Their desperate, hungry stares were fixed on Luca's newly healed form.

My heart beat a heavy drum in my ears as I stood to shield him from the swarming citizens. They would touch him over my dead body. A woman rushed forward and fell at my feet. Her blistered fingers grabbed the hem of my pants. "Please, heal me!" she pleaded, pawing at my legs.

Instinctively, my hands reached out to her, but the crowd surged forward like a horde of crazed zombies, reaching out for me. I cried out and tripped on Luca's outstretched legs, falling onto a sharp piece of concrete and cutting my palm.

Alena pulled a pistol from her waistband and shot into the sky. "Back up!" she commanded. The authority of her voice crackled in the nuclear air. Leveling the gun at the crowd, she forced the desperate back, but only for a moment. A man from behind rushed forward, taking advantage of Alena's turned back. Zoeya turned and pulled a gun from her holster. She shot the ground near the man's feet, and he sprang back with a cry, his eyes wild with desperation.

"Don't make me shoot you, man," Zoeya warned. Her hand visibly shook, but her gaze held firm. "Seriously, back off!"

Tears stung my eyes as I watched them struggle in pain, desperate to be healed. My hands itched to reach out to them. How could I not do something when it was in my power to take away their pain? But their rabid expressions held me back.

The people were dying and beyond reason. They would tear me apart before I healed them.

A fire in a nearby building suddenly surged, and the structure began to collapse, spraying sparks and rubble into the street. I threw myself over Luca, shielding him from flying debris. The crowd, mindless from fear and panic, scrambled in all directions, thoughtlessly trampling the dead beneath their heels. The fire was quickly devouring the city around us and the heat singed my already burned skin. We had to move quickly.

"Help me get him up," I yelled to Alena. She holstered her gun, and together, we pulled Luca to his feet. Draping his arms over our shoulders, we hobbled out of the now-empty city square down a side street lined with fire. Zoeya took up the rear, gun still raised in defense.

We hobbled several city blocks before Luca's waning energy finally gave out. "I need to rest," he rasped, his chest heaving from the effort of staying upright.

I chewed on my bottom lip, reluctant to stop while still within the city limits. Though we'd put distance between us and the destruction, the fire from the epicenter was quickly spreading. If we stopped now, we could easily find ourselves trapped by the flames. Then there were the rabid survivors from the square to worry about. Who knew where they were?

Alena and I shared a look past Luca's shoulders. She shook her head. "We can't stop here. It isn't safe."

"Can you go a bit further?" I asked him. His lips pressed into a tight line, but he nodded once. Alena and I readjusted

Luca's arms over our shoulders and tightened our grip on his waist. We limped forward, carrying most of his weight.

Some time later, when the heat of the fires was finally at our backs, we helped Luca to the ground, leaning him against a blackened brick wall. His head fell back, and he promptly fell asleep. I felt guilty for pushing him so hard. His body needed rest to recover, but it wasn't safe to stay in one place for long. I collapsed next to him, my shoulders screaming from carrying his weight. Wrapping my fingers around his wrist, I felt for the beat of his pulse and the warmth of his skin, taking neither for granted. The grief of watching him die was still fresh.

The streets in this part of town were cleaner, and although the buildings' windows had been blown out, the walls were still erect. Thankfully, there were also fewer people, both living and dead. I could sense that the energy field here was weaker, suggesting we were nearly out of the range of radiation.

With a grunt, Alena slid down the wall next to me, clearly in as much pain as I was. Luca was lean, but his muscles made him as heavy as stone. Zoeya remained standing. Her shoulders were rigid as she scanned the surrounding buildings, gun at the ready. Anxious energy radiated off her in waves.

My head fell back against the brick wall as my mind tried to process the events of the past few hours. My arms and legs began to shake as the adrenaline drained from my body. We'd failed to deactivate the bomb. The Order must have altered its countdown. How many others had also failed their missions? How many people had lost their lives that day, and how many would follow? With or without The Void's interference, nuclear winter would soon set in, and many more would die.

Not that it mattered. Based on what I'd seen so far, humanity would quickly destroy itself before then.

As the sun sank lower in the sky, I gazed out at the darkening street littered with debris and death. An empty shoe lying in the last ray of sunlight caught my attention. I stared at it despondently, knowing the owner likely didn't need it anymore. A cool breeze whistled down the street, carrying with it the stench of death. It was as though we'd been transported into a hellscape where there was no hope, no light at the end of the tunnel. The road ahead only ended in death.

I turned my free hand over and stared at my bleeding palm. I pulled a little energy from the fallout, and sealed the wound shut. I ran a finger over the smooth skin there, marveling at the immense power that lived within the cells of my body. Luca had *died,* and I'd brought him back to life with that power. My eyes traveled over the ruined city. But what good was it in the face of such destruction? My abilities were useless in the end. I turned to Alena, who looked as empty as I felt.

"We should have healed those people back there," I murmured. My voice sounded dead to my own ears.

Alena shot me a sidelong glare. "And then what? Assuming they didn't tear us limb from limb, the radiation would only make them sick again. Besides, look around you." She gestured to the devastation. "What are you saving them for? Death would be better than living in *this* hell."

She had a point. What was there left to live for when everything and everyone would soon be gone? Still, I hated feeling so helpless. "But shouldn't we help the injured if we can?" I argued.

"The only thing we should be doing is getting the hell out of here." Alena's retort lacked her usual level of heat, exhaustion and shock still clearly weighing her down.

Zoeya pointed to a newly developed sore on her forearm. "She's right. We need to get further away from ground zero. The radiation will continue to degrade our cells the longer we stay."

We'd been running from the radiation zone for hours with no clear destination or objective beyond survival. At any moment, we could run into looters. Or worse, The Void could return. We were in no condition to defend ourselves. We were running around in the dark, unable to see the pitfalls ahead.

I balled my fists in frustration. "Where are we supposed to go? Mentmore Towers is too far away to reach on foot, and we can't stay here. What are we even doing?" We had no plan nor direction and help was *not* on the way. Hot tears stung my eyes as the full weight of our situation threatened to bury me.

Zoeya knelt in front of us, her arms resting on her knees. "So let's make a plan. The first thing we need to do is find a satellite phone since ours was destroyed in the blast. Then, we'll contact Mr. Bellamy. He'll give us orders from there." She spoke with the patience of a much older woman. Zoeya had always seemed so full of youth and personality that I hadn't seen the maturity there.

Alena's mouth turned down. "And where are we going to find a satellite phone?"

"I remember seeing a military base a few miles to the northeast on the map. It's far enough from the blast that it likely survived," Zoeya said, pointing a finger in that direction. "They're sure to have a sat phone there."

Alena pushed to her feet with a grunt. "Okay, fearless leader. Lead the way."

"Luca." I gently shook him awake. "Time to get going." He complied without comment, and I worried about his silence.

We trudged slowly through the suburbs of Watford. The sun disappeared behind the skeletal remains of the high-rises as we made our way down ruined city streets. The going was slow as we dragged Luca along. At first, we could hear cries for help from the nearby alleyways and windows, but they slowly quieted as more victims succumbed to their injuries. Thankfully, the few remaining survivors still able to run had scattered in their mad flight from the poisonous city. I dragged my feet, reluctant to leave the dying behind. But Alena was right. Even if I could heal them all, they'd simply just become ill again from the radiation.

Several miles outside Watford, the air grew lighter and fresher. Zoeya pointed to a two-story clothing shop that was still intact. "Let's rest here," she said, shooting Luca worried glances.

We stumbled through the glass doors. Racks of clothes lay on their sides as if the store had simply been hit by an earthquake. A whimper came from the front counter. Guns held at the ready, we rounded it, and found a middle-aged man huddled behind the register, shaking violently likely from pain and shock. His clothes were ripped and white with ash. Open sores, yellow and red around the edges, marred his skin. I approached him slowly. My heart twisted in my chest, and fresh tears stung my eyes as I watched him struggle to breathe. He was about the same age and build as my stepdad, Barry. A powerful urge to stop his suffering came over me. I knelt beside him and crinkled my nose as the smell of singed flesh assaulted me. Pulling from the energy in the air, I lifted my glowing hands to his chest. The man's vacant eyes reflected my light.

"Kirie." Alena said on a sigh. "We talked about this. He's too far gone. Even if you heal him now, he'll only die a gruesome death later."

She was right, of course. Likely, none of us was making it out of this alive. Healing this man would only condemn him to days of additional horror as the Earth died. But as I watched this Barry look-alike struggle to live, I knew I couldn't simply walk away. Perhaps it was selfish of me, but in some way, I felt as though healing this man from The Void's cruelty might begin to heal the old Kirie, who was too weak and untrained to save her mother and stepfather from Donovan's knife. So I sent a steady flow of healing current into his chest. The man sighed in relief as his sores closed and his skin regained its healthy tone. His eyes cleared, and he stared at me in wonder as I helped him to his feet.

"What did you do to me?" he asked, his gaze full of wonder.

I shrugged and stepped back, uncomfortable with his awe. "I did what I could. I'm sorry I couldn't do more."

The man's face fell, and he looked around the small clothing shop in confusion. "W-what happened?"

My heart filled with compassion for the man. The bomb must have been a complete surprise to him. He'd have no idea what had caused the blast, let alone how much damage it had done. I reached out to him, hoping to offer comfort. "There was a bomb," I began.

The man suddenly cried out and looked around frantically. "Felicia! Where's Felicia?" He turned and ran out the glass doors. My eyes stung as I watched him race down the street, screaming his loved one's name in a blind panic. There was little hope his Felicia had survived. Alena was right. My compassion was useless here. I hadn't saved that man; I'd simply condemned him to a short life full of terror and grief.

I felt a light hand on my shoulder and turned to meet Alena's sad, caramel eyes. "No more healing, okay?"

A knot formed in my throat, and I nodded. "No more healing."

Chapter 23

Kirie

We stayed in the shop only long enough to heal our fresh wounds and catch our breath. We slogged through the night, taking few breaks to rest our eyes and feet. My legs were numb from walking. By the time we reached the military base, the sun was just peeking over the horizon, and I thanked the universe that we'd made it through the night without being attacked or succumbing to radiation poisoning.

The base was an old, two-story red brick building surrounded by a metal fence. "Barnet Army Reserve" was written on the front. It was clear we weren't the only survivors who thought to gather there. Several white tents had been erected in the street, surrounded by temporary chain-link fences. As we got closer, I realized they were medical tents. There were rows of cots set up inside, all occupied by the injured. Hundreds more lay in the street, waiting for a bed. The line stretched back several city blocks. Nurses and doctors rushed between cots, doing what they could. Their faces and bodies were already showing signs of exhaustion.

My tired eyes ran over the crowd. Most were barefoot and wore nothing more than their pajamas as the attack had happened before any of them had gotten out of bed. Some, had avoided the worst of the blast, but many more appeared to be on the brink of death.

"Come on," Zoeya said, limping toward the base. "Let's find a satellite phone."

Uniformed guards flanked the base's gate. They lifted their rifles a few inches as we approached.

"The line for medical attention is over there," the guard said, pointing toward the tents with the tip of his rifle. "Get in line like the rest."

The man had dark circles beneath his eyes, and his shoulders slumped as if he, too, had stayed up all night.

"We're not injured. We just need to use a satellite phone," Zoeya said.

"Sorry, military equipment is for military purposes only," the guard said. "Now move along."

"Please, it's very important." Zoeya pouted up at the guard and tears appeared in her wide, brown eyes.

The man shifted uncomfortably. "Fine, whatever," he grunted. The guard disappeared for several minutes and came back holding a bulky rectangular phone. Zoeya reached out for it, but he pulled it back, glaring down at her. "You have two minutes. Stay where I can see you."

"Yes, sir." She nodded.

We turned our backs on the soldiers and huddled close together. Zoeya handed me the phone, and I quickly dialed Finn's number.

"Hello?" I nearly cried as Finn's familiar voice crackled over the line.

"Finn, it's me."

"Oh, thank God. Are you okay?"

Tears clogged my throat, and I struggled to answer. Was I okay? Were any of us okay? I looked back at the desperate, ash-covered faces of the survivors lining the street, and I worried none of us would ever be okay again.

"We're alive," I finally got out. "How is everyone there?"

"We're alive," he parroted. "Where are you now?"

Luca leaned over my shoulder and spoke for me. "We're at the Barnet Army Base."

"Okay. Stay where you are. I'm coming to you."

"Finn, things are pretty bad out here. Be careful," I warned.

"You just worry about you. Stay where you are and keep your guard up. I'll be right there," he assured and hung up.

I returned to the gate where the soldier stood waiting. His uniform was wrinkled and his skin was pale and lifeless. He couldn't be older that twenty-two, yet his hunched form made him appear much older. The poor guy was probably on post through the night, doing what he could to maintain order amid the chaos. I may not be able to heal everyone, but I could ease some of this one man's burden. When I held the phone out to him, I let our fingers touch, sending a small flow of energy through the contact. His shoulders strengthened and the circles beneath his eyes brightened as if he'd just woken from a good night's sleep. He stared down at me, mouth agape.

"Thank you for your service," I said with a smile, backing away quickly.

"Y-yes, ma'am. Good luck out there," the soldier called after me.

My heart felt lighter as I returned to the group. I wrapped my arm around Luca's waist again, and he leaned into me with a sigh. "Finn's on his way."

Alena shifted on her feet. "Did he say anything about Arabella?" Her voice trembled a little as if she were afraid of the answer.

"Everyone is safe at Mentmore Towers," I assured her. Alena let out a breath of relief.

Zoeya clapped her hands. "Great. Let's find a place to rest. I can't feel my legs."

We limped across the street and sat, huddled together beneath a small grouping of trees. I leaned my head on Luca's shoulder, and he rested his over mine. I grabbed his hand, desperate to anchor him to my side, but his grip lacked its normal strength. Through our bond, I could feel how deep his exhaustion truly went. Luca needed a meal, a bed, and about a month-long nap to fully recover. I doubted any of us would live that long. I pushed my darker thoughts away and sank into Luca's side. For now, we had each other. We were keeping out promise. That would have to be enough. My heavy eyes drooped closed.

Sometime later, a hand touched my shoulder, and I jolted awake. Finn's face came into view, framed by the rising sun. I couldn't help the tears that began pouring down my cheeks.

"Dad," I cried. I jumped up and threw my arms around his neck. Finn froze a moment before returning my embrace. He patted my back as I sobbed.

Finn finally pulled back and faced the others. "I'm happy to see you're all alive."

Alena folded her arms and glared at Finn. "We should have had more time to intercept the bomb. What happened?"

He rocked back on his heels and ran a hand over his tired face. "I honestly don't know. My best guess is that The Order found out that Donovan gave us the list of locations, and they moved the delivery time up a few hours."

"That tracks, actually," Luca said with a heavy sigh. "They made sure we were close enough to kill, but not close enough to intercept the bomb. Bloody bastards."

Finn looked over us, his brow deeply furrowed as he took in our ash covered clothes and tattered hair. "How did you all survive the bomb? You must have been only a few miles away from the detonation site.”

“We didn’t,” I said. Finn squinted at me in confusion. “All survive, that is.”

“I’m sorry, I don’t quite understand,” Finn began, looking at each of us in turn. “Who died?”

“Luca did, but only for a minute,” Alena said in a flippant tone. “But Kirie brought him back to life.” She hooked a thumb in my direction.

“No,” I said, putting my hands up. “I didn’t bring him back; we did. You and Zoeya helped remember?”

Alena rolled her eyes and tossed her filthy ponytail over her shoulder. “Fine. We brought Luca back to life, and then we healed ourselves.”

Finn stared at us, slack-jawed. “H-how is that possible? No Agent of Light has ever brought someone back from the dead before.”

“Turns out a nuclear bomb creates a shit ton of energy,” Zoeya said with a shrug as if that explained everything.

Finn crouched in front of Luca, who was still visibly pale and weak. “Is it true?” Luca simply nodded, his green eyes dull and heavy with exhaustion. Finn put a steadying hand over Luca’s shoulder as if he were afraid he might fall over at any moment. “How are you feeling?”

“Like death warmed over,” Luca replied with a half smile, but the joke fell flat.

Finn squeezed his eyes shut and shook his head. "Okay, we'll talk about this later. First, let's get you home."

Though my aching legs protested, I pushed myself to follow as Finn led us away from the army base and medical tents.

"I had to park a few blocks away because of the crowd," he called over his shoulder.

The hair on my arms suddenly stood on end, and a chill crept down my spine. I came to a sudden stop. Turning back to the base, fresh dread washed over me. The sun was quickly fading behind a gigantic thundercloud.

"You guys, look." I pointed to the darkening sky. Luca, Finn, Alena, and Zoeya stopped and stared at the horizon with equal looks of dread.

The crowd fell silent as a thundercloud covered the sky at an unnatural pace. A familiar presence enveloped me in its cold embrace. Within seconds, daylight was snuffed out like a candle flame.

"Be on guard!" Finn yelled.

In unison, we called forth our power and lifted our shining hands, illuminating The Void's spindly form. It stood high above the army base, crouching low as if preparing to devour its entirely.

Several soldiers inside the base's gates yelled, and a volley of shots rang out as they began an assault on the otherworldly threat. The bullets passed right through The Void's noncorporeal body. They continued their attack to no avail, for The Void was dark energy, not flesh and bone.

A voice, deep as the ocean, wide as the Grand Canyon, blanketed the land.

My children. My Darklings.

The soldiers dropped their weapons, and every head on the city block lifted in unison. I gaped at the crowd as they stared at The Void, not with fear, but with rapt attention. Did they…No. Luca and I were the only ones who could hear The Void's voice, the only ones made to endure its taunts and demands, its visions of destruction. Was it possible they heard its voice, too?

Fear not. I am your liberation from this cursed world.

Several people from the crowd gasped, confirming my fears. The Void was in the mind of every survivor. Luca grabbed my hand as the same realization hit him.

Rejoice! Your pain and suffering are at an end. Today, I welcome you back into my embrace.

The Void had taken on a god-like tone full benevolence and compassion. Every head bowed, and every knee bent. They lowered themselves to the ground as supplicants. I stared in horror at their bent forms as The Void worked its way into their minds. Its argument, when proposed to a grief-riddled mind, would sound like reason and kindness. For the first time since meeting The Void, I realized that it truly believed it was doing humanity a favor by eradicating it. It believed light and life were infections that must be cured.

I looked around at the pain and suffering surrounding me. The Void was right about one thing. Being human was hard. It meant experiencing an array of emotions, many of which were difficult to endure. In the wake of war and destruction, darkness's embrace may sound like a blessed release to these people, as it once had to me.

My heart broke as the survivors leaned toward The Void's long, spidery arms, like an injured child to its mother. They were vulnerable, broken, and easily swayed by The Void's enticements. But submitting to its dark embrace, willingly slipping into nothingness, wasn't a solution. It was an ending.

My heart pounded in my chest, and I cried out, "Don't listen! Don't give in!"

Lightning cracked across the sky, framing The Void's massive form as its sightless gaze fell on me. A gust of frigid air slammed into me. Inside it, I felt The Void's frustration and malice. It flexed its talon-like fingers and surged forward, pressing its oppressive Darkness down upon the crowd. I fell back onto the pavement, the breath forced from my lungs. I struggled to breathe, but the pressure was too much. Beside me, the others thrashed and gasped like landed fish as the The Void's dark force pressed down on us. We were being buried alive.

Like so many times before, whispers filled my mind, saying there was no use in fighting. We were already dead. The Earth would never recover. Those who survived were doomed to short, terror-filled days. It was better to give up now. I gritted my teeth and fought against the whispers. I knew they were nothing but lies, thick tar meant to entrap.

Luca cried out my name, and his clammy hand slipped into mine. Though his body shook from exhaustion, our energy combined and we began to glow. The sightless eyes in the crowd turned our way, and my breath caught in my throat. Their pupils were so dilated from The Void's artificial night, they could easily have passed for Shadowmen. It was as though we were surrounded by a sea of zombies. Within only a matter of seconds, The Void had been able to subdue hundreds of people. They hadn't even tried to fight back.

In desperation, I reached over and grabbed Alena's hand, and our light grew, but it was still no match for The Void's dark whisperings. The people were still under its menacing spell.

"Look to the light!" I cried. The survivors' brows knit in confusion, seemingly torn between the seductive voice and our radiant light.

Slowly, their survival instincts kicked in, and they moved toward our halo, forming a circle around us. They huddled together in a mass of desperation and fear, as The Void bellowed it's disapproval above us. Dozens became hundreds, until our light could no longer touch all who flocked to us. Their fear and confusion fed The Void's oppressive force, and it pressed back against our light with renewed force.

"We need more energy," I said through gritted teeth.

"On it." Luca reached back and grabbed Zoeya's hand, who linked hands with Finn. Once again, the force of our light grew.

Submit to me! The Void roared, and the people cowered, some covering their heads and crying out. The darkness pressed down on our circle of light, threatening to suffocate it like a flame.

"It's not enough," I cried. "We can't create enough light to break through the darkness."

I searched the crowded street, looking for some form of energy. There was no sun and not enough ambient nuclear power this far from ground zero to feed us. I clenched my teeth in frustration. There had to be another way to increase our output. But after the EMP destroyed the power grid, the only source of energy was coming from the people. My eyes grew wide. The people! They were made of energy!

"Finn! Grab that man's hand," I yelled, pointing to the half-dead young man standing behind him. "Tell him to form a chain."

Without question, Finn grabbed the survivor's hand and instructed him to do the same. The command was repeated until it became a thousand echoes down the street.

I crawled to my feet, still holding on to Luca's and Alena's hands. I lifted my chin and raised my voice. "I know you're scared right now. I'm scared, too. We've all lost so much." My voice cracked. The faces of our dead filled my mind. Mom, Bert, Arin, and Bodhi. The millions of citizens around the world who had been reduced to radioactive dust. So much death. So much loss. Grief threatened to cripple me, but I fought against the tears. This was what The Void wanted—our fear and misery. We couldn't willingly grant them to him no matter how much we'd lost. I swallowed down the lump in my throat and pressed on. "The darkness feeds on grief and despair. You must not lose hope."

Hands continued to meet, and with each new source of energy, the light around us grew. People cried out as wounds began to stitch together, and their minds began to clear. Our light steadily spread through each connected source.

Luca and my light glowed brighter until our eyes glowed white, and our skin was pure light. Our feet began to leave the ground, and Alena and Zoeya tightened their grip on us, anchoring us to the earth.

Luca stared at me in wonder. A lone tear carved a path through the blood and dirt on his cheek. "I don't understand. How is this happening?"

"We might be The Children of Light, but we're not the only ones with light within us. Look at them." I nodded to the people surrounding us. A slight glow radiated from each of their bodies. "The sun, the Earth, every living thing is made of energy. We are simply greater conduits of that light," I explained.

Luca nodded slowly, as if the concept had never occurred to him. "You're right. Of course, you're right."

Luca and the other agents hadn't seen it because they'd been raised in a world with only Bright Ones and Shadowmen. Everyday humans weren't a part of their worldview. I, on the other hand, had only known the care and comfort of average citizens, or so they were called. But they were just as heroic and bright as any Agent of Light. In my darkest hours, Rylie's family had been my lighthouse. They took me in and treated me like their own. My own mother, though ordinary by The Society of Light's standards, had kept the Darkness at bay until the day she died. We were all made of the same energy, connecting us in a way The Void in its solitary darkness couldn't understand. A smile spread across my lips, and my light intensified as hope and vindication warmed my chest.

The Void had no idea what he was up against.

It thought we were weak. It thought we were small. And maybe alone, we were. But together, we could defeat the darkness. Together, we could light up the world!

Alena and Zoeya held us to the ground as Luca and I became more energy than human. Our hair whipped around our faces as the energy built to a crescendo. A brilliant light, full of all the colors on the spectrum, radiated from our chests as our energy merged into one. I was Luca, and Luca was me.

I locked eyes with my other half, my perfect pair. Luca was as radiant as the sun and far more beautiful. My love for him only served to increase our light. My mortal body strained against the pressure of so much power, and it felt as though I would soon explode.

"Release it!" Finn cried. His voice sounded as though it were a million miles away. "Let go!" he yelled.

Luca smiled, and I nodded. It was time. With twin cries, we released the energy, shooting it straight into the heart of Darkness. The Void screamed in pain as pure energy continued to flow through us and into it. The light tore at The Void's body, ripping it apart bit by bit. The dark monster fought back, reforming its broken pieces as quickly as the light destroyed them.

"Keep going, don't let go!" Finn ordered. "Everyone, think joyful thoughts!"

Faces all around us strained as they fought against The Void's poisonous mind tricks. Luca and my light suddenly surged, and an immense burst of light exploded from our chests. The Void cried out one last time as its body disintegrated, subatomic molecule by subatomic molecule, until there was nothing left.

My vision went black, and we fell to the ground, utterly spent.

When my eyes finally cleared, I was staring into the perfect English blue sky.

(War Time)
There will come soft rains and the smell of the
ground,
And swallows circling with their shimmering
sound;

And frogs in the pools singing at night,
And wild plum trees in tremulous white,

Robins will wear their feathery fire
Whistling their whims on a low fence-wire;

And not one will know of the war, not one
Will care at last when it is done.

Not one would mind, neither bird nor tree
If mankind perished utterly;

And Spring herself, when she woke at dawn,
Would scarcely know that we were gone.

"There Will Come Soft Rains" by Sara Teasdale

Chapter 24

Kirie

The green grass tickled my toes as I stood before twin headstones in the overgrown lawn. In the background was the *chih, chih, chih,* of a sprinkler. I squinted up at the sun beating down on my head. A bead of sweat ran down my spine. I'd forgotten how intense the sun was in the Mile High City. A warm breeze caressed my bare shoulders, and I welcomed the momentary respite from the heat.

I placed my palm on the sunbaked headstone and ran my fingers across the words etched into granite. Claire Sorenson.

"Hi, Mom," I whispered.

My heart was heavy as I stood before my mother's grave. I hadn't been back since their funeral, and seeing their gravestones reminded me of that awful day. Even now, watching them lower my parents into the ground was one of the hardest things I'd ever had to do. But it had also been the day I'd officially met Luca and Alena. I knew my life had changed back then, I just didn't know how much.

Thunder clouds slowly rolled in from the east, as they always did in summer along the Rocky Mountain Front Range. As I breathed in the scent of oncoming rain and the freshly cut grass, an old memory worked its way to the surface of my mind. Rylie and I were playing in the community pool. We were nine years old that summer. Like clockwork, an afternoon storm had rolled in. When the skies began to weep, we quickly climbed up the metal pool stairs and ran screaming for cover under the pavilion, never considering the fact that we were already wet. We huddled together, our damp beach towels wrapped around our shivering shoulders. Cold water dripped down our backs from our stringy, pool water hair. The moment the skies cleared, we promptly discarded our towels on the wet concrete deck and cannonballed back into the pool, amid the lifeguards' shrill whistles and yells to stop running.

The innocence and joy of that memory healed my tattered soul a little. I wondered where Rylie was at that moment. Agents were able to disable most of the bombs planted across the US, but not all. Two had detonated on the west coast alone, one in Dallas, the other in L.A., and the resulting fallout had been devastating. The United States was in a rare moment of unity. It was a beautiful thing. But like all beautiful things, I feared it wouldn't last. Humans were fickle creatures.

Behind me, Luca leaned against a black sedan, waiting with his hands in his pockets. He wore aviators and a black shirt that strained across his broad shoulders and defined chest. He looked healthier, the stain of death on his skin less pronounced. He caught me staring, and he smiled. My heart swelled in my chest. I'd almost lost that man, had lost him. But by some miracle, I got to live a life with him. My eyes stung with tears of gratitude.

I took a deep breath and motioned him over. We were taking a big step in our relationship. After going to hell and back, it was time to introduce him to the parents. He crossed the lawn, weaving in and out of headstones.

"Mom, this is Luca." I placed a hand on his arm. "Luca, this is my mom, Claire Sorenson."

Luca dipped his head. "It's a pleasure to meet you."

We sat on the grass, and I told him stories of my childhood. I'd been so angry at my mom for hiding things from me that I'd forgotten all the good times. I regretted that now.

"Do you think she would have liked me?" Luca asked.

"She would have thought you were trouble and warned me away from you, for sure," I said with a laugh.

"Damn. That's harsh," he grumbled.

"Well, you did kidnap me and take me to Paris."

Luca laughed. "That I did."

I patted his arm. "But she would have come around eventually. It's hard not to love you."

Luca pulled me closer and kissed the top of my head. "Love you, too."

I leaned forward and pressed a kiss to my mother's grave and turned back to Luca. "Come on. Finn's waiting."

"Ah, yes. Let's go see your other disapproving parent," Luca said with a sarcastic grin.

I snorted out a laugh. "I think he's warming up to you."

"Bullocks! That man glares at me every time I come in the room."

I laughed again because it was true. Luca took hold of my hand, and we walked back to the car. A private plane was waiting for us in Denver to take us to Washington D.C. Thankfully, only the cities hosting Centers of Light were hit with the EMPs. The electric grids in all other cities remained untouched, so many cars, phones, and planes continued to function.

When Mr. Daiko provided the centers' locations to The Order, Shadowmen wasted no time deploying the grid-destroying devices in an effort to halt or, at very least, stall communications between Society agents. It was all part of their plan of chaos and destruction. What Daiko and The Order hadn't counted on was Finn's paranoia. Anticipating The Order's plans, Finn had placed EMP-proof cages in safe houses near key centers across the globe, allowing him to communicate with trusted agents and rally the troops quickly. Turned out, paranoia came in pretty handy at the end of the world.

Over half of the bombs were detonated early, destroying cities such as London, Los Angeles, Chicago, and Beijing; though, many of the cities on the doomsday map still stood. Agents of Light saved millions of lives, but millions of others were lost. Those who were too far gone didn't rise. Those too far from our light remained in the dark embrace of death. It was the greatest loss of life the world had ever known.

The survivors moved into the country, away from the toxic cities, and were receiving care. Surprisingly, residents had opened their homes and community centers with open arms, and the best of humanity was on full display. Alena, Arabella, and Zoeya chose to stay at Mentmore with Nora who was, at the end of it all, still dedicated to restoring a house she hated.

The brightest minds in the world, both from The Society of Light and the public sector, were working on a way to neutralize the radiation. Atmospheric domes had already been constructed over the bomb sites, containing the worst of the radiation.

The battle at Barnet Army Reserve taught us that by directing blasts of concentrated light at the sky, we were able to disperse the dense smoke caused by the bombs that would otherwise spread across the planet. Thus, preventing nuclear winter from setting in.

Though the EMP strike ensured that no one was able to use their cell phones to record the moment we defeated The Void, people talked, and news of what happened in London spread. After thousands of years of operating in secret, The Society of Light was exposed to the world. No more operating behind curtains, no more pulling strings behind the scenes. For better or worse, The Children of Light would finally live in the light. Of course, that also meant governments, news outlets, and everyday citizens had entered the chat. The Society would no longer be able to direct world change without external oversight or input. It would have driven Daiko crazy had he not defected and died.

Mrs. Delgado, co-leader of The Society of Light, had announced to the world that it would address the surviving members of the public from the White House front lawn that very day, and Luca and I were determined not to miss it. We met Finn at the D.C. airport, and after giving Luca his signature glare, he drove us to our nation's capital.

Elena Delgado, the leader of The Society of Light, stood alone at the podium on the White House lawn as she faced a sober crowd and delivered her speech with proud shoulders. Finn remained stoically by my side.

"Our world has suffered a great loss," she said with a grim voice. "The Order—an ancient organization that works in secret against the public good—placed hundreds of nuclear bombs in the world's largest cities for the sole purpose of killing as many humans as possible. Though many of the bombs did detonate, our agents were able to disable the majority of the weapons of mass destruction. Unfortunately, millions of Earth's citizens still lost their lives in the attack and the resulting fallout. It was not just an attack on our world, but an attack on all light and knowledge. They wanted to eradicate us from this planet and plunge the universe into eternal darkness. I am proud to say they failed!" She raised a fist in the air, and the crowd exploded in applause.

"As we go forward as a human race, we are dedicated to forming a unified republic, one that honors and respects all the

Earth's inhabitants, not just the privileged few. Gone are the days of division between nations and parties. Gone are the ideologies of hate and suppression. We will form a worldwide coalition. Country lines will be dissolved, and districts will be formed in their stead. Every corner of this planet will have representation and a seat at the table." Delgado's body began to glow in her conviction, and many in the crowd cried out, having never encountered a Bright One before. She continued undeterred. "Delegates will be chosen, not for how much money they have, but for what they can offer to the world. Instead of crooked politicians, only the brightest minds and forward thinkers will lead us into a new age."

Despite their awe and fear of her glowing skin, the crowd cheered, caught up in her words. Cautious optimism filled my chest. Delgado painted the perfect picture of a perfect world. A world in which I might be able to live openly as a Child of Light. A world where oppression and discrimination were no longer accepted norms. It was everything The Society of Light had fought for thousands of years. I wanted to believe mankind was ready for such a system, ready to accept those who were different, but I struggled to believe mankind had learned its lesson. Still, I wanted to have hope.

Finn listened in silence as Delgado continued her speech. Mere hours after the fight was won, Finn had quit his position as co-leader of The Society of Light, claiming he'd lost faith in the organization. Perhaps like our light ability, skepticism ran in our DNA.

Finn touched my arm lightly. "Come on, let's go. I have something I want to talk to you about."

I turned to Luca. "I'll be right back."

"Alright." He gave me a quick kiss and turned back to the stage.

Finn led me to a bench facing the National Mall. It was nearly May, and the trees were in full bloom, and the grass was green. I was thankful again that the agents assigned to this location had successfully disabled their bomb, and the nation's capital was still intact. One couldn't say the same for the American Government. It had only taken twelve hours for the United States to fall since most of the politicians and leaders had betrayed their country and were killed in bunkers of their own. I couldn't muster sympathy for them.

Finn settled his arm over the back of the bench. "I looked into the strange connection you and Mr. Durrant share, and I think I have an answer as to why it occurred."

"You can call him Luca, you know," I said, rolling my eyes. "If you're going to be a part of my life, you're going to have to get used to him."

Finn grunted. "Fine. Can we get back to my findings?"

I saluted him. "Yes, sir! Continue."

Finn laughed and shook his head. "As I was saying, I did a little research on your connection, and I have a theory. Have you heard of the phrase 'quantum entanglement?'"

I pursed my lips and squinted into the distance. The theory sounded familiar, but physics wasn't my field of science. "Given its name, I assume it has something to do with quantum physics."

"Very astute," Finn said, rolling his eyes. "Quantum entanglement is a phenomenon where two or more particles come together and become linked. This link can remain even over vast distances. Albert Einstein called it 'Spooky action at a distance.'"

Come together to form a link? I thought of the online messages between Parisxxxi8 and me. I'd formed a connection with Luca months before I met him or knew his real name. "Do you mean the bond was formed by a physical connection?"

He nodded. "In theory, yes."

"But Luca and I bonded before we ever met in person. How would we have formed an entanglement over the internet?"

He sat forward, eyes bright. "That's where things get interesting. I believe you and Luca met before."

I squinted at him in confusion. "Before, what?"

"As you know, energy is neither created nor destroyed," Finn explained.

"Yeah, the Law of Conservation," I said with a wave of my hand. It was common knowledge for any Bright One, as it explained where our unnatural gifts of Light originated.

He nodded again. "Which means all living things existed in some form or another. Therefore, it stands to reason that in some previous existence, the two of you met and formed a quantum entanglement."

I chewed on that for a bit. If energy always existed, and we were only on Earth for a short time, then we had to exist in some form or another before our human lives. Was it possible that Luca and I physically interacted with one another in some energetic form before our births? The idea sounded too fanciful to be scientific. Still, it was possible, wasn't it? But if Luca and I had met before, then we weren't the only ones. Our energies would likely have interacted with hundreds, if not millions, of other energy fields. Why was our connection so unique?

"If particles form connections when they come together or touch, why don't I share the same connection with you or anybody I so much as shake hands with?"

Finn shrugged. "It's an uncommon phenomenon. The pairing must have a perfect correlation. You and Luca have especially strong energy signatures. Perhaps you're bonded because you're both perfectly unique. There are no two others quite like you."

My brows rose. "Like soul mates?"

"Like soul mates. I believe you would have found one another no matter the distance, no matter the circumstance. Your energies are drawn to each other." Finn's eyes looked out in the distance, and his face took on a wistful sadness as if he were reliving a bittersweet memory.

"Did you feel that way about my mom?" I guessed.

His mouth lifted in a sad smile. "Claire might not have been a Child of Light, but she was the sun to me." He paused, swallowing hard. "Leaving her behind was extraordinarily difficult."

I looped my arm through his and lay my head on his shoulder. "You know, I don't think she ever stopped loving you."

"Nor I her." Finn cleared his throat and patted my hand. "At least I have something left of her. I have you." The crowd erupted into applause once more and then began to break away. Delgado's speech must have ended.

"What happens next?" I asked.

"Lunch, I suppose. Though I'm not sure the restaurants are open," he joked.

I slapped his arm. "Stop. You know what I mean. What do I do now that The Order is gone and the world is in shambles?"

"I have plenty of houses across the world that survived the attack. Pick one. As for direction, we're going to need some good scientists to help heal this world and its citizens. I seem to remember you have a particular interest in biophotonics. I'd say you've got a bright future ahead of you," Finn said, emphasizing the word bright unnecessarily.

I looked up at him in surprise, squinting in the afternoon sun. "Did you just make your first dad joke?"

Finn looked down at me and smiled. "Maybe. How did I do?"

I snorted. "Terrible."

J.B. Tucker is a novelist and short-story writer living in the Rocky Mountains with her bearded husband, three game-loving teenagers, and a small pack of doxies that follow her every move.

She has a master's degree in English (cohort in creative writing). By day, she teaches high schoolers how to read and write, and by night, she crafts complex worlds and characters in both long and short forms. Darkest Dawn is the final installment in The War Scroll Series, a YA Urban fantasy trilogy that explores an apocalyptic world through the lens of ancient prophecy.

Please visit her website at **jbtuckerbooks.com**